Alphonso A. (Alphonso Alva) Hopkins

The triumphs of duty : or, the merchant prince and his heir. A tale for the world

Alphonso A. (Alphonso Alva) Hopkins

The triumphs of duty : or, the merchant prince and his heir. A tale for the world

ISBN/EAN: 9783741163937

Manufactured in Europe, USA, Canada, Australia, Japa

Cover: Foto ©Andreas Hilbeck / pixelio.de

Manufactured and distributed by brebook publishing software
(www.brebook.com)

Alphonso A. (Alphonso Alva) Hopkins

The triumphs of duty : or, the merchant prince and his heir. A tale for the world

THE

TRIUMPHS OF DUTY;

OR,

THE MERCHANT PRINCE AND HIS HEIR.

A Tale for the World.

BY THE AUTHOR OF

"GERALDINE," "A TALE OF CONSCIENCE," ETC.

BOSTON:

PUBLISHED BY PATRICK DONAHOE,
23 FRANKLIN STREET.
1863.

Stereotyped by
J. E. FARWELL AND COMPANY,
37 Congress Street, Boston.

CONTENTS.

THE TRIUMPHS OF DUTY.

CHAPTER I.

THE GRANDSIRE AND HIS HEIR.

IT was a fine evening in the cheerful busy city of
Marseilles, on the 10th of June, 1850. The windows of a certain first floor were thrown open on a
balcony commanding a view of the ever-varying scene
of the port. The hum of a peaceful multitude, re-
creating after the toils of the day, gave additional
value to the luxury of a solitude seldom enjoyed,
while something more than these external aids to
happiness—something of the sunshine of the breast,
outshining the luminary of the skies—was reflected
on the countenance of a fine old gentleman of sixty-
seven, as alone, yet expecting a beloved guest, he sat
in his arm-chair beside a small table, on which were
lying several parchments and papers.

The dining-table, at a little distance, was arranged
for two persons, and in a short time the well-known

step was heard, and affectionate greetings were exchanged between the grandfather and his only grandson and heir, Arthur Bryce. The grandsire's welcome was in pure English, to which the youth responded with perfect facility, but with a slight French accent.

"My sixty-seventh birthday passed off well and merrily, did it not, Arthur?"

"Indeed it did, sir; and I have to return you many thanks for having chosen your dinner guests to please me, not yourself. What nonsense, we must all have talked, we young Marseillais, in our supposed wisdom, when the good wine had circulated a little!"

"Yes, you did all talk nonsense, to my notions. Young France as well as young Italy is to me like children blowing bubbles."

"And yet, sir, you sat leaning back in your chair, and smiling as benevolently as you are doing now. You did not even shrug your shoulders."

"My dear boy, the torrent of nationalities must rush on at present. The result will sober you all. It is in vain for old people to endeavor to convince you young ones by theory. One theory, until put to the test, may be as good as another. Neither will an appeal to history avail; for great men, great actions, great sacrifices, have adorned each opposed side. The best state of mind to maintain," added the venerable merchant of Marseilles, "and which

I think my own, is to have a confirmed preference, from having seen and proved what is best; to remain faithful to this conviction, yet to believe that an equally intelligent and honest mind may, by the same test of thought and experience, have arrived at a totally opposite conclusion. The true test of a conviction, is to make willing sacrifices for it. I have done this. The last thirty years of my life, have been a sacrifice to my convictions, social and political."

At this final and solemn assertion, the young Arthur gazed astonished at his grandfather. Respect prevented his openly laughing, but a smile curled his mouth, and twinkled in his dark eye as he replied:

" Pardon me, sir, if I find it difficult to conceive how a much-respected and three-fold millionaire, whose every speculation has been successful during these thirty years, can speak of the spirit of sacrifice; nay, of the fact of sacrifice, through all that golden time."

" You speak thus," said Mr. Bryce, " because that which is a sacrifice to one man is not so to another. But now come to dinner. Let us defer the long explanation I am prepared to give you until after the restoration we both require."

The removal of a step or two brought the loving pair to the now well-furnished table, where for more than half an hour more good things were eaten than said; and when the conversation recommenced, it fell more to young Arthur than to his grandfather to enliven it by sportive anecdotes and projects for the coming autumn. At length, however, Mr. Bryce, starting from some deep musings, returned with a resolute step to his former corner, saying: "Come Arthur, this is the hour long appointed for making a disclosure to you — an astounding disclosure. To defer it would be weakness. Sit down — sit down here."

Arthur recalled from an excursion he had been planning aloud, half playfully, — half in earnest, to the bay of Naples, now looked with sudden alarm at his grandfather. The young man had not been displeased to be known throughout the city, as the sole heir to the immense sum realized by the prosperous industry of his grandfather. He now concluded that some heavy loss was to be revealed to him, and he said faintly:

"To what extent, sir?"

"Ha!" cried Mr. Bryce, "you think you are a ruined man? No! my boy, not that; quite the reverse."

"Quite the reverse!" repeated Arthur. "Oh, well, sir," added he, smiling, "I have no objection to your being a four-fold millionaire."

"You mercantile fellow," said his grandfather, "the disclosure I am about to make to you has nothing to do with money. Look here," continued he, unrolling a parchment, on which were long lists

of names, coats of arms, coronets, crests, and supporters; in fact, all the usual routine of a long and
noble pedigree. Arthur looked, and felt both relieved and disappointed.

"Oh, sir!" cried he, "if you did but know how
little I care for such things. I acknowledge no nobility, but nobility of soul. I am aware that you
are originally of good family, and have some claim
or other to an estate in England, but I hope you
do not require me to study all this grand family history?"

"I require you merely to read it through," said
Mr. Bryce.

Arthur glanced at some historical names at the
top of the page, then rapidly descended to the last
of them — the Earl of Charleton — saying, "What
have we to do with this last personage?"

"He has the honor of addressing you," replied
the grandfather, smiling, as he bowed to the astonished grandson.

"You the Earl of Charleton?"

"Exactly so."

"Then who am I?"

"Since the death of your father, in 1832, you
are Viscount Stanmore."

"Well, sir, I mean my lord, I am, indeed, as
much surprised, and my mind thrown into as great
a state of chaos as you could possibly have anticipated. And is Bryce an imagined name?"

" No; it became one of the family names, though not the primary one, at the marriage of my father, your great-grandfather, to Augusta Bryce, an heiress. The old family name is Woolton."

" Then my second and supposed baptism name is really that of my family, and I am now, as ever, Arthur Dieudonné Woolton Bryce or Arthur Dieudonné Bryce Woolton? "

" The latter will be, henceforth, the more correct," replied the grandfather.

And now a long pause ensued. The fact just announced to Arthur was sufficient to occupy his mind without reference to past or future. In these first moments he did not perceive any weight of responsibility lowering in the distance, from the acquisition of high rank in addition to the immense fortune to which he was the heir — no sacrifice appeared to beckon to him, with conscience sternly urging him on — still a feeling of antagonism against the aristocracy made him nourish a sort of proud disdain of that which had just been announced to him.

" Well, Arthur," at length inquired Lord Charleton, " have you no inquiries to make? Can you now form some idea of what I implied by the term ' sacrifice,' in speaking of the thirty years I have spent as a merchant of Marseilles? "

" Perhaps so, my dear grandfather; but I cannot feel as you do all at once. I have been perfectly happy hitherto in the rank of a well-educated commoner, and it will remain to be proved whether I shall gain in true happiness by the change."

"True happiness," said Lord Charleton, "is the *reward* of conscientious duty. It *follows* our having done our duty in that state of life to which it has pleased God to call us."

"It is now explained to me," said Arthur, "why, in the spite of the railleries of the other merchants in Marseilles, you have given me an education so much more varied and extensive than that of my associates here."

"And surely you do not consider your education to be finished," continued Lord Charleton. "You are not yet eighteen; you must now give three years to whatever finishing studies you may require, including a classical tour to Greece and Italy, and you will, at one-and-twenty, be fully able to compete with your peers, although the shades of neither Eaton nor Oxford have nourished your early lore."

"I should like to study in Paris," said Arthur.

"I can trust you; you may go."

"Thank you," cried Arthur, brightly. I begin to like the good news well enough; I shall be very happy. But I should now like to hear your history, my dear grandfather, and that of my parents, if you are prepared to relate them to me?"

"Sorrow may endure for a night, but joy cometh in the morning, said Lord Charleton, musingly. "You are that 'morning' to me, my dear boy."

CHAPTER II.

THE FAMILY HISTORY.

"I was born in the year 1783, in the ancient family mansion of Woolton Court in Westmorland; a lovely spot on one of those smaller and sequestered lakes unknown to ordinary tourists. All around the shores of the lake had been hereditary property since the battle of Agincourt. I was born unexpectedly, to the great joy of my parents, when they were advanced in life; other children followed me, but did not survive their birth. My father had two brothers, the elder of whom, having expected to succeed to everything, had no scruple in contracting debts, and even in bringing a mortgage on the estate which, at the death of my father, was discovered to the great disadvantage of the family. My unsuspecting father had left these two uncles my sole guardians, and when I came of age the fatal truth became known to me that the family had become bankrupt in funds, in land, in reputation, in honor, — in all that nobility holds most dear."

"In all that an honest man of any rank holds most dear," interrupted the grandson. "These two scamps of uncles are not calculated to warm my feeling towards this grand hereditary line since the battle of Agincourt."

" The hereditary *lands* of Woolton date from the battle of Agincourt," explained the grandfather; "for they were then given and held of the crown under the great Charter, for valiant deeds on the battle-field, by Philip de Voulton, first Lord Woolton, but the family can be traced in perfect descent to Gaston de Voulton Chatelain de Gours in Dauphiné, before the conquest. However, as you do not yet care for these researches into antiquity, I will proceed to recount, as briefly as possible, the departure of both uncles for America; a departure made so secretly that fresh dishonor fell on the family. I had but one friend after the death of my excellent mother; but he was a true one, and from a class of men who have great power for good or ill. This friend was the family lawyer. My mother's jointure had been the half of her own fortune. This alone was rescued from the wreck of all else. I retired at the age of two-and-twenty to Caen in Normandy, retaining my title, and with sufficient to support it in a provincial city. I married the daughter of the Baron de Rambullieré, with whom I lived happily during the reign of the first Napoleon, and whose family I accompanied to Paris on the return of the royal Bourbons in 1814. My fortune, however, having been all placed in the French funds, was gone. I had three children, I was in the vigor of manhood, I saw around me those of the first nobility, who, during their emigration, had labored with the pen, the pencil, or as teachers of French. I was inspired to emulate these examples of cheerful courage. I became English clerk in a great mercantile house in Paris, connected with this in Marseilles. I dropped, however, my title, and bore my mother's name, that by which I have been so long known. After some years I was offered a partnership in the house here, which I accepted, and by patient industry and an undeviating adherence to a prudent line of action I have become rich. The senior partners have been some years dead. I effected a separation of risks from the house in Paris, and associated no partner to myself here. I remain the sole possessor of wealth securely funded in the Bank of England, and have already signed the papers which, in six months hence, transfer, for an immense sum, the vessels, the warehouses, and the credit of Mr. Bryce, general merchant, to Messrs. Luisond, brothers, our old acquaintances here in Marseilles. This is a rapid sketch of my own life. Details can be given at leisure. You naturally wish to hear something of your immediate parents, and I turn from myself to them.

" Your father was the only one of my three children who survived his infancy, and he, to my sorrow, was of an extremely delicate constitution. He had a private tutor, and studied only as his health permitted. At the age of three-and-twenty, a marriage took place between him and the daughter of the Count and Countess de Courtrai, a younger branch of the great Ducal House of Courtrai. It was all arranged for him in the French manner. He was married by his proper name and title, in the Church of St. Sulpice in Paris, and then remained with the parents of his bride at Versailles, during the first year of their marriage ;. which, alas ! was the last of his life. He had thus stayed in the centre of France, instead of returning to Marseilles, on account of a projected visit to England, should he happily expect to become a father. He knew my ever-strengthening hopes of finally regaining the estate of my ancestors, and often filially lamented that his weak health prevented his sharing in the labors to which, for that end, I had devoted my life. It was in the autumn of 1832, that I received the joyful news of the intended journey to England ; but this was followed, a week after, by a letter from Calais, announcing the opinion of the medical friend who had travelled with the young couple, that, in the precarious state of my son's health, he ought not to risk the passage to Dover. I instantly started by the mail for Paris, and thence to Calais, where I arrived just in time to witness his edifying death, and receive his desolate widow to my heart. My son was buried in the country of his birth, but his unborn child must see the light in England, or be an alien. You are aware that such is the law for the second generation born abroad. I did not appeal in vain to the courage of your young mother. Although but seventeen she had given tokens of the heroic power of her principle of duty. I bore her from the grave of her husband to your birth-place, in the outskirts of Dover. Her mother, Madame de Courtrai, had joined her but two days when, in the midst of all our sorrow, you came, like a sunbeam, to cheer and.console. Your mother rejoiced to give birth to an heir, but felt some natural regret that you bore but little resemblance, in those early days, to him she had lost; while I, knowing the strength of constitution as well as firmness of mind of her who bore you, preferred to trace in your infant face the dark eye and determined little mouth of your mother, for by those tokens I felt more assurance of your being spared to reward my long labors. From consideration for my daughter-in-law, I left her with her parents at Versailles and you with her, until your fourth year, when I fetched you both to my house here at Marseilles. During the week of convalescence at Dover I visited London, where I conferred with my ever-kind friend, Mr. Oldham, then a very aged man. He resigned some valuable documents to me, and introduced his nephew, whom he had made acquainted with all the affairs of the Woolton property. It is with this nephew I have corresponded during the last seventeen years. He is considerably my junior, and therefore I trust will be sufficiently active to advise and befriend you, when you, Arthur, in your turn, shall visit England."

During Lord Charleton's narrative, his grandson had drawn from a hidden fold near his heart a double portrait suspended by a chain round his neck. These miniatures on ivory, worn since childhood, were now gazed on with fresh and tearful interest. They had been bridal presents exchanged between the young bridegroom of three-and-twenty and his little bride of sixteen. Arthur perceived, as if for the first time, in his father's countenance high intellectual capacity, without physical power to render it available; something also of patient suffering and of a hope beyond this earth, gave a sacred character to the fair Anglo-Saxon head. Arthur pressed it reverentially to his lips, then turned his eyes on the bright, keen, impetuous mother, whom he could remember to have hugged and played with, and whom he had wept over with clamorous unappeasable sorrow.

" How well she retained her youthful expression," said he, smiling. Then with a sudden gush of tears, " Oh! how impossible it seems that some persons should ever die!"

CHAPTER III.

THE OLD MANOR COURT HOUSE.

THREE years after the disclosures made in our first chapters, our young hero, having finished with great success his studies in Paris, and his classical tour with a tutor, then visited England, in the spring of 1853. Some weeks were devoted to pleasant sight-seeing round the coast, some more to investigation of all the principal dockyards, harbors, and arsenals, then more weeks to manufactures and mining districts, and still Arthur was not wearied.

England continued a land of poetry and romance in contrast to France, which being the country of all the prose reality of his life, he loved in a deep, earnest, and a practical manner, as the Arthur Bryce of Marseilles. This name he was obliged still to retain in its simplicity, for reasons which will declare themselves in due time. London had been seen merely in passing from one railway station to another, but now he was to visit and reside for some months in our immense metropolis, where, after seeing with deliberate attention, the many objects of the great capital, he was to finish his education by the study of as much law, as Mr. Oldham, the family lawyer, might judge proper. This substantial elderly gentleman continued to be the only person to whom Arthur was permitted to give his confidence ; for Lord Charleton, anticipating the time when his grandson could select his young friends from his true position in life, bade him content himself for the present with guides, directors, inspectors, and all official persons ; and, with the above exception, to outpour his feelings in letters to himself alone. Arthur had been residing in London about four months, when Mr. Oldham imparted to him that, after the most apparently capricious conduct, the present owner of Woolton Court seemed determined to dispose at once of the property, and had requested Mr. Oldham, by letter, to go immediately to confer with him on the spot. " Now, sir," added Mr. Oldham, " I have written, in reply, that I will have the honor of waiting on Mr. Sanderson on the evening of the twenty-fifth of this month of August, and of remaining one whole day at Woolton Court. That as his invitation was to remain ten days or a fortnight, to clear up some complicated affairs, with which request it was impossible for me to comply in my own person, I proposed bringing with me a gentleman who would remain to act for me, in all that Mr. Sanderson wished to intrust to my skill and zeal."

" And that profound lawyer is Mr. Arthur Bryce ?" said our hero, smiling.

" It is," replied Mr. Oldham. ' " Your grandfather wishes you to see the place, and I think this appears a good opportunity. As for depth of law required in arranging Mr. Sanderson's papers, you have acquired knowledge more profound than those will require; besides, you can write and consult me about any difficulty that may prolong your stay. This is the 19th of the month. In six days, then, I shall have the honor of conducting you to Woolton."

Mr. Oldham departed, and Arthur soliloquized: " Yes, this is England! romantic, dreary England! What an unreal life mine is? Do I wish this to continue, or to end? I know not? I may say with Hamlet, ' To be, or not to be, that is the question!' "

A letter from Mr. Oldham to Mr. Bryce, senior, at Marseilles, imparted the approaching visit to Woolton Court. He thus concluded: " It is still quite as necessary as ever, to keep the secret of the name and history of him who wishes to possess the place. Mr. Sanderson is one of those gentlemen, who have a jealous antipathy to those in a still higher class of society. He has also a nervous dread of being advised and persuaded into any measure; so that, however favorably inclined he may be to a project, he will relinquish it if advised, — still more if urged to remain constant to it. I have fully apprized Mr. Arthur Bryce of this bias of character in the present owner of Woolton Court, &c." The next letter received by the venerable merchant of Marseilles was from Arthur, as follows:

" My dear grandfather, to know that you will read with emotion the fact, that I am at Woolton Court, gives me a sympathetic feeling, from the reverence and affection I bear you. From your description, I have identified many parts of the house and grounds. It all strikes me as solidly grand, and noble, and worthy of you. As for myself, as connected with this place, I cannot believe it. The future is too uncertain — the present too unreal. But I must relate the facts of our arrival. Mr. Oldham, and 'Mr. Arthur Bryce, an intelligent lawyer,' recommended by him, travelled together from London by railway, as far as Congleden. Thence in a vehicle, misnamed a ' Fly,' to the entrance lodge of Woolton Court. We had ascended gradually for the last mile or more, and now we descended still more slowly the inner side of the mountain, or hill, into the little valley of Woolton — a scene of great beauty. Alternate rock and verdure ; higher mountains in the distance ; the peaceful little lake, nestling in the depths ; a great variety of fine timber ; and, abruptly rising from the valley, on a platform rock of its own, the mansion of Woolton Court. The natural causeway from this rock to the side of the mountain, which we were descending, brought us on level ground, and our poor little fly then flew with some speed, till we found ourselves before the huge portals of the outer archway of the court. We were expected, and immediately admitted, through inner courts, and halls, and

ante-rooms, to the comfortable little parlor, wherein
sate the domestic trio of Mr. Sanderson and his two
sisters.   Rather pleasant and kind people, especially
the elder sister.   But there is in the house a most
charming person; a daughter or sister of the Marquis of Seaham, who lives near, and comes from
time to time to Woolton, to copy some of the pic-
·tures in this gallery, for her own family seat in
Cheshire.   The cottage they have on Windermere, is,
I hear, very well worth seeing.   You have, I think,
mentioned that family when talking of old times.
The family name is Chamberlayne.   I leave Mr.
Oldham to report progress, should there be any,
towards the re-possession of this place.   The conversation last night seemed favorable; but this morning Mr. Oldham's looks did not betoken much advance; indeed, he was so inwardly fretted that he
was compelled to vent it on his dry toast at breakfast, by scraping and stabbing it, as though it had
been the effigy of Mr. Sanderson's irresolute self-
will.   In a few days I will write again, &c.'

On the third morning of Arthur's visit to Woolton, he rose early, and with some vague feeling of
expected pleasure in viewing the living as well as
departed beauties in the great picture gallery, bent
his steps that way.   He perceived Lady Clara Chamberlayne already seated at her easel, and he gradually
made his way towards her, preserving, however, after
the first compliments of respectful greeting, a pro-

found silence. Lady Clara had passed that first bloom which is supposed to hover between fifteen and five-and-twenty, but a consequent increase of intelligence and dignity, had given to her beauty a still greater charm. Amongst her many talents the art of portrait painting in oils had been one of the most cultivated; and Arthur beheld with admiration the fidelity with which she conveyed to her own canvas the lovely original, a Lady Sybilla Woolton, in the costume and style of Sir Peter Lely. At length the natural polite inquiry of whether his admiring gaze on her work were intrusive occurred to Arthur, and received the courteous reply, that it would be very acceptable to an amateur to hear the observations of one who, from his visits to foreign galleries, and the instructions he had received from the first masters, must be a good judge of pictures, especially heads. Then followed an animated conversation on the comparative merits of the galleries of Dresden and Florence, in the first of which Lady Clara had studied, in the latter, Arthur. At length he ventured to observe that, beautiful as was the picture her ladyship was copying of the fair Sybilla, there were others in the gallery that he would have preferred to possess.

"I do not copy the Lady Sybilla because she is beautiful, but because she belongs to our family as well as the Wooltons, and ought to hang in our gallery at Marsden. She is labelled here the Lady

Sybilla Woolton, for Sir Peter Lely must have painted her when very young. She afterwards married my great grandfather, the fifth Marquis of Seaham, and there is a melancholy pleasure in securing that all shall not be forgotten of the Earls of Charleton."

"That is very kind, very generous in you, Lady Clara," exclaimed the young man, energetically. *You* are not one to trample on the fallen. The line of Woolton can boast of dauntless courage, of heroic endurance. I have heard of the last of that race — the last known in England. My grandfather was intimate with him abroad. Oh! how I wish you knew him."

Lady Clara looked at the speaker with a smile of intelligence, then laying aside her brush, she gave a small book open into his hand, saying, as she pointed to the various names of the owner on the blank leaf. "I thank you much for the perusal of this work. I would have detained it longer, had I not already thought it better to warn you, that, although to the world in general, Arthur *William* Bryce may be the more obvious interpretation of the initial ' W.,' yet in this house, especially in this gallery, where the Wooltons can never be forgotten, you risk the discovery of your secret."

" Have I a secret?" said Arthur, prudently.

Lady Clara replied, " You had better trust me. You will never repent it."

Arthur seized the hand she extended to him, and pressed it to his lips, exclaiming, "I do trust you; I am a Woolton;" then added, "but tell me, how do you know me?"

"I own that I am puzzled," replied Lady Clara. "The last Lord Charleton has been traced — not in the spirit of bailiffs and constables, but with the purest motives of friendship — to Caen, to Paris. The marriage of his son, as Viscount Stanmore, proved that the earl still lived in 1831. But that son died childless in 1832. His bereaved father can no longer be traced. I must suppose you to be the descendant of one of the two younger sons of the ninth Earl of Charleton, who fled to America in the beginning of this century, as is recorded in certain family annals at our old place in Cheshire, setting forth how Gilbert Woolton wooed a certain Lady Jacqueline Chamberlayne, and how the gay deceiver fled from his word and his love to the woods and wilds of America; and how the Lady Jacqueline wrote verses, Oh! Gilbert, Gilbert, in rhyme to filbert, and far-fetched Mechlin to Jacqueline, giving a clue to otherwise mysterious emblems in her portrait at Marsden."

"The scoundrel!" cried Arthur, "he is even worse than I thought him. Thank heaven, I am not descended from him."

"You shall tell me from whom at another time," said Lady Clara, suddenly resuming her painting.

3

" The present owners of Woolton Court will expect Mr. Bryce, the lawyer, to attend the breakfast-table. The bell is sounding, and my most punctual attendant is advancing with my little tray."

" But when," demanded Arthur, " shall we again meet without interruption? Will you finish your sketch from the lake this evening?"

" I will, provided I can prevail upon my hospitable friends here to have an early dinner. You shall row me to the spot. Of course, you can row, and swim, and dive, like a proper Ligurian?"

" Do you wish me to perform all those feats?" inquired Arthur, laughing; " because if you do, I should like to be in proper costume."

" Mr. Bryce," said Lady Clara, with a grave warning look, as the maid arrived by the easel, " I will accept with pleasure your professional assistance, but only for the first point mentioned; and I beg you will receive my thanks for the information you have already conveyed to me in this book." Arthur, recalled to prudence, bowed with respect, and received his little book of legal hints, which might, or might not, be discovered by readers in general in Lamartine's beautiful poems. With spirits raised by the conversation of the morning, and its hoped-for renewal in the evening, he descended to the family breakfast.

CHAPTER IV.

INDECISION.

It was more than a week since the return of Mr. Oldham to London, during which our hero had to undergo the penalty of being so able and rising a young lawyer, by remaining closeted each day, after breakfast, with Mr. Sanderson, during a couple of hours, looking over the same papers, and hearing the same observations.

A few days more, however, and from some domestic cause, unknown beyond the family trio, the owner of the dwelling determined to remove; and commissioned Mr. Oldham by letter to close with the offer made by his correspondent, the English gentleman in France. Arthur had to make a copy of this letter—a light task he performed most willingly; and with greater courage foresaw another wet day that would postpone the row on the lake, the sketch, and the history of the three last heirs of the estate.

The following day, still a soft interminable rain. Arthur buried himself in the library, for Lady Clara had deserted the picture gallery. The evenings, however, were always pleasant, and as Arthur was convinced that Mr. Oldham would reply by return of post, he obeyed with alacrity the summons on the following morning to the study, where he found the expected letter open in the hand of Mr. Sanderson.

" So — well, pray Mr. Bryce, have you received any letter yourself from Mr. Oldham? No — really — because I do not much relish the fast way in which he is driving on, just as if I had definitely made up my mind to the thing. Here he is respectfully offering his congratulations on the unheard-of offer he has closed with for Woolton Court-house and lands. Why, sir, no one can force me to sign the transfer against my will. There is nothing definitely done. There can be nothing done without my signature. Why, sir, no one can force me to sell the place ! "

" Most assuredly not," said Mr. Bryce.

" It seems exactly," continued Mr. Sanderson, " as if the old families of the neighborhood had combined to get one of their own set into the place, and were helping him with the cash to make a tempting offer."

" This might possibly occur with reason to you, sir," observed the confidential lawyer, " had you been the first to occupy the estate, after the departure of the hereditary owners ; but I am informed that two different families preceded you here. That of the Berkeley Westons, being the immediate purchasers from the last Earl of Charleton, who remained here sixteen years ; and the family of Sir Errol Leigh, who were here thirty years, and laid out much money on the place."

"So should I, sir; I should have done just as much for the place as did Sir Errol Leigh; perhaps more — yes, certainly more, if I had not been going, ever since I came."

"That was a pity," said Arthur, involuntarily.

"Pity!" echoed Mr. Sanderson; "as if a man were not the master of his own actions. Why, sir, the Leigh family all died off of consumption. That was the recompense for living here those thirty years. All, all but the two youngest girls, now elderly women, who are living in the South of France; a rather different climate, where you can combine health and beauty. Now, here in our country, unless you can find a place to suit you in Devonshire — and Devonshire is relaxing — you have to pay too high a tax for beauty. This Woolton is unhealthy. It is a decided fact. It is too shady. You cannot see the sun till the very time you would rather be without him; that is, at mid-day, darting down his vertical rays on your brains. No sun-rise — no sun-set. The mist from the lake rising to your throat like the grasp of an assassin. No; nothing will do at this Woolton Court but closed doors and windows, a roaring fire in every room, plenty of port wine, Peruvian bark, and the house full of company. I have read in the *Times* this morning, of a house that may suit me in Hampshire. There is one, also, that I have long thought of, near Windsor. But I shall prefer the one in Hampshire. Fine sea view — distant glimpse of the Isle of Wight. Good neighborhood, without any nonsense of pedigree. Yet how can one possibly judge of a place until one lives in it."

" Very true," sighed the wearied Arthur.

" Therefore I have thought," continued Mr. Sanderson, " of seeing the two places myself, and we could travel up together to London ; see Mr. Oldham, and then take a run down first to one place, then to the other. Of course I frank your expenses, and pay for your time. And your time here, Mr. Bryce——."

" Oh, sir," cried Arthur, nearly laughing aloud, " I feel extremely obliged to you, but I must totally decline any remuneration. I have, on the contrary, to express my thanks for the hospitality I have received in this house ; a visit which I shall ever consider with grateful pleasure, as one of the happiest of my life."

" Indeed, sir — very strange — I am sure it has been easy to make you happy ; very strange. Well, as to this journey to London ? I think of going the day after to-morrow."

" You are very kind, Mr. Sanderson, but my instructions from Mr. Oldham are to visit on business, quite in an opposite direction."

" Well, then, I will take my sisters, Bell and

Susan. They will enjoy it; and Lady Clara, as she came self-invited, must not take it ill. The fact is, I am not a marrying man. Why, what is the matter, Mr. Bryce? Ha! the cramp. But you must not stamp so violently; do you know you may break one of the smaller fibres. This is the case sometimes. But it *is* a painful thing, the cramp. Walking up and down, which you are now doing, is very good — very."

" I wish you good morning, sir," cried the infuriated Arthur, who rushed from the house into the grounds, exclaiming, " the cool, conceited coxcomb ! "

The afternoon proved splendidly fine; the early dinner was politely agreed to by the Sanderson family, during which the highly spasmodic, neuralgic, rheumatic character of the place, as exemplified by cramp, in a highly developed form, was expatiated on by the master of the house, and fully assented to by Miss Susan. The two sisters could not join the boating sketching party, for visitors arrived to see the flower gardens ; therefore, at the appointed hour, Lady Clara and her elderly attendant, bearing shawls and sketch-book, descended to the landing steps of the lake, and were conveyed by the practised and willing arms of our hero to the point selected, whence the old mansion was seen to the best advantage. The preliminaries of the drawing were soon arranged, and Lady Clara said with much gravity :

"Your proposal, Mr. Bryce, that I should become acquainted with that certain point in law I accept most willingly, but as I am aware that you can explain it better in French, I beg you will do so without scruple, as I have brought a book to beguile the time to my attendant." She then added with the same formality in French, " my maid does not understand the language in which you will recount your history, but she is very intelligent in the interpretation of looks and gestures."

Arthur bowed, and commenced the history in the calmest manner possible; the self-control of the listener was equally admirable. The sketch was the victim. It would have been highly dangerous for the Sanderson family to have inhabited a mansion so far from the perpendicular.

The following morning, after breakfast, our hero, instead of a summons to the private study of Mr. Sanderson, was invited by the elder sister to the flower-garden, and thence to an alcove, where she sweetly, yet gravely, bespoke his attention and advice. Arthur could promise with zeal and truth to do all that lay in his power for a lady who deserved his respectful feeling; partly from a strong likeness to one in France who had been maternally kind to him when a child, a Mrs. Colville, partly from her own good qualities and strong practical sense. Something of this he expressed, to which Miss Sanderson replied :

" I am about to put this good opinion of me to rather a severe test, especially the encomium of ' good sense ; ' but I must risk it, for I require your assistance. During the first years of our residence here, my brother was much on the continent, and had given us the commission to let the place and join him. We were not able to succeed according to the terms he thought right, and at length he came to reside here with us. Then commenced the persecution, if such it be, that has with some few intervals, tormented us ever since. This persecution is in the mode of nocturnal sounds, proceeding from that part of the house where formerly the religious services of the family were celebrated ; the family chapel, beneath which are the family vaults, and behind which is what is called a mortuary chamber, where the mortal remains of any member of the family lay until brought into the chapel for the funeral services, and thence to the vaults. I have been over all that part, except the vaults. But soon after my brother's return, he ordered the chapel to be locked up. These sounds do not come from below, they are rather above the bed-room floor. One striking fact I must mention, for it may assist your investigations. Whenever we are really preparing to leave the place these nocturnal sounds cease ; and, on the contrary, whenever we seem to have made up our minds to remain they recommence. They are not terrific — they are wailing, pathetic, and most mournful sounds, producing exactly the effect that these sly enemies propose, that of the grief and lamentation that strangers should occupy these halls.   Now to convince you of all this I will speak to my brother and sister, and we will conduct the conversation at dinner so as to make it appear that we have renounced all idea of removing.   I will also, on the plea of your feeling cold on the north side of the house, order the bed to be prepared in a room where the sounds are heard the most plainly; a room, in fact, where no one of the household will now sleep, and where we never place strangers.   I will order a good fire, as the room has been so long unoccupied.   I shall then have done all that my sagacity can achieve, and must leave to the superior penetration of the lawyer to dive deeper into the mystery."

" Have you ever made an investigation at the very moment of these sounds?" inquired Arthur.

" We have not; we felt so much convinced of the ill-will of those who contrived them, that we feared to expose ourselves at midnight alone to their power.   We have confided in no one, for fear of ridicule."

" That was prudent; but to-night you will not be alone.   I shall remain up, reading in the room you have selected for me, expecting you to fetch me directly the sounds are distinguishable."

" The room you will occupy," said Miss Sanderson, " is the very nearest to the sounds.   It will not be necessary to meet in the night; you will merely listen to them, and in the morning we will again confer together."

All was arranged in the order proposed by the lady of the house. The counter-mine was sprung at dinner. Mr. Sanderson, in high spirits, contradicted himself and every one else, till the whole scheme would have failed but for the watchful presence of mind of his sister. Lady Clara, who was not in the secret, looked polite astonishment at the sudden abandonment of the trip southward, and then resigned herself to her own thoughts. When the party broke up for the night, the servant who conducted Arthur to his new room, civilly regretted that his former apartment had proved too cold, raised the fire to a cheerful blaze, lit a second taper, and, with a sacred glance round the room, departed. Arthur admired the form and furniture of his new and spacious apartment, and at length, after more careful observation, found a fresh interest which, for a while, superseded that for which he was its occupant. He recognized, from a description repeated by letter since his arrival at Woolton, that he was in the room of the last Earl of Charleton, his own loved grandfather.

CHAPTER V.

MYSTERIES AND ENCOUNTERS.

His mind filled with thoughts of "days of yore," Arthur remained by the fire till it occurred to him to look forth on the same scenery over which his grandfather must so often have gazed in those young days when hope and joy and tender love were his. There was sufficient moonlight to enable Arthur to distinguish the route by which he had entered the valley of Woolton, and the distant heights round Windermere. "Oh! will *he* ever retrace that path?" thought he. "Will he ever again stand at this window, not as I do, a stranger, but once more lord of this rich domain?" The reply to this was in the first tremulous notes of the nocturnal wail. Roused at once, and shaking off all sinister impressions, Arthur stood intently listening. He was soon convinced that he heard no human voice, however disguised, nor could he identify the sound in connection with any instrument he had ever heard. Passionately fond of music in every grade, from the wildest to the most scientific, he had, as a boy, fastened an æolian harp in his window, and the sea-breeze had modulated its chords of harmony as he lay on his mid-day couch in the summer siesta. But this was not quite the æolian harp, some notes were more like the flute. At length he proceeded to another investigation — that of sight, and endeavored to penetrate the secret in every way his piqued curiosity could suggest. All in vain; he had proved that no communication existed between the room and the aerial sounds, but that was all. He softly opened the door into the rooms that formed the complete suite to the one he occupied; and as he passed from the dressing-room into the sitting-room, the immense thickness of that inner wall, as compared with the others, struck him as an architect, for Arthur had studied that art. A shallow closet occupied the thickness of the wall, but he felt assured that behind it ran a narrow passage to the mysterious choir. This once ascertained, almost to conviction, Arthur betook himself to rest, and recalling all that had been confided to him, dozed into a sound sleep amid the sounds that, he felt assured, portended no evil to the ancient possessors of Woolton Court.

The mutual confidences on the following morning may be easily surmised; but the conjectured passage behind the china closet was imparted to Miss Sanderson alone. Arthur promised to remain at Woolton, after a confidential visit elsewhere, and Mr. Sanderson and his sisters, anxious to travel beyond hearing of the, to them, fatal sounds, departed

4

some days after for London and the coast of Hampshire.

Arthur started the same evening for the tour of the lakes. He had not been able to see Lady Clara, and was uncertain whether she had left Woolton before or after the Sandersons. He determined, however, to console himself for this disappointment by a visit to Windermere as soon as a letter from Mr. Oldham should release him from his forced incognito. The miniature beauties of our English lakes he fully appreciated, but he returned to Woolton a day sooner than he would otherwise have done, being desirous to " come of age," in the halls of his ancestors; their eventual re-possession, however, lay in the balance of an irresolute and prejudiced mind, on which to rely for sympathy with an exiled race of patricians, would be to rashly close the portals against them forever.

Absorbed in many conflicting thoughts, Arthur remained waiting a considerable time after the first peal had been given at the entrance tower of the court. He rang again, with an almost equal time for solitary musings, before a servant appeared.

" Oh, Mr. Bryce; so it 's you, — yes. Mr. Sanderson said you were to return and stop till you had made out some accounts for him. I suppose you would like his study? and a new bed-room from the last ? "

" I prefer the library, and whatever bed-room is

most convenient," said Arthur, walking across the court in that direction, while the servant closed and barred the gate of the tower.

"Oh, very well," said the man, "it is all the same. Have you dined, sir?"

"I have," replied Arthur; "but I should be glad to have a light supper towards night, and to send some man or boy to the village coach-office for my portmanteau."

This commission being accompanied by the remuneration in advance, the servant volunteered to go himself that minute, and our hero, relieved to be alone, walked leisurely into the great hall, and gazed with the eye of a critic—yet a partial critic—on the fine oak pannelling, the lofty vaulted ceiling, the broad staircase, parting at the first flight into two branches, and the stained-glass windows, still bearing the crest of the Wooltons, and part of the armorial bearings; the crest of the coat of arms having been repaired at various times, with good arrangement of colors, but without heed to correct quarterings. Arthur then gazed on the rusty armor, and other trophies of an obsolete warfare, and was finally about to seek the library, when, remembering that some of the happiest moments he had spent in that house, had been opposite the picture of the Lady Sybilla in the picture gallery, he mounted the stairs, and, for the sake of these reminiscences, passed through the open door at the east end of the gallery,

which extended the whole length of the north façade
of the mansion. The portrait of the Lady Sybilla
was at nearly the west end ; and Arthur, whose time
was his own, slowly passed up the gallery from picture to picture on the contrary side, till he recognized a certain knight in armor, which he remembered to hang exactly opposite the picture of happy
associations. He turned, and beheld, with a mo-
mentary terror, succeeded by a transport of joy, the
living form of Lady Clara, who was gazing with
equal surprise at him. In the distance she had supposed Arthur to be some stranger, admitted to view
the pictures. She was painting, as when he had first
known her, but the copy was nearly completed. She
seemed more beautiful, — more interesting than ever.
Her sudden recognition evinced pleasure the most
encouraging ; so, in the impulse of the moment,
darting forward, and bending one knee to his liege
lady, the young viscount poured forth his vows of
fealty, and passionately entreated a return.

Lady Clara did not reply. It appeared as if emotion prevented speech ; at length a few large tears
slowly trickled down her cheeks, and she said, —

" Lord Stanmore, this meeting has not been
sought by either of us ; neither is to blame. Before
we parted you told me your history. I will now tell
you mine ; it will soften the refusal I am compelled
to give. It is so painful to inflict pain. I am betrothed to another. I am to be soon married to one

who possesses claims on my heart that no other can ever equal. He is blind."

"Good heavens!" exclaimed Arthur. "Then you are, indeed, lost to me."

"Oh, how well you understand me," said Lady Clara. "But," returned he, "how well, at the same time, I feel the value of all I have lost. Oh! angel of a woman, why — why have I to feel it is too late. To-day I know, for the first time in my life, what sorrow is. To-day, the 2nd of October, I am twenty-one. In bitter sorrow have I come of age."

"Do not say 'bitter,'" interposed Lady Clara, with gentleness. "There is no sting where there is no self-reproach. You were free, — you believed me free. I do not wish that my engagement and approaching marriage should sever the ties of friendship and family connection between us. Would it not interest you to hear something of my future life?"

"*Mon Dieu, non,*" exclaimed Arthur, proceeding unconsciously and rapidly in the language most familiar to him. "At all events not now; I could bear nothing now."

"Believing that you would devote a much longer time to a view of our beautiful scenery, especially round Keswick, I wrote to my brother to invite you to his cottage on Windermere, and to direct his letter to the lawyer at Keswick, where you had purposed to remain some days. I wish you to know and appreciate my brother, and I wish him to know and appreciate your venerable grandfather and yourself. No one more fitted than my brother to understand and value the laborious thirty years of Lord Charleton, for he has of late years had plenty of mental labors himself. You are aware that he has been in the ministry ever since the formation of the present cabinet."

"You mean your elder brother, the Marquis of Seaham?"

"Yes,—Hugh. He is at present in office for the colonies; but Claud is also engaged in serving his country. He is in the foreign office, and is just now under Sir Stuart Gorman, at Munich. It is possible that Claud may be sent to England this autumn, and join us for a short holiday here at the lakes. We do not remove into Cheshire till near Christmas. Now, if you are not recalled into France by duty to Lord Charleton, and can spend the Christmas at Marsden, having previously visited us here at Rockley, you will become insensibly attracted, by all you hear around you, to the service of your country."

"I do not feel in the least attracted to that service at present," sighed Arthur. "Perhaps I might, under other circumstances; but now I have no stimulus to exertion."

"Have you not that of love of country?"

"But I am not clear that England is that country.

I believe I love France much better. I *could* have loved England, — I could have loved this Woolton Court; but now I am quite prepared to hear by post that Mr. Sanderson has finally made up his mind to die here of cramp or sore throat, I shall then return to France, or more probably roam the world over."

"For what purpose?"

"For no purpose, but to forget that ever I saw you, heard you, adored you; to forget my own identity, my own existence."

"A very mistaken purpose for an intelligent and responsible being. Shall I propose for you something far better, that will make you far happier? Shall I? Shall I? *Do* say *yes*. You shall begin by calling me 'Clara,' while I will call you 'Arthur.' You shall confide your thoughts and plans to me as to a true and affectionate cousin. You shall prepare, in a subordinate office, under my brother, to rise gradually in the service of your country, till your eloquent and effective speeches shall attract your cousin, Clara, first to the ventilator of the house of commons, next to the peeresses box in the house of lords."

"What am *I* fit for?" said he, gloomily.

"That remains to be proved, not altogether by the test of your own abilities, but also by the demand that may be made of the special kind possessed by you alone. For instance, in the midst of a galaxy of talent, you alone may be found to possess a talent for finance, and the Marquis of Seaham, minister for the colonies, may have to cede you to Lord Gratmore, minister of finance, to the total disappointment of Sir Drake Bruce, of the board of trade."

Arthur could not smile, but he just said—

" And what next?"

" Some years of patient toil and investigation, and sacrifice of self to the public good; a high tone of feeling, with great urbanity of manner, and at length the Earl of Charleton will be sent for by the august lady at the head of the state, and will return with the portfolio and seals of office, to form a cabinet of his own views in Downing-street.

CHAPTER VI.

CONSOLATIONS.

THE picture-gallery at Woolton Court was visited early on the following morning by Lord Stanmore; but some workmen, removing a picture-case, and the absence of all painting apparatus, told him that his happy interviews with Lady Clara were now to be classed among the reminiscences of his minority. He felt as if the last few hours had added years to his life. Much of what had fallen from her lips he retained with respectful tenderness, and they formed subjects for deep consideration, as he wandered through the grounds that lonely day.

At dinner he asked, in as careless a tone as he could assume, at what hour Lady Clara Chamberlayne had left the house, and was informed that her ladyship and attendant had departed in a hired carriage the evening before, having given directions for the picture to be forwarded to Marsden, the family residence in Cheshire. In the evening, by the cross-country post, the letter arrived from the Marquis of Seaham, forwarded from Keswick. It contained a more than polite, — a cordial invitation to Mr. Arthur Bryce to spend as many days as his professional duties would permit at Rocksley, the "holiday cottage" on Windermere. A ray of something like consolation gleamed across the desolate heart of our hero, as he drew the implements of writing towards him, and responded gratefully to the invitation. He was convinced that the secret of his identity had not been divulged to the marquis, and therefore comprehended more fully the confidence that the brother must repose in the taste and judgment of the sister to so immediately accede to her request. There was much in this thought to soften the pain of his position.

Arthur had accepted the invitation of the marquis for the 6th October. It was then the third of the month. On the ensuing day, after devoting some time to completing the arrangement of Mr. Sanderson's papers, he rowed to the spot where he had related his history to Lady Clara, and gave a turn to his pensive regrets by taking an exact sketch of the mansion, its platform, causeway, and back-ground of mountains. On his return to the house he made two copies, one for Lady Clara, one for himself. The original, which he carefully worked up, he enclosed in a letter to Marseilles, which he endeavored to make cheerful, but his own hopes had fallen so low, respecting the re-possession of the Woolton property, that he could scarcely dwell on the topic. He preferred filling his letter with inquiries about persons and places in the city of his early happy youth; so, promising to write soon again, he was closing the envelope when the servant brought two letters with the London post-mark. He recognized the handwriting of Mr. Oldham, and he thought he could pronounce the other to be from Mr. Sanderson. Weariness and disgust filled his mind. The upper servants had informed him that day that they had no doubt of the return of the family, and he thought he might well defer opening the letters till the morrow. The still unsealed letter to Marseilles, however, and long-taught habits of attention to correspondents, urged him to read first the lawyer's, then Mr. Sanderson's, not only once, but several times; for it was difficult to awake from the passive endurance of disappointment to the actual realization of his brightest hopes. Mr. Sanderson, in a fit of antagonism against a competitor for the Hampshire property, had determined in favor of that place, to the great joy of his amiable sisters. He had therefore closed, beyond power of retraction, with Mr. Oldham for the property in Westmorland, for he had actually signed away the house and lands of Woolton Court; and the document, or rather two-fold document, was then on its way to Marseilles, to be countersigned by the hitherto nameless friend of the lawyer. When Arthur had fully comprehended the fact that his grandfather's signature was the only formality required, except that of an order on the Bank of England for a hundred and fifteen thousand pounds sterling to Mr. Sanderson, he fell on his knees with eyes and hands raised to heaven ; he then burst into tears, and kissed the ground of his home. After some time he turned his eyes on his own dull letter to Marseilles, full of forced questions, to which, in the first emotions of the announcement from London, his grandfather would find it irksome to reply. He tore it up, and still enclosing the drawing, wrote some rapid lines of congratulation, putting the important question, at what point of the route from Marseilles to Dover, and on what day, the happy meeting should take place. It was late in the night before he closed his eyes. He had not expected to sleep ; but the having written to Marseilles, added to all the other soothing influences of the evening, produced a slumber, deep and prolonged, which bore him far into the morning of the following day.

Arthur had resolved to consult the Marquis of Seaham on the expediency of continuing to bear the name of " Bryce " until the arrival of Lord Charleton. To do this it would be necessary to see the marquis in private, and briefly relate his history. The cross-country between the little private lake of Woolton and the far-famed Windermere was quite unknown to him ; he, therefore, thought of procuring a guide and two horses, in preference to taking the circuitous route by the public coach. He started on the fifth, intending to sleep at the little inn on the lake of Windermere, described to him by the guide, and present himself on the ensuing morning about ten o'clock at the residence of the marquis. All this was easily accomplished, and our hero being immediately admittēd to the private study of Lord Seaham divulged his secret, and was greeted not only by a warm-grasp of the hand, but even folded in a cousinly embrace by the celebrated statesman.

Had Arthur not seen the Marquis of Seaham in this advantageous moment, he might afterwards have been annoyed or repulsed by certain characteristics. The marquis spoke little, but he made others talk, and would suddenly pounce down from his heights of abstraction on the weak points of information or argument that had caught his attention in the circle of his guests. Again, his voracity for information, could only be equalled by the skill with which he drew it forth from the often unwilling giver. He had no compassion for that desire of repose or relaxation, which often leads public or professional men to prefer any other subjects in their leisure hours to that which is their daily labor. His brother ministers might laugh and escape from him; but not so the subordinates in office, who could scarcely risk offending him. Still less the military and naval applicant for his favor, the renowned poet, or artist, or scientific man, who found himself under the falcon-eye, and firm mental grasp of the master-spirit of the day.

5

The only but marked exception to this devouring element, was made in the society of the fair and weaker sex; the active, acquiring dominant mind, was then, for awhile, content to repose, refresh, and recreate. After a morning spent in snapping at and humiliating half-a-dozen secretaries, or terrifying out of all technical memory some candidate for his patronage, this portentous examiner of other men's wits was, in the evening circle in St. James's Square, his suburban villa, or hereditary mansion in Cheshire, the bland and courteous host, the gently-playful brother, and, as years rolled on, the tenderly approving father.

Arthur's intelligent mind watched all these phases during his sojourn on the banks of Windermere. He also submitted to be passed through the ordeal, and had come forth with the encomium, " Good head."

The first dinner and evening at Rockley Cottage gave Arthur a sample of the rest, although the guests were always changing, with the exception of himself and one or two family friends. He perceived that the brother's house was Lady Clara's home; and this, in itself, gave a charm to the visit, although they seldom conversed together. The marquis had advised him to continue the name of Bryce, until the expected letter should arrive from his grandfather, and during the interval to remain his most welcome guest at the cottage. Arthur consented, and, after taking all precautions necessary for the safe and speedy transmission of his letters, fell into the habits of those around him, as easily and happily as though he had passed his life among them. At dinner, the chief lady guest was, of course, at the right hand of the marquis, while Lady Clara, with her cavalier,— whoever he might be, — sat opposite. The table was oval, and this quartett occupied the centre of the sides, as in France, which contributed to make our hero feel at home. The chair on the left hand of the marquis, was always left vacant till a certain period of the repast; and the question, " why is this?" occupied Arthur during the first dinner without any solution until the last course, when a beautiful girl of fourteen, the only child of the marquis, came in. She bowed around with ease and grace, and gliding her right hand into the left of her father, began immediately to converse with him, or with whoever addressed her, in a bright intelligent manner, worthy of *his* daughter and the niece of Lady Clara. Our hero who, as Mr. Bryce, had to yield precedence to apparently greater people, was seated at one of the ends of the oval table, and could, therefore, see and watch at an equal advantage the aunt and the niece. For the first time since his arrival, he was aware that Lady Clara was also turning a scrutinizing glance again and again on his countenance. At length, their eyes encountering more than once, she said, smilling:

" Yes, there *is* a great resemblance as between a mother and her child."

"Mr. Bryce, said the marquis, "you will become a great favorite with Violet, if you think her like her aunt. She is her model for all female excellence, as she well may be."

"Dearest brother," said Lady Clara, "you have the wisdom, given from above, of supporting the weak, and casting the halo of your own genius on those you wish to honor."

CHAPTER VII.

ANNOUNCEMENTS.

A FORTNIGHT had elapsed since the departure of Arthur's letter to Marseilles, when the answer arrived, stating that the signature had been affixed to the papers sent by Mr. Oldham of London, bearing the full names and titles of Philip Henry Bryce Woolton, Earl of Charleton, Viscount Stanmore, Baron Woolton of Woolton, &c. Arthur was required to sign his full name and title beneath those of his grandfather. The letter also signified that Mr. Oldham would be the bearer of these papers to Woolton Court, where Arthur would sign them, retaining one copy; Mr. Sanderson would receive the other from Mr. Oldham, on the latter's return from Westmorland. The earl requested that his grandson would remain at Woolton until his return, of the date of which he would apprise him in his next letter. He thanks his dear Arthur for the sketch of the old mansion, and for his offer to meet him wherever he should appoint; but he prefers to travel alone, and to be received back to the halls of his ancestors by a welcome such as Arthur could best prepare for him.

"Lord Charleton is quite right," said the marquis, to whom Arthur imparted the contents of his letter. "After so long an exile there should be a good welcome home. We must devise something to be remembered and recorded in the archives of Woolton Court. The ladies are admirable in their suggestions on these occasions. From the time of the Crusades to the welcome back from Hyderabad and Moodkee, our fair ones have honored the brave. And is *he* not brave — is *he* not a hero who fights and conquers the weird sisters Poverty, Toil, and Exile? Come! let us consult Clara and Violet."

The dinner-table that day happened to be unusually well filled with guests; for some had been invited from the immediate neighborhood, in addition to the party in the house. The order of precedence was also a little out of the usual course. The marquis led forth the first lady present, who happened that day to be the Dowager Duchess of Peterworth; but, after the other couples had been adjudged to each other, Lady Clara, for the first time, invited the escort of the unknown Mr. Bryce, who accordingly formed one of the supreme quartett in the centre of the table. Lady Violet, at the usual time, or perhaps a little earlier, occupied the vacant seat and glided her little hand into that of her father, bowing around as usual, but looking as grave in her excitement as though a *coup d'etat* were projected, that would plunge all England into consternation.

" My friends," at length began the marquis, " I have to request your kind attention to one of the most interesting histories of moral courage that, perhaps, has ever passed under your notice. It has been said there is no romance equal to that drawn from real life; and the history I am about to relate will verify that assertion, especially as we are hoping to welcome in a few days the veteran hero of my tale in triumph back to his home."

The perfect silence that ensued enabled the marquis to proceed in the gently modulated tone suited to a private and closely approximated audience to narrate the exile and subsequent labors of the Earl of Charleton in so interesting, moving, and attractive a manner, that even Arthur, well as he knew how to appreciate all those family details, felt as if new lights and shadows were thrown over each scene described by the gifted orator. He had been prepared to be shown forth at the end as the second hero of the piece; but Lord Seaham had either deliberately changed his mind or was borne by the enthusiasm of the moment to declare the fact of his young friend's presence before the time appointed; for, just when Arthur had been won to forget where he was and all around him — just when the auditors were almost equally effected by the death-bed at Calais, the heroism of the young widow, and the birth at Dover, the speaker exclaimed — himself much excited —

" *This* is that infant, justly named God-given, Dieudonné! This is the Viscount Stanmore!"

Exclamations, congratulations followed, and every one felt so enthusiastic, that the narrative continued more in the style of Pinnock's Catechisms than with any continuous flow. The task of responding to questions and cross-questions fell to our hero, whilst the marquis leaned back in his chair, smiling, complacently, and tasting the marmalade recommended by Violet. After the little stir of pleasure excitement was passed, Viscount Stanmore arose to return thanks to the company in general, and to the Marquis of Seaham in particular. Arthur was naturally eloquent and his action graceful. He had been educated in a country where example had taught him the true politeness that is born of charity and appreciation of others, and this quick perception of their feelings, with a generous confidence in a kindly return, made him ever self-possessed, polite, and elegantly gay. His chief thanks were given to the marquis, with a just tribute to the heart and head of their most noble host; and Violet at the close, evinced her gratitude by exclaiming —

" Oh! papa, do you not think Lord Stanmore will make very eloquent speeches in Parliament? He will be a great man some day, *I* think!"

" There again, cousin Arthur," said Lady Clara

aside to Lord Stanmore, " you perceive that your future career is foreseen by Violet as by myself."

" Marquis ! " cried the dowager duchess, " permit me to move the resolution that we do all adjourn together to the drawing-room. I have something in my mind that will make a final scene of the most vivid interest."

All arose, and in French style left the dining-room in the same procession with which they had entered, and formed a circle in the drawing-room, with her grace in the centre."

"Now, most noble Marquis of Seaham," said she, " you, who are toiling for the interests of your country, yet are wise enough to be aware that well-ordered charity begins at home, — I appeal to that zeal, that wisdom, that charity, to enact that on this twenty-second day of October, in the year of grace 1853, the Viscount Stanmore, future Earl of Charleton, shall, in your presence, and that of this goodly company, be betrothed to the Lady Violet Chamberlayne, your only child, and heiress to this very property of Rockley, on the Lake of Windermere !"

Fortunately for our hero, he did not lose his presence of mind. What Frenchman ever does? He had supposed the intention of the duchess, and whispered to Lady Clara — " Do you wish it?"

The reply was, " I do," and he was just in time to step forward to the duchess, call her his " good angel," and trust that her mediation in his favor would be crowned with success.

" Success ! " cried she.   " Yes, to be sure, success !   I never made a bad match for myself or any one.   Now, you, Lord Stanmore, are accustomed in France to marriages arranged by friends, and you are wisely determined to consent to the same.   You, therefore, deserve to have a good wife.   Lady Violet, you will make a good wife if you get the right man — and this is the right man, Dieudonné, given by God.   Marquis, this is a betrothal only — not a marriage.   So you must consent that the old fairy or the good angel shall produce the rings.   Here, Arthur, Viscount Stanmore, take this for the moment ; and you, Lady Violet Chamberlayne, hold this one.   Now, marquis, is not this the proper winding up ? "

" Violet ? " said the father.

"Papa, I cannot tell yet.   I do not know whether Lord Stanmore really —— "

But Arthur dropped on one knee, with gentle violence exchanged the rings, and now pressed the little jeweled hand to his lips.   Violet blushed, then turned so pale that her father came to her relief, saying —

" Duchess, the curtain may drop ; I should conclude, and the dramatis personæ — as their final act — seek the repose they require."

CHAPTER VIII.

On the following morning, after an early breakfast *tête-a-tête* with his host, our hero returned to Woolton Court. He had entreated with so much earnestness and truth to be permitted to consider the exchange of rings as binding on himself, while he left the Lady Violet free, that the marquis consented, and Arthur returned full of thought to his home. Gazing on the diamond ring, which just fitted the little finger of his right hand, his mind first turned to Lady Clara, and he ejaculated, "*She* wishes it." Then he thought of the young and slender flowret, that seemed almost too precocious to live.

"Can all things glide on so smoothly?" considered he. "Can my life continue so to differ from that of my grandfather and father? Does not all this prosperity include immense responsibility?"

On entering the Court of Woolton, Lord Stanmore turned his thoughts exclusively on the preparation to be made for the joyful event of his grandfather's return. The marquis had truly remarked that the fair sex are good suggesters on these occa-

sions; and Arthur, recalling all the aunt and niece
had said, resolved to carry out their wishes, partly
to prove his gallantry, partly because he really admired their taste.   He retired to the library to make
notes of all he wished to order, after which he rang,
and desired that workmen might be sent for to receive orders for certain preparations to be made for
a grand festival, to take place, within a fortnight, at
Woolton Court.

" Are you aware," said he to the head servant,
" whether any one in the village remembers the old
family?   Those who lived here fifty years ago?   The
Earls of Charleton?

" Yes, sir — I mean my lord.   We all know who
you really are, Mr. Bryce.   You are the grandson
of the present earl, who is coming back through
France, overland from India, prodigious rich, having
been away fifty years.   I beg pardon, my lord, but
I should be much obliged if you would write down
your title here on this card."

Arthur did so, and after arranging to accept all
the servants who desired it, he repeated his request
to see some aged person from the village, who could
remember the old times in Woolton Court.

" There are two old men, great friends, my lord,
who are fond of remembering the great days here.
They have always kept much together, talking over
the old family.   One used to be the gardener, the
other a house carpenter, always employed about the

odd jobs, and seems quite wound up in the family secrets. The secrets you know, Mr. Bryce, I mean my lord, the mystery, you understand — those queer sounds at night — that have sent every other family away. I suppose we shall not hear them now. Well to return to these two old men, I think they have their own notions about that part of Woolton Court. Permit me to refer to the card. Yes, Viscount Stanmore, you'll judge for yourself. I'll step down to the village myself. Seeing one is seeing both. They'll be sure to come up together whenever you please to mention; this evening or to-morrow morning. Which shall I say, my lord?"

Arthur had fallen into a fit of musing, caused by the butler's opening comments on the two old villagers, and he could not be roused to give an answer to the question, so the volunteer quietly withdrew to fetch the old friends from the village, and the solitary musings continued somewhat in the following mode —

"What can all this mean? How totally I had forgotten this plot, this trick. How disgraceful to appear mixed up or even to profit by this now obvious scheme of these old retainers to keep the house for the old family. Had that sagacious Miss Sanderson any suspicions? Yes, she evidently had. I remember it all now. But I was not personally implicated. To her I was simply Mr. Bryce the lawyer. Yet when she knows the whole, or rather the surface

6 .

of things, what will she not suspect? This thing is certain, that for my own honor's sake, I am bound to probe the matter to the bottom, with caution, however, and with some merciful feeling for the poor old souls, who have, doubtless, thought themselves justified in all they have done."

In about an hour, Grainger, the butler, returned, introducing the two old villagers as James Turner and Thomas Jenkins, whose countenances gave a favorable impression of their general candor and honesty, especially that of the former gardener, James Turner. But the sturdy retainers seemed to require more substantial evidence than they had yet obtained that the noble looking youth before them was really the heir of Woolton Court house and lands.

" Why, sir," said one, " if you be the grandson of the earl, you ought to be the honorable Arthur Woolton, and not call yourself Viscount Stanmore, which title belongs to the son of the earl, the eldest son only. Ah, I knows all about these matters."

" My father, alas! is dead," said Lord Stanmore; " I am his only child, and he was the only surviving child of my grandfather; I am given to console the long years of sorrow and adversity of the Earl of Charleton, therefore did he name me Godgiven Dieudonné."

" How old were you at the time he left this house?"

" I was just the earl's own age," replied Turner,

"and my friend Jenkins two years younger. We were therefore two-and-twenty,—that is, I was, and he twenty. We therefore remember all and everything most perfectly, more particularly that we always loved the young earl, both for himself and his father's sake, and for his great misfortunes; above all, that of having so extravagant and careless a guardian in his uncle, the honorable or dishonorable Gilbert Woolton."

"He was a pleasant gentleman, though," interposed Jenkins, the carpenter, "and a wonderful taste for improvements and decorations and elegancies had he, this Mr. Gilbert; a most finished-up nobleman, both for beauty and manners. He broke hearts in this neighborhood, as he broke the county bank, all in the same bowing, pleasant way, till he could be favored no longer by any one, and the bailiffs were so close upon him, that he and I had to change coats and hats, and he went to my saw-pit, quite easy like, while I ran, on purpose, in full view of the bailiffs, into the woods by the lake. I threw the coat and the hat into the water at the first opportunity, climbed up into a tree, and at night came down, and went a round-about way to our place of meeting, after getting all he wanted at the house, and seeing by the window the crowd by the lake dragging the water for his body. He laughed in his pleasant way at it all, and went up to London, and then to America, by the help and contrivance of friends. He was still young,—not more than thirty-six, for there was a great difference between the sons of the two marriages of the old earl of all."

" But there was another and younger uncle of my grandfather," said Lord Stanmore. " You do not mention him. What became of him?"

The two villagers looked at each other; at last Turner said, with some hesitation, —

" The younger brother died."

" Well, I conclude he died," observed Lord Stanmore, " or he must now be past eighty, even allowing for the great difference of age between my great grandfather and his younger brothers. Tell me something of Uncle Tristam?"

" He did not go to America, as was generally supposed," said Jenkins; but Turner gave him a nudge, and added, — " Mr. Grainger says that you have orders, sir, for great doings here to welcome back the earl. I humbly beg to say that we shall be proud to help in any way that lies in our power."

" The best way, the only way in which you can possibly assist, at your time of life," said Lord Stanmore, " is by recalling to mind and informing me of the precise way in which the corridors and rooms lay at the time of my grandfather's departure. He has himself described to me much of the interior disposition of the house. I have recognized his own suite of rooms. I have slept in his bed-room; but I am stopped at the entrance of a narrow corridor in that suite by a closet, an artificial, or rather a modern closet. The entrance to the chapel below is also closed, but only closed; it will be easily opened by proper workmen, and that will be our first care. I wish the chapel to be opened to-morrow."

Lord Stanmore watched the countenances of the two old men as he addressed them, and perceived they were startled by the mention of the little blocked-up passage ; while they recovered themselves at the order given to open the chapel, and eagerly proposed to investigate it at the moment. To this Lord Stanmore agreed, being convinced that the time had not yet arrived for obtaining their confidence, and inwardly resolved to open the corridor by other means than theirs.

On the following morning, while Lord Stanmore was at breakfast, the village veterans arrived with younger workmen, and awaited his good pleasure in the hall. Before giving orders to open the great entrance to the chapel, he sent for the butler, and inquired whether it was there Mr. Sanderson had left his own furniture, to be removed at a future period.

"Oh, no, my lord," replied the butler; "the inventory was verified by Mr. Sanderson's agent, and all that furniture removed while you was stopping at the Marquis of Seaham's."

"Then let the workmen open the chapel directly, but carefully," said Lord Stanmore, silently recalling to mind the fact of the chapel having been so com-

6*

pletely closed by the late owners of the place. The slender wall of masonry was soon demolished that had filled up the depth of the ancient wall beyond the thick oaken doors. The men had worked carefully; the doors would require no more than cleaning and polishing; they were locked, but that difficulty had been provided against, and in a few instants Lord Stanmore was within, and, at his request, alone within the sacred spot. All was in good repair, though faded, and he looked around with the deepest interest. He heard the retreating footsteps of the workpeople, and closing the door, knelt at the foot of the long-deserted altar.

"The remains of my forefathers lie in the vaults beneath," thought he, "and the hidden Lord of glory has, in the old days, blest this shrine. Here must be the culminating point of welcome to the long-exiled lord of Woolton Court!"

The daylight was employed in viewing the various parts of the premises, and giving orders for the approaching fête. But these preparations for the joyful return of the Earl of Charleton, did not prevent Lord Stanmore from writing to Miss Sanderson an account, not only of the progress made towards a discovery of the nocturnal sounds, but also of the motives of honor that bound him to unravel a plot of too exaggerated a devotion for the ancient possessors of Woolton Court. In the evening, a letter was written to the Marquis of Seaham, giving the whole confidence, and intreating it in return, on the subject of the mysterious music, or plaint, in the southwest angle of Woolton Court; mentioning also the blocked-up corridor, and the two old villagers with their traditions. In a few days the answer arrived, and was as follows:

"My dear lord, the mysteries of Udolpho are revived in those of Woolton Court. I have listened to their legends from my boyhood. Of course, I have never heard nor seen anything myself, having visited the mansion by daylight only, in gay company, talking and laughing enough to scare away any ghost, even that of Tristam Woolton, your collateral ancestor, who is said to haunt the house. To be serious, I uphold your resolve to probe the matter to the bottom, with the prudence, firmness, and sagacity, so truly your own. Should you wish for a confidential companion at midnight, that flesh and blood may sympathize in your encounters with restless spirits, or designing mortals, ride over here and I will return with you on the following day. I am at liberty this week, but cannot promise beyond. Yours faithfully,

SEAHAM."

Our hero accepted this proposal most gladly, and the two friends found themselves on the last day of October comfortably seated by a blazing fire in the library at Woolton Court, discussing every possible topic of interest, except the projected onslaught at midnight on the secrets of the south-west corner of the mansion.

CHAPTER IX.

MORE MYSTERIOUS SECRETS.

THE marquis enjoyed his *tête-a-tête* evening extremely; the more so that he was secure from all intrusion. He had even forbidden that any letters should be forwarded from Rockley; and now, extending his limbs before the genial blaze, he fully entered into his favorite pastime of drawing largely on the mental funds of his companion. Arthur could supply abundantly and freely, so the night insensibly advanced, and wine was brought, and servants retired for the night, and Bouchier, the marquis' valet, was informed that his services would be dispensed with. This with any other but the marquis might have excited some curiosity; but the valet was accustomed to his lord's vigils, and on this occasion glided into the room with some quires of paper and other requisites for despatches, also with night-slippers and scent-bottle. It was now considerably past eleven o'clock: in a short time every domestic in the house would be asleep, and the marquis observed that it was full time to withdraw his thoughts from the insurrection in New Zealand to affairs at home.

" Are we to use these pretty little weapons ?" demanded he, taking up one of the pair of pocket-pistols which lay already loaded on the chimney-piece.

" No," replied Arthur, " I keep these by me on the defensive against house-breakers, or other assailants; but I think a good cudgelling is all we need inflict to-night on the musicians of the south-west wing."

" Are you certain that the entrance by the little passage has been effected without causing suspicion ? "

" I think so. I took care to throw that clearance on Grainger, without entering into that part of the house myself. I told him to enable me to assure Lord Charleton in my letter of this evening that his suite of rooms was restored to what he remembered them. Grainger informed me, just before we sat down to dinner, that the closet had been cleared away, and the rubbish removed by the workmen, adding that it was by that time getting too dark for any woman alone, or in company, to be prevailed on to undertake the final purification of the corridor. But I should not dislike having caused a little alarm, because then you will hear the sounds."

" Come, then," said the marquis, " I will follow you in silence, with this good cane, holding my taper in the left hand."

" Stay, my lord," said Arthur, " a taper is soon

blown out by a concealed adversary. My French
habits have fortunately provided me with a little
lamp; the glass globe will protect the flame.   One
will suffice for both.   I will precede you, as in duty
bound."

Accordingly the two friends left the library by a
door which communicated with stairs leading to the
suite of rooms above, at the northwest end of the
mansion, one of which was occupied by the marquis.
Thence they passed through galleries and corridors,
by the top of the great staircase, to the one principal
communication with the southwest end of the dwelling. They had scarcely closed the double-baized door
which divided this large passage from the centre of
the house, when both stopped and looked significantly
at each other, then proceeded with still greater caution, while the soft tremulous sounds became more
and more distinct, to the great satisfaction of Lord
Stanmore, and the excited wonderment of his visitor.
They soon stood at the entrance, so long concealed,
of the little private passage belonging to the suite of
rooms once occupied by the lord of the mansion, and
with redoubled interest penetrated through it to the
actual region of the mysterious plaint, — a room, or
loft, immediately above the mortuary chamber, both
being at the back of the sanctuary of the chapel.
The two friends cast searching glances around, while
the sweet, melancholy sounds wailed across them, as
they stood amazed. Suddenly their eyes fell on the

same object, and they simultaneously grasped each other's hand. It was a long coffin, placed on low tressels, uncovered by any pall, and without inscription. Arthur knelt by the side, and commenced some prayers for the dead, amid the sympathetic strains, while the marquis, seizing the lamp, continued the investigation of every part of the room with still greater minuteness. The window was placed beyond his reach; a ladder or steps would be needed, which could only be brought by the servants in the full daylight. There was also a shallow closet with shelves. On one of these was a portfolio leaning against the back of the closet, and in good preservation. As Arthur rose from his knees the marquis made a sign for him to take possession of what might prove a clue to the mysteries of the place. They then ascertained that this room had once been used as a sort of tribune, or private gallery to the chapel, in case of indisposition or late rising; for a window-shutter, fastened with nails, was on the chapel side. Here, for the time, terminated their discoveries, and in a few minutes the Marquis of Seaham and Lord Stanmore were stirring the fire in the library, and pledging each other in a glass of Madeira.

They had seemed to have been long away; but it was scarcely one o'clock in the morning. Time is spun out when much is done and felt, as objects at various intervals in a landscape increase the prospective distance.

"Oh! no, I cannot yet go to bed," replied the marquis to an offer from Arthur to that effect. "We will lay our heads down in an hour from this time. Much can be done in an hour. That coffin must contain the remains of — who?"

"My great-grand uncle, Tristam Woolton," said Arthur.

"Exactly so. I had arrived at the same conclusion. The body was never found in the lake. It was suspected that he never went to America, but kept himself concealed on the old premises. What we have seen to-night corroborates all this."

Arthur then related the carpenter's narrative, and found that the confusion made in the history of the two brothers had led to the belief that Tristam had drowned himself in the lake, and that his restless spirit haunted the house.

"There are, doubtless, two living witnesses in the gardener and carpenter, to prove that the body of Uncle Tristam lies in that coffin," observed Lord Stanmore, "and thus free his memory from the stigma of suicide. Ah! what a victim he must have been to the dominant spirit and unprincipled mind of his brother Gilbert. Let us look into the portfolio." But the contents, although interesting, disappointed Lord Stanmore with respect to the personal history of his collateral ancestor. There were the long pedigrees and alliances of the Wooltons, and several portraits in water-colors and pencil.

One very beautifully executed of the two brothers, Gilbert and Tristam : one in the arms and the other leaning on the knee of their young mother, the second wife of the seventh Earl of Charleton.

"Can anything be more sad and affecting," said the marquis, "than to watch the innocent faces of children who are destined to break the hearts or ruin the fortunes of their families?"

"They are not destined to do this," objected Arthur.

"Let the word pass for to-night," continued the marquis. "Look at that villain Gilbert. What an eye! what a mouth! And so these old men remember him, with all this seductive beauty, and with the additional curse given him of expensive tastes without principle of restraint — I will not say without *power* of restraint, for fear of a second amendment from the noble lord opposite, on my proposition in favor of fatalism."

"He was the Benjamin of his father's old age, I conclude," said Arthur; "or, more correctly, the Joseph; and Tristam the Benjamin. With an aged father and a young mother, these beautiful boys were spoiled. Gilbert was the more mischievous, because he had more mental power : he must have overawed and governed the weaker Tristam."

"Who is this, think you?" said the marquis, turning over another and equally well executed portrait. "This is evidently by the same artist; and as it
7

represents a fine youth, while the others are young children, it must be their elder brother by the first marriage; your great-grandfather, the eighth Earl of Charleton."

"Yes," said Arthur, "I recognize the features, although the picture my grandfather took abroad with him is of a man advanced in life. We must be thankful that the loving and confiding elder brother died ignorant of the conduct of the younger. How placid is that brow, how serene the smile!"

"Here we differ," observed the marquis; "better that the brow be knit and furrowed, and the mouth compressed with grief and indignation, than that he should have left so fatal a will."

"Ah, yes, you are right," said Arthur; "we do not differ. Had my great-grandfather known the truth in time to have altered his will in favor of other guardians to his heir, how smoothly all would have glided on at Woolton Court. However," added he, gayly," it is perhaps by great crimes — certainly by great misfortunes — that great virtues are brought to light. Therefore I will regret nothing that has made the present Earl of Charleton what he is. All I have to pray for is, that prosperity may not spoil his heir."

"We have had one good damper to-night to the pride of success," observed the marquis, smiling. "We cannot make out this ghostly music."

"But we will to-morrow — or rather to-day, by

sunlight," replied Lord Stanmore. "Let us now go to rest, and rise with that in view before your ride back to Rockley."

"Not *my* ride back, but *our* ride back," said the marquis. "Are you not to return with me?"

"Ah, no; my duty lies here. I am hoping to welcome here all the dear inmates of Rockley, to assist me in fitly receiving the long absent lord of Woolton. . Will you promise me that it shall be so arranged. Will you, dear marquis, select the suites of rooms for the ladies Clara and Violet?"

"We will be here. We will do all in our power to show respect and honor where it is so due " replied Lord Seaham; "but I decline selecting any suites of rooms, having perfect reliance on the good taste of our host."

It was late in the forenoon before the friends again met; and when they did so, and coolly talked the matter over, they each felt a delicacy in introducing servants and workmen into a room where lay the body of the unfortunate Tristam. It was agreed to lock the room until the arrival of the Earl of Charleton.

The next few days were agreeably occupied in giving a hospitable welcome to that true friend of the Wooltons, Mr. Oldham, and in signing the documents mentioned in the letter of the Earl of Charleton.

CHAPTER X.

THE WELCOME HOME.

WHILE many interesting preparations occupied the mind of the heir of Woolton, the venerable merchant of Marseilles, having carefully terminated all his worldly affairs in that city, was returning thanks to Heaven for having blessed his many years of toil, and opened a bright path for his return to his native land. His charities had always been commensurate with his increasing wealth; and now, in farewell, he left to each public institute a two-fold donation, and still a larger bequest to the fund for " those who had known better days." This class of deserving persons had, in attracting his especial sympathy, partaken the most largely of his charity.

After a farewell visit to the bishop, and a parting dinner to his late brother merchants of the city, the long-exiled Englishman bent his steps, on the eve of his departure from Marseilles, to the shrine of Notre Dame de la Garde. Besides rich benefactions, he now bore a votive offering in the form of the seal with which, during thirty years, he had secured all his mercantile correspondence. The duplicate of this seal he intended to take with him to England, as a remembrance of his labors, and of God's blessing on them. It was a beautiful southern evening, that 28th of October, 1853. Even on the heights, where stood the chapel, the gentlest of zephyrs played. Vessels of every size lay on the calm azure of the lake-like sea: the sunset glow tinting the white sails pink, and the brown sails a still warmer hue. One of these vessels, just entering the port, had been his; and he smiled as he watched it, saying, "He maketh their corn and wine and oil to increase." He had often ascended during his adversity to the friendly beacon of Our Lady de la Garde, and had gained strength at that once poor and humble altar. Now, like himself, the chapel had become enriched, and a band of holy missionaries ministered within its strengthened and decorated walls. The devout merchant had aided in this, as in most other good works in the city of Marseilles, and with thankful heart descended the slopes, and wended his solitary way to the hotel, there to await the hour of departure. He had already visited the tomb, in the cathedral, of his daughter-in-law, the mother of Arthur, for whom he had ever felt a strong and justly deserved parental affection and esteem.

The next hour of solitary emotion was spent in the church at Caen, by the vault where lay his wife and her parents, with his infant children, recalling those first years of exile, when domestic affections and congenial friends had lulled him into an indolently happy life, forgetful of past or future. Passing thence to Calais, he had to unite action to prayer. Twenty-one years had passed since he had laid his only son in the grave, but he had long resolved to raise the coffin, and bear it with him to the vaults of his ancestral home. As this intention had been previously signified to the authorities, and the exact date adhered to, Lord Charleton found all in readiness. He went on board in the early morning of the 6th of November, the body of the late viscount having been placed in its allotted cabin during the night. The passage was calm and rapid, and the living and the dead proceeded to London, and thence to Lancaster with the same speed. Here, by previous arrangement, in the mortuary chapel of the Catholic burying-ground, the body was to remain until sent for from Woolton Court. From this town the earl travelled on, accompanied solely by his faithful personal attendant, Monsieur Julien.

" They that sow in tears shall reap in joy. Going they went and wept, casting their seed; but returning they shall come with joy, bearing their sheaves."

These were the joyful words of the chorus, that, borne on a favorable wind, were at first faintly distinguishable, then heard in accents loud and full, as a carriage and four at full speed, brought the long-exiled Earl of Charleton to his home, on the 8th of

November, 1853. The avenue, and still more, the old gateway, with open portals, was in a blaze of light; and as the earl passed into the court, and was folded in the embrace of his grandson, the cords of an illuminated balloon were cut, and the globe of light, ascending high in air, gave notice, far and near, of this auspicious return. Through the hall and great corridor to the chapel, a line of guests on either side strewed flowers. The chorus from the outer court was now succeeded by the strains of the organ, with voices singing from the eightieth psalm—

"How lovely are Thy tabernacles, Oh, Lord of Hosts! my soul longeth and fainteth for the courts of the Lord. For better is one day in Thy courts above thousands. Oh, Lord of Hosts! blessed is the man that trusteth in Thee."

Then followed the function - of the benediction, during which the suppressed emotion of the two chief assistants found relief, unseen by mortal eye. The psalm of thanksgiving closed the service:— "Oh! praise the Lord all ye nations: praise Him all ye people, for his mercy is confirmed upon us, and the truth of the Lord remaineth forever." Lord Charleton then leaning on the arm of his grandson, left the chapel, followed by all the congregation, and returning to the hall, ascended the great staircase to the picture gallery, where was spread the banquet. All had been previously arranged with the minutest attention to order and precedence; so that, on standing at the head of the first table, while the chaplain gave thanks and blessed the viands, the earl found himself in the midst of friends. On his right hand was one ever kindly remembered — the dowager Duchess of Peterworth, supported by the Marquis of Seaham, his distant relation, and the son of early playmates. On his left Lady Clara Chamberlayne, with Lord Stanmore and Lady Violet. The *vis-a-vis* to Lady Violet, next to the Marquis of Seaham, was the newly-inaugurated family chaplain. Other families of the neighborhood followed, and " below the salt" were seated the delighted tenants of the estate. The banquet table sparkled with precious metal, cut glass, and flowers, nor were the substantial parts omitted. The various wines, also, " gladdening the heart of man," were successful in their accredited use, and very soon, to the silent grasp of the hand, and short sentences at intervals of compliment or emotion, succeeded " the feast of reason and the flow of soul." The band of music took the hint. From the stirring overture and triumphant march, the succeeding airs were softened to a tone the most subordinate. At length, at a signal, the music ceased, and the Earl of Charleton thus addressed his guests : —

" My friends, I thank you for your cordial welcome home, and in my turn I most cordially welcome you all to Woolton Court. Joy is social ; it expands first to the Almighty bestower of all good, and then seeks the sympathy of man. If the woman in the Gospel, on finding the lost piece of money, calls around her the neighbors to rejoice, much more should *he* do so, who, having lost the inheritance of his fathers, has now regained it. But I bid you not only to rejoice and give thanks with me, but also to bear witness that house and lands thus recovered are considered by me, their earthly owner, as doubly held in trust for the service of the Divine Giver."

Lord Charleton did not look on himself as an orator, but many a one might have learned of him the rare and happy art of expressing briefly what he felt strongly, and of leaving his subject before it had left him, or, in other words, knowing where to stop. To the acclamations and health drinking, which, especially at the further end of the tables, was most inspiringly vivacious, other speeches succeeded. The marquis, as before at his own house, gave the history of the earl in exile; and if Arthur had then admired the eloquence of the speaker, and at length had been carried from the actual scene to those described, his enjoyment, on the present occasion, was fully equal in watching the effect produced on others; for the marquis, doubly inspired by the presence both of grandsire and heir, surpassed himself. Lord Charleton was deeply affected, and at the conclusion, when his grandson arose to return thanks, in a self-possessed, manly, and heartfelt tribute to both the orator and the subject of his praise, he felt that earth could give no more.

Two other short and effective speeches followed —
one from Squire Gelliott, a warm-hearted neighbor,
who desired to represent the gentry of the county,
the other from the reverend chaplain, whose speech
concluded by returning thanks to Heaven, during
which all the company rose, the music recommenced,
and by a private door at the top of the banquet gallery the guests at the high table passed, with their
hosts, to the drawing-rooms.

CHAPTER XI.

PAST AND FUTURE.

"How delicious is this calm," said the marquis to Lord Stanmore, as they stood together in the centre drawing-room; "one is the more aware of it from the distant hum of enjoyment of the crowd on the terrace, and in the scarcely perceptible movement of the more refined company in the rooms above."

As the marquis spoke, his eye fell on one of the chief objects in that centre room, a beautiful harp that stood beside a pianoforte, of the most approved modern construction. This tribute to the expected presence of Lady Violet did not pass unnoticed by the gratified father.

"I do not remember that a harp entered into our programme, made at Rockley, for the fête at Woolton Court," observed he, smiling.

"But an appendix was added during my ride home," returned Lord Stanmore, in the same strain, "and perhaps the Lady Violet will ascertain how the instrument has borne the journey on springs from London."

"Shall it be to-night or to-morrow, Violet?" asked the father.

"To-morrow, papa. Oh, papa, is it not a pity to disregard all that Lord Stanmore is doing to honor his grandfather? *We* never thought of an illuminated vessel on the lake. And those beautiful fire-works? Lord Charleton is standing at a window in the next room with the duchess; so is aunt Clara. Do come, papa, to this window here with me."

"Where did you learn the secret of that magic ship?" inquired the marquis, as they moved towards a vacant window.

"Where I learned many things, nautical and scientific," replied Lord Stanmore, "on the Ligurian coast. It was not, however, at Marseilles, but before the little port of Nice that I first saw and admired an illuminated vessel."

Seeing that Lady Violet was fully engaging her father's attention to the really attractive scene, which a dark but fine night showed off to great advantage, Lord Stanmore now passed to the first drawing-room, at one window of which were stationed his grandfather and his old friend the Duchess of Peter-worth, and at the other Lady Clara Chamberlayne. In the vacant part of this last-mentioned window our hero planted himself in silence. Some instants passed before he said:

"You are thinking of one far away?"

"I am," was the reply.

"Do you wish him to be here?"

"Not at this moment, although he would, as he

always does, enjoy our description of what is beautiful; but I should like him to have heard the speeches at the banquet."

"Ah, true; but you will soon relate them to him; and they will gain in eloquence and in interest by passing those lips."

"They will be transmitted to him by my pen."

"Your pen! and by whom read?"

"By his reader, a young man who is devoted to him, and who reads remarkably well. It will not be his fault if these speeches fail in interest."

"And so all your correspondence has to pass under the eyes of this third person; but of course it could not be otherwise. When do you expect to meet?"

"Immediately on leaving the lakes, which is, I believe, fixed to be to-morrow week. We then go direct into Cheshire. My brother will be obliged to make short visits to London, during the interval before Christmas; but at Christmas we shall, please God, be a large and happy party at Marsden."

"Shall you still be Lady Clara Chamberlayne?"

"I believe not."

A long pause ensued. At length Lord Stanmore said, with emotion:

"You proposed once, in this house, to tell me the history—your history—in return for one I related to you on the lake. I could not then bear it. I will endeavor now to think only of your happiness. I

·have never inquired the name even of the man who, notwithstanding his physical deprivation, I consider to be the happiest on earth."

" Sir Henry Moreland *is* a happy man," said Lady Clara; " not because he is soon to marry the woman of his choice, but because he has, in many difficult circumstances, done his duty both to God and man; because he receives his calamity as the one privation, amid many blessings, decreed for him by an almighty, all-wise, and loving Father; and because he knows, in true faith, that a sure reward is in store for him; he knows that 'eye hath not seen what God has prepared for those who love Him;'—far beyond," continued Lady Clara, " far beyond even the beautiful scene of to-night, in which there is so much of the mysterious blended with the beautiful that I have been greatly delighted. And now, my cousin Arthur," added she, turning more fully towards him, " let me assure you, that although at the moment you asked me the question I was really thinking of Sir Henry, yet, before and since, I have thought of those around me, and more especially of yourself. You do not know,—you do not believe in the affectionate interest I take in you."

" Oh, yes, as your future nephew. As the good young man who is to do all you tell him to do; whose life is to be portioned out by a set of duties. At one-and-twenty I cannot feel much disposed to a life full of mere dull duties."

"The duties of life *are* life," observed Lady Clara. "for what is life without them. You are describing duty as a dull, monotonous thing, but your practice disproves your theory; for your duty was to welcome back your grandfather, and instead of feeling and making him and others perceive it to be a dull affair, can anything have been more joyous?"

At this moment the closing beauty of the fireworks arose in the form of the nosegay, well known, but always beautiful; and when at length the spectators turned from the windows, the conversation became more general. The venerable earl looked at each of the group with silent interest, especially on the young and lovely Violet. It was apparent that he had approved and assented to the betrothal between the youthful pair.

One anxiety had troubled the Marquis of Seaham, which he had wished to impart to Lord Stanmore before the earl should retire to his apartments; yet, as is often the case, it' had escaped his memory while they were alone together. He shuddered at the idea of the effect that might be. produced on the mind of the long-exiled lord of the mansion should the mysterious music recommence its wail. It was true that both he and Lord Stanmore had become convinced that the contrivers of the plot were friendly to the old family; yet the uneasiness continued, and he resolved to make the opportunity that he had permitted to escape him. Hitherto the only servants who had entered the drawing-rooms had been the butler, Grainger, and the earl's own valet; but now, just when the marquis had crossed the room to draw away Arthur to a private conference, two footmen entered in the heavy and gorgeous livery of the Wooltons, without bearing refreshments, or any apparent motive for their presence. They advanced together with great formality and respect, till they found themselves directly opposite Lord Charleton, who was seated in an arm-chair near a sofa, on which sat the Duchess of Peterworth and the two other ladies.

" Earl of Charleton," commenced a voice that Arthur recognized to be that of the old gardener, " I first wore this here livery fifty-two years ago, being then eighteen years of age, and I have kept it in a box under my bed all these years, and it has served as a pattern for all the rest to be in order on this state occasion. I could not have got into it all the years of my hearty manhood; but now, at seventy, I've shrunk back, and it fits me very well; don't it ma'am ? "

" Incomparably well," cried the duchess, quite delighted.

" Now here is my friend, Tom Jenkins, that's only two years younger than me and the earl; he has been as faithful as me to the old times, and we remembers all the afflictions of the young earl, as you was then, my lord, and we hopes you remembers us, the gardener's son, Jim, and the carpenter's son, Tom, that used to be proud to row you on the lake, and take letters for you to that pretty, grand lady, who lived at Eagle's Crag; and when you had to go off with the old lawyer, Oldham, we took your horses to meet you at the turn of the road up to Eagle's Crag, and there you was, not seeing us, nor minding the danger of stopping there; and there was the pretty young lady not heeding us neither, in her grief; and says she, 'You're my first love,' says she, 'and if they part us for ever, I'll never forget you, Charleton,' says she; and then we two makes a noise, and off she flies, and we hurries you off to the chaise waiting with Mr. Oldham, the old 'un. And all these long years we two helped with our contrivances that no other family should stop for long here at Woolton Court. We'll tell you all about that, my lord, another day. What we come for, now, is to beg while we live we may come and go freely from our little cottages to the servants' hall, here, and on great days may do, as we used to do and have done to-day, wear the state livery of the Earls of Charleton, and wait on the company."

"That you shall freely do, my old and faithful friends," said the earl. "I remember you both perfectly, and the incidents to which you allude as perfectly. The only part I do not comprehend is that you have assisted, it appears, to keep the lawful purchasers of this place from the enjoyment of their property."

"Come, my good man," said the marquis, advancing, "give us your word that the magic music shall cease from this time."

"As far as I have the power it shall," replied James Turner; "for it has answered its purpose."

"And you, too, Mr. Carpenter," continued Lord Seaham, "give your promise, also, that the noble earl may enjoy a good eight hours sleep, after the excitement and fatigue of this propitious day."

"I makes the same promise as my friend," replied Jenkins, "that, as far as lies in my power, the house will be still to-night."

As soon as the two old men had quitted the room, the duchess arose from the sofa, and said, —

"My dear friends, on the last occasion of our meeting in a happy group, I fulfilled my promise to wind up by a final scene that should interest you all. That scene was a betrothal. On this momentous day, I propose winding up by a public confession, that shall strengthen that betrothal. I am, or rather was, that imprudent girl who loved not wisely, but too well; who made promises she was forced to break. At sixty-five I may own my first preference for a man now seventy. So, my dears, you see him in the hero of this fête. The Earl of Charleton is he; and if I have been bound by other ties to forget him during the greater part of my life, I am now, in my old age, at full liberty to love him as much as I please, and his son's son, till time shall be no more."

As the duchess paused, Lord Charleton raised her hand to his lips, saying, —

"Ever the same!"

CHAPTER XII.

THE BALL.

At how late an hour the several breakfasts were
served to the guests, on the second day of the festival
at Woolton Court, has not transpired. The chief
point of interest was to be the ball; and although
there was riding and driving, and walking and boating, not to mention luncheon and dinner, all was
made subservient to the approaching night.

"I expected that Stanmore would open the ball
with Violet," said Lord Seaham to the duchess;
"but after the disclosures of last night, perhaps,
as you were once the finest dancer of your day, and
Lord Charleton has declared you to be 'ever the
same,' he will solicit your hand for a polonaise."

"Lord Charleton has never done a ridiculous
thing yet," replied the duchess; "and God forbid
I should tempt him to forget the dignity of his age
and mine."

"But I only suggested a polonaise," continued the
marquis. "Claude will tell you of the German courts,
where grand dukes and even emperors of the age of
the noble earl lead forth the lady whom they wish to

honor. The polonaise is only walking gracefully to a measured strain."

"They had better do so by deputy," returned the duchess; " and my substitute is your own graceful Violet, the future lady of Woolton Court. As for Lord Charleton, where can he find a better substitute than his grandson, a truly fine youth, whom I loved from the first time I saw him."

This little interchange of opinion between two friends who well understood each other, was in the twilight, checkered by firelight, of that late autumn day, while Lady Violet was tuning the harp in the adjoining room, and Lord Stanmore was, in a subdued voice, relating and hearing much of deep interest in a conversation with his grandfather.

The subject that had the most occupied the attention and touched the feelings of Lord Charleton had been the history related to him that morning, by old Turner, of the last years of his uncle, the Honorable Tristam Woolton, who, having failed, or been averse to escape with his brother, Gilbert, to America, had remained during eight years, a voluntary prisoner in the mansion of his birth, sometimes enjoying the range of all the top floors of the house, and walking at night in the grounds; sometimes, and especially latterly, confined to the room and corridor, which the vigilance of his humble friends had secured from intrusion. When years had past, and the gradual payment of all debts had rendered this seclusion unnecessary, Tristam had become so habituated to the life, that he could bear no other. Naturally shy and timid, with strong family affections, he dwelt morbidly on the past; and, notwithstanding the devoted care and attention of his two family retainers, would have finally sunk some years sooner but for the soothing influence of music. For this beautiful art he possessed a genius that, in an humbler class of life, or connected with a greater energy of character, might have redeemed his fortunes. He played most exquisitely on the flute, and before the property had found a purchaser, solaced his solitude by strains that, like the perfume of the desert rose, fell on no human sympathies. As the alteration in his health became apparent to his faithful friends, they consulted the medical advisers, who agreed in forbidding the flute. Tristam could, with his genius, have mastered the violin, but he had always preferred wind instruments, and now a thought occurred to him which, with feverish eagerness, he carried to an extraordinary perfection, aided by the mechanical skill of the faithful Thomas Jenkins. Tristam made a model of what Thomas either bought or executed, and afterwards placed in the cornice and ornamental groining of the ceiling of the room, which cornice, owing to some change in the destination of the room, perhaps from an humble lumber-room to a decorated tribune, had been an after-thought, and was, therefore, made easily to accommodate the musical apparatus of the unfortunate young nobleman; for young he might still be deemed, although he lingered to the age of forty-one, solaced in his last hours by strains which he associated with those of the heavenly choir.

Whatever faults poor Tristam had left unchecked —for natural faults we all possess — they were not those of malice. He received the last consolations of the church, and was laid in his coffin in the room which latterly had been his sole retreat. His overwrought feelings, which continued even to the last, on the subject of the occupation of his home by strangers, contributed to excite the already indignant antagonism of his two humble friends against all new-comers, and they determined, as Miss Sanderson had suspected, to bring in the aid of nocturnal mysteries to drive them away. The superstitious terrors of the neighborhood assisted their project. It was believed that Tristam had drowned himself in the lake; and his appearance occasionally, either in the grounds at night, or passing an open window, had never undeceived the terrified spectators. The tubes of the scattered organ or panspipes had been originally supplied by bellows, and when access to the room threatened to become difficult, if not impossible, Jenkins, the carpenter, continued, by means of a rope attached to the handle, and conveyed outside the chapel, concealed by trees, to enable Turner, the gardener, to supply the tubes with air. No melody was produced, but a succession of wild and plaintive sounds, which, connected, as they were, with a melancholy and terrific fiction, had rendered Woolton Court an unenviable and transitory possession. Its hereditary lord, however, as times drew on, frequently permitted the trusty Turner and Jenkins to wake the echoes of his uncle Tristam's wail.

The harp was now attuned to satisfy the delicately correct ear of the young Violet, and as if she were —as doubtless she was—awaiting the moment when her niece might expect her nearer presence, Lady Clara quitted the writing that had occupied her, and took a chair close to the harp. A plaintive air with brilliant variations was the first choice of the young harpist, and the surprise and pleasure of those who had not yet heard her were duly expressed. She then whispered, " let us sing together : something I have often sung with you ; never mind its not being new. Let us sing ' Go where glory awaits thee ! ' "

" Yes, Violet," said her father, " you have made a good choice ; sing that with your aunt."

The two voices blended and thrilled as family voices best do, and Lord Charleton said to his grandson, " What angelic voices ! Heaven is doing much for you, my boy ! "

" Ah, my lord," replied Arthur, in a low tone, " I have no secrets from you. My heart is, alas ! with the elder angel, in spite of the double barrier between us. My mind requires such a mind as Lady Clara's. I prefer a woman of my own age or more. She piques me beyond measure, without knowing it; for she is no coquet. "She ——" but here Arthur caught the fixed and fiery eye of the marquis, for the singing had recommenced, and he gave the same devoted attention that he had bestowed on the first song, feeling as then that each word uttered by the "elder angel" was united in thought with his absent rival. The *duo* was this time in Italian, and sung with the same perfect taste and feeling. Both Lord Charleton and Arthur, with Lord Seaham, were attracted to the fair vocalists; and while the aged nobleman assured Lady Clara, whom he purposely engaged, that he had rarely heard such expressive notes, the younger auditor was pouring forth a volley of well-deserved compliments to Lady Violet, in unconscious French, of which he became aware only on her saying in the same language,

"If you prefer speaking to me in French, pray do so; I like that language very much, and have known it since I have known anything."

The conversation continued. Violet consented to open the ball, although her extreme youth had prevented her from being present at anything of the kind beyond children's dances and fêtes champetres.

The marquis heard the arrangement, as he passed to and fro, and the party dispersed in the most harmonious dispositions.

"Do you not intend to add some ornaments to

your dinner-dress?" said the duchess to Lady Clara, as they retired from the dining-room.

" Ah! no," replied she, " I am saved, by your grace's presence, the necessity of appearing as chaperon to Violet, at the ball. From the time of my engagement, which was that of the departure of Sir Henry for scenes of danger, I could dance no more. Since his return, under the bereavement of sight, I feel the same reluctance to any amusement no longer in sympathy with his feelings. I go willingly to concerts, for music he can still—nay, more than ever—enjoy. I am sure, duchess, you are one to fully understand my feelings."

" Perfectly, my dear. The betrothed of a blind hero to be skipping about, or exposing herself to the importunities of rejected partners, would evince bad taste, if not bad feeling. Sir Henry deserves that delicate perception of the most perfect, which is peculiarly yours."

" These beautiful scenes always make me think of heaven," said Lady Violet to the duchess, as they entered the brilliant saloon, formerly the banquet hall, and were conducted by Lord Charleton to their seats at the head of the room. The venerable earl then left them to make the tour of the room, in polite welcome to his guests, and Violet continued — " Do you not feel this, duchess, you who have seen such magnificent and beautiful entertainments?"

" God bless you, my sweet girl! Well, I suppose

that heaven will appear, to those who are so happy as to enter it, just according to the tastes and feelings they have received from Nature; and also, perhaps, according to their age. It is very natural that you should associate with heaven the lights and flowers, and brilliant dresses, and cheerful movement, not to mention the soul-stirring music, which imparts positive happiness. To you, in your innocent girlhood, this ball-room may fitly convey an emblem of heaven, for all seems joy, and peace, and love."

"And is it not so, duchess? Where are the thorns in this rosy bower? How happy every one looks, even before the dancing begins? Can all this be deceit?"

"Oh, no; I do not say this. I believe that every one, or almost every one, here to-night is prepared to cast off care, and do honor to the occasion by happy looks, and even happy hearts. But, my dear child, life cannot continue one brilliant festive scene. We will talk this over to-morrow. It would be out of place now, and make you look too grave when Lord Stanmore comes to claim your promise to open the ball with him."

"I suppose he dances very beautifully," said Lady Violet, "as he has been brought up in France. So I must do my best."

"And that best will be very beautiful, my little Violet," said her father, who had broken off his conversation with the earl, and was now beginning to

feel outraged at the non-appearance of Arthur.
" If," whispered he to the duchess, " he is aiming
at effect— if he is aping royalty, he should remember
that *our* royalty is ever punctual."

" Some disaster of the toilet, I should conjecture,"
suggested the duchess, in the same tone.

The musicians were doing their best to prevent a
too evident delay ; but it had become apparent to all,
save Lord Charleton and Violet, who were occupied
in the innocent enjoyment of the music and the brilliant scene before them. Suddenly, from a side door,
his eyes sparkling, and his cheeks glowing with anger,
not at his toilet, which was perfect, but at the refusal
of Lady Clara to be present, a discovery connected
with his tardy entrance, Lord Stanmore rushed
towards Violet, and, with all the rebounding force
of a heart rejected by another, exclaimed—

" Is it possible that I have kept *you* waiting ; you,
my angel ! "

This was in French, and heard by all the group.
The emphasis on the repetition of the word " you "
unfurled the gathered furrows on Lord Seaham's
brow, deepened the smile on Lord Charleton's mouth,
and the roses on the cheek of Violet. The dance
commenced — a dance often recalled in after-months
of separation and vicissitude, then gazed on with fond
admiration by the partial relatives. The hilarity extended over the whole room, and lasted till the early
hours of the morning.

CHAPTER XIII.

PARTINGS AND MEETINGS.

THE third day of festivity at Woolton Court was entirely of a popular nature, and on the same scale of magnificence and beauty. The nearest barn had been emptied and decorated, to rival in effect the saloon of the mansion. The band was the same, and the supper more abundant, if not more refined. Mr. Grainger, the butler, did the honors with Mrs. Tartson, the housekeeper, and the reduced family party within the mansion contented themselves with the hired services, at their late dinner, of the respectable waiters from the hotel in the village. On the following day " farewell " was said for a while, and keepsakes were exchanged, and promises made of portraits and letters ; and Violet endeavored not to weep, and was strengthened in her courage by the discovery that although the Earl of Charleton could not be won from his home and domestic family at the approaching Christmas, and that Lord Stanmore must, in filial affection, remain with him over the actual solemnity ; yet he had accepted the invitation

9*

to Marsden for New Year's Day, where he would remain till after the holidays.

"There will be no partings in heaven, thank God," cried the duchess; "but on earth they are useful; for but for them we should find this 'the best of all possible worlds,' as the French infidel really called it."

"Ah, duchess, what are we to do without you?" cried Lord Seaham. "I will not say, 'we could better spare a better woman,' because a better does not exist; but we shall sadly miss your windings up, your dramatic surprises, your final scenes. Twenty years hence Clara may, in her own way, supply your place. She has genius enough now, but with her discriminating good sense she sees that her age, and in her actual position, retirement is the more dignified and graceful. So you see, duchess, you are absolutely necessary, like the last bright touches in a picture, to our Christmas holidays at Marsden. Will you come?"

"Do not tempt me, marquis; my duty at Christmas does not lie at Marsden, but in a certain arm-chair in Leicestershire, among step-children and step-grandchildren at Polhill Towers, who, having received me forty-six years ago, when I was nineteen, and they little children, as their own mother, deserve to be treated as my flesh and blood."

"But cannot you combine the two good things?" pleaded the marquis. "Cannot you divide the Christmas, part in Leicestershire, part in Cheshire?"

"I will write to you," replied she; "I will ascertain whether the division can be effected without causing pain. If not, it ought not to be attempted. We hear of coolness and estrangement in families: the fault lies with the one who first let it be perceived that the family circle is twined outside his heart instead of within it; but my carriage is first at the door, I understand, so all the wise things I have yet to say on that head shall be given on paper."

"Come, Lady Clara, let us walk through the rooms together, for I shall not see you again till you are the soldier's wife. A little box of jewelry is already packed up with yours, which I hope you will wear some day during the honeymoon, in remembrance of your mother's old friend. Kiss me, Violet; remember to ride on horseback and practise the harp alternate days, that your figure may remain as perfect as God made it. Good-bye — good-bye — all —all."

Lord Charleton was on the steps of the portal, and handed the warm-hearted duchess to the carriage: she had not remarked the exact number of the steps in descent, and risked falling, but recovered herself, assisted by her venerable cavalier, who, in his anxiety, called out, "Take care, Emma."

In another hour, Arthur and his grandfather were seated together, for the first time alone at the dinner-table, since their familiar home at Marseilles.

"These festive days must have fatigued you, my

lord," observed Arthur, when the servants had retired.

"They would have done so," replied Lord Charleton, "had not everything been so well organized, that there was no anxiety,—no confusion."

"Thank you, my dear lord,—thank you, my own best-loved grandfather!" And Arthur, resting his face on his hands, wept in a sudden outburst of emotion that surprised even himself. The venerable grandfather did not arrest this salutary relief; but changed the current of Arthur's thoughts by saying:

"These festivities over, we have in duty to welcome a different guest,—one whom we receive in faith, that the body sown in corruption shall rise to a joyful immortality. I expect the body of my son and your father, on Friday next at nightfall. I do not wish the funeral rites to be in secret. On the contrary, I rather court publicity, for reasons I will unfold to you at another time. I wish a procession to go the length of the causeway to meet the body, composed of the household servants and those immediate settlers on the estate who have been accustomed, in the old times, to wear the livery, on state occasions, of Woolton Court. Each will bear a torch and receive a long black scarf. I desire that you will act as chief mourner. I shall receive you,—both"— here the voice faltered—"both my living and dead treasures in the chapel of my fathers." After a short pause the earl added: "After the solemn interment of my son, I wish that of my uncle. But the false report of his suicide will require witnesses to prove its falsity, that he may receive Christian burial. It is, therefore, doubtful whether a long delay may not occur, — that is, a delay beyond Friday next."

"Why, Turner and Jenkins can attest that he was alive long after his supposed suicide," observed Lord Stanmore.

"Yes, but it appears that Turner and Jenkins have themselves become suspected by their over-wrought zeal, and that their word, when given for the advantage of the old family, would not be deemed sufficient. There must be the medical at-testation. This can be procured; for, the medical gentleman who attended my uncle is still alive, but removed to a distant town. I shall have the desired attestation by post."

The interval between the joyful festivities of the earl's return and the solemnities of Christmas was occupied by these two obsequies, which were duly performed according to the pious wishes of the Lord of Woolton. Then followed the holy season of the wondrous birth, — the crib of Bethlehem, and all its tender and grateful associations. It was also a sea-son of benefactions to the poor; and Christmas week passed swiftly thus in sacred deeds for God and man till new-year's eve, when, at the earl's express desire, Arthur fulfilled the engagement to join the family party of the Marquis of Seaham, at Marsden Park,

Cheshire. Thanks to cross-country railroads, our hero arrived the same day to a late dinner, and, by an expeditious toilet, contrived to be one of the first in the drawing-room, where Lord Seaham greeted him warmly, and introduced his brother, Lord Claud Chamberlayne, who had arrived just before Christmas from the court of Munich. There was a strong likeness between the brothers, and evidently a perfect understanding between them: this was a pleasing dispelling of prejudice in Arthur's mind against presumptive heirs. The dinner party consisted of Sir Henry and Lady Clara Moorland, a dowager Countess Silbrook, and Miss Tolman, her granddaughter, Lord Claud Chamberlayne, a Colonel Harris, and the private secretary to the Marquis of Seaham, a Mr. Pemble. The conversation during the short interval that occurred before dinner was chiefly between the marquis and his new brother-in-law, Sir Henry Moorland, with occasional sounds of merriment from Lord Claud and a group whom he was entertaining by a description from a clever French work,* and his own experience of the excitement in the streets of Munich, at two intense and all-absorbing epochs of the day, — an excitement which, continuing throughout the year, never abated, was ever up at fever-point, and extended to the hidden aristocracy as well as to the visible and active body

---

* By the Baron Thibault.

called " the people." This was the rush from all the private dwellings, including palace and hovel, with mugs and jugs to fetch beer from the enormous tuns stationed at the accredited venders only; the which tuns, immovable in their vastness and solidity, might, in contrast to the agitation around them, fitly represent the passive sublime. " For ' beer,'" continued Lord Claud, "' beer' takes a position in Germany unknown even in England. It makes its importance be felt; it forms one of the grave topics of the day; it ranks with prime ministers, influences foreign diplomacy, keeps up friendly relations, cements the Germanic Union, and, finally, is quaffed by the Queen of Bavaria, every night at supper."

Dinner being then announced, the marquis, inviting Lord Stanmore to follow with Lady Clara, led the Countess Silbrook to the centre of the table, as at Rockley. Sir Henry Moorland, with the aid of Lord Claud, who yielded his precedency, offered his arm to Miss Tolman: the group of gentlemen followed. Lord Stanmore cast his eyes on the vacant . chair to the left hand of the marquis, and, smiling, said :

" I am glad to see that nothing is changed from the dear cottage by the lake of Windermere." He then continued in a low tone to Lady Clara, as the voices around permitted him, " for your marriage has changed nothing to me, — we met too late. I admire Sir Henry Moorland extremely, — a fine martial figure, with a most expressive countenance; no one would detect his misfortune. But he must be on the shady side of forty, therefore considerably your senior."

Lady Clara merely observed, " I feel assured that you will appreciate each other, and become great friends."

After this the conversation became general on the approaching meeting of Parliament, and the consequent removal after the Christmas holidays, from Marsden Park to St. James's Square.

At the usual moment, in the last course, Lady Violet, gliding to the vacant chair, and protected by her father's hand, looked, and bowed, and smiled all her innocent pleasure at seeing Lord Stanmore once again; and it not unfrequently happened, during the following half-hour, that where the right-hand would, on other days, have been employed, it was now the left that handed the sweetmeats to her father, or raised the wine-glass to her lips; that left delicate hand, on which rested, in fidelity, the emerald ring of her betrothal. In the evening there was music. The ladies also worked, partly in compliment to Lady Silbrook, who was one of those surviving ladies of the court of Queen Adelaide, who worked as indefatigably as in the days of Queen Matilda and the tapestry history of the Conquest. The marquis had seated himself by Lady Silbrook's little work-table, and, unperceived by her, was concentrating all his attention on the open page of a book before him. For the first time since his early boyhood, the great man was puzzled, — hopelessly puzzled, — and must have retired as crestfallen as any of those incompetent applicants for office whom he had dismissed, had his country imperatively exacted his scientific and practical knowledge of its contents.

" Claud," said he at length, as his brother passed him, " just look at this. Can you form any idea of its meaning and intention? There is neither preface nor title-page to guide to the solution of its mysteries ; and yet it seems to be English, and we might well be expected to have some knowledge, however superficial, of the scientific terms of our country."

" How delicious it is to be a little puzzled in this commonplace world?" said Lord Claud, taking the book. " No, I cannot make this out: ' Perl two, turn over, drop one, take up the ribs,' — this seems surgical, — ' cast off, — repeat.' Oh, here is a clue, ' knit five plain rows.' "

" Oh ! it is my knitting-book, or rather part of my book," cried Lady Silbrook. " I have given all the first part to a friend, who is somewhat my pupil in fancy knitting. Just imagine my possessing a book understood by my poor weak mind, and beyond the capacity of two such geniuses, and learned geniuses, too."

" So this is a printed direction for lady's work," said Lord Seaham, examining the little book ; " what
10

an extraordinary production ! Your mind, I perceive, Lady Silbrook, is perfectly engrossed by these minute changes. You have also to count, knit eighty-four rows ; leave two ribs. No wonder your ladyship has become so silent. You are rendered, by this all-engrossing work, perfectly independent of the society of your fellow-creatures. It would be a great alleviation to a prisoner in solitary confinement, to be taught this work ; " and taking out his pocket-book, the memorandum was made : " a work easily learned, that absorbs the mind from all sense of loneliness, — solitary prisoner, — Countess of Silbrook, — books written to instruct."

As the marquis closed his pocket-book, his attention was arrested by a conversation between Sir Henry Moorland and Lord Claud Chamberlayne ; so laying down the knitting-book by the silently-counting Lady Silbrook, who could only bow and smile, he approached the animated speakers.

CHAPTER XIV.

"WHAT was the last wise thing you were saying, Claud?" demanded the marquis, seating himself near his brother.

"We were speaking of political exaggerations," replied Lord Claud, "and their consequent reaction; and whether it were not better to let all violent movements rush on without control, in the certainty that all exaggerations must become too palpably mischievous not to disgust in the end, and produce a reaction almost but not quite as violent, till at length, like the gradually lessening motion of a suspended object, a vibrating pendulum, the action ceases, and all is calm, and, were it a question of inert matter, stagnant; but a human population cannot stagnate."

"That is very true," said Lord Seaham, "one of the best faculties given to man is his power of mental equilibrium; he sees, ponders, compares, adjusts, and chooses at length the solid best; that is to say, a moral and durable good. Can you say as much for your favorite Armstrong gun, general?" added he, turning to Sir Henry, who replied, that as man was born a pugnacious animal, and was prone, as they had just determined, to violent impulses, in the desire to secure for himself a solid and durable good, he must constantly fight."

" Well," continued the general, " if man must fight his fellow-man to obtain this good, and the science of his country has brought this means of success within his reach, is he not wise and patriotic to secure it, by giving science and practice every advantage possible?"

" Certainly," said the marquis ; " science and mechanical art, laborious experiments, and constant practice of a newly-invented means of defence, are due to the love of country. We may lament the necessity of war; but if war be inevitable, we are bound to be grateful for every fresh aid to success. Still, no gun is a moral and durable good, and therefore all the pomp and glitter of the army is not to be compared to the meek influence of diplomacy, which, by no other weapon than the tongue or the pen, calms all these exaggerations, these national jealousies, these pugnacious propensities, or rather their furious development ; and, at length, leads the wolf to lie down with the lamb."

Sir Henry observed, smiling, " that with many an honest man the term ' deceit ' and the term ' diplomacy ' were synonymous."

" There is something certainly more straightforward in the blow of a cannon-ball," said the marquis, "but observe and acknowledge this,—that if in reconciling friends in private life you are justified in concealing all that could keep alive or cause fresh irritation, and you charitably dwell on the good qualities, and still more on the high opinion each has of the other, how much more when whole nations are involved in the questions of war and peace. We diplomatists have high authority on our side; 'Blessed are the peace-makers.'"

"The first battle, however, that we hear of," said Sir Henry, "was in heaven; and if the angels had not fought bravely, their diplomacy would have availed them little."

"Well," returned the marquis, "we are agreed that fighting must take place so long as there is evil. War is a sad necessity, because of the imperfections of all things here below. The test that war is an evil is, that in heaven there will be no more fighting, but an eternal reign of peace."

"And no more diplomacy," persisted the general: "where there is an eternal peace, no peace-makers are required."

"They are eternally and gloriously rewarded," said the marquis.

"And so is the heroic soldier," continued Sir Henry, "greater love hath no man than that he lay down his life for his friends. So highly do the army chaplains abroad think of the sacrifice of life that a soldier makes from duty, that if he be otherwise in a fit state to die, that is, in a state of grace, they consider it a martyrdom by which he immediately enters heaven. Now they do not pronounce in this way on the diplomatist. I think they consider rather that the great man has probably to wait some time in the ante-rooms above before gaining admittance : ' faire l'ante-chambre,' as our neighbors say."

"Come, my dear decorated general," said the marquis, "if you make the diplomatist remain in the ante-chambers of the heavenly court, because of the dross of wordly honors, what do you intend for a soldier who does *not* die on the battle-field?"

"He has died for his country by desire, and by exposure and risk," said Sir Henry, "and the sin which causes fighting to be a necessary evil no more takes from the merit of the sacrifice, than in the case of actual martyrdom, when idolatrous and wicked judges condemned the early Christians."

"That is a very good argument," observed Lady Clara.

"It is," said her brother. "This soldier of yours, Clara, is worth grappling with. You do not think, however, that we have finished the argument, do you ? because I have further to observe, that as mind is superior to matter, and soul to body, the diplomatist, that is, the peaceful statesman, who loves his country more than his party, and yet sees that his party is, when united, of the greatest service to his country ;

when that statesman cannot conscientiously vote with his party, and foresees, nevertheless, that his not doing so will break up the most generally upright and useful cabinet that has ever been formed—this crisis of self-sacrifice, of desertion of friends, of mental agony—this is martyrdom. We know from history and biography," continued Lord Seaham, "that when several of these conflicts occur in the career of a statesman, and that he is gifted or cursed with a delicate sense of honor, strong affections, and feelings too acute, we know that in the end the seat of reason has lost its equilibrium, and suicide has ended all."

"Alas! not ended!" said Lady Clara, "his eternity but then begins."

"I understand and feel all you say," observed Sir Henry, "in which you mean, doubtless, to include the being misjudged and misrepresented, not only by the public at large, but also by the statesman's own personal friends?"

"Yes, indeed," continued the marquis; "this last hidden blow has, perhaps, been the one to strike fatally both heart and brain."

"And are there no culminating hours for the soldier?" said Sir Henry. "Is there not an awful responsibility in giving a word of command that shall decide the slaughter of thousands—send the souls of thousands into the presence of their Maker? Then, again, is it nothing to lose a battle; to sound a retreat; to know that stupidity, or cowardice, or treachery has ruined the best tactics and the finest army in the world? To know that, in her first disappointment, the mother country may utter words that will become historical, and all against you? That the triumphant welcome home is to be exchanged for a private return in small numbers at a time; and that at head-quarters some polite and well-meant words will alone greet you, such as, 'Well, general, these are the chances of war. Cannot expect all to be Marlboroughs and Wellingtons. Eh!—Did your best. No more can be asked of any man,' &c."

"Yours was a very different reception, Moorland," observed the marquis. "I saw the actual emotion in the royal personages who bestowed, or witnessed the bestowal of your decorations, and I heard the gracious words. There were many there that day who would gladly, for such historical words, have compromised for your privation; who would literally 'have given their eyes' for their monarch's and their country's thanks and praise."

CHAPTER XV.

TÊTE-À-TÊTE CONVERSATIONS.

THE following morning Lord Stanmore and Sir Henry Moorland became personally acquainted; and during a tête-à-tête conversation, which led gradually to the information the former desired to obtain, he said:

"If it be not intrusive, Sir Henry, I should feel much interested to know which of the two accounts published is the correct one respecting your loss of sight. At first it was said to have been on the battle-field, then that it was owing to indiscreet bleeding."

"Both are correct," replied the general. "It was at the moment of victory I fell, not from a wound, but from a stroke of apoplexy. I was carried off and carefully tended, but, perhaps, not skilfully. However, these things are in the hand of God. I suffered very little pain. I received the same reward as for the loss of limbs, and — my affianced bride was faithful."

No one better knew the truth of that last assertion than he to whom Sir Henry, unconsciously, addressed it. Lord Stanmore, after a little pause, continued:

" All that you described last night in your argument with the marquis, as proving the tension of mind, the anguish of doubt, the final resolve of the general of an army to be equal to that of a minister of state — all that emotion fully accounts for the apoplexy which destroyed your sight. You were seized in the moment of victory: the revulsion of feeling from painful doubt to joyful certainty gave the stroke. The retreat of the enemy from the field of battle was the last your eyes beheld. This is, then, the truth; and I pray God you may preserve in your present cheerful courage, until you behold the final battle of the great Field-Marshal, St. Michael, against our common enemy, Lucifer, and hear that first-rate band — the nine choirs of angels — sounding victory?"

" Thank you, thank you," said the general, warmly. " And in my turn, let me wish you, my lord, in the opening of your public life, true patriotism, and the same cheerful courage you wish me, with the wisdom of the serpent and the innocence of the dove."

" You speak of the opening of my public life," said Lord Stanmore; " and it is true that the marquis wishes me to represent in parliament the little town of Helkington, near here; but the people know me only through his lordship's report, and may not be disposed to accept me."

" They, virtually speaking, cannot refuse the marquis," said Sir Henry. "He can command the votes: Helkington may be termed a family borough!"

"Why that is what is called a rotten borough!"

"Exactly so," said the Marquis of Seaham, who had approached just near enough to hear this last exclamation. "Now, would you like to hear me defend a rotten borough?"

"Yes, indeed. I like to hear you grappling with a difficult subject, the more so that I know you have sufficient candor to pardon a listener who remains unconvinced."

"To begin, then; you are aware of all the fundamentals of our glorious constitution, the equilibrium of kings, lords, and commons, in threefold power; and that any undue increase, even involuntary, on one part, must be met by a moral barrier on the part of the two other powers, to stay the progress of this encroachment. Now, rotten boroughs form the barrier on the part of the aristocracy against the encroaching power of the commons; — Helkington is a case in point. My brother, Lord Claud, who is a commoner, and I, who am a peer, agree perfectly in politics; therefore he would, without scruple, accept to be placed, by my interest, in the house of commons, where he would vote for the same measures as I do in the house of lords, and with all the other members of family boroughs keep the proper equipoise of power against the preponderance of the commons. My brother cannot yet enter parliament.

He will be for many years in foreign courts ; I have, therefore, thought of you, — hoped for you ; for in our many conversations together, I have ascertained that we think and feel alike on all subjects likely to engage the attention of parliament."

" And if," said Lord Stanmore, " we should, in the course of the session, find some unexpected subject on which we cannot agree ? "

" Why, then, you can pair off with some honorable member of the opposition, and not vote at all."

" And suppose I should discover, as my knowledge and experience extended, that we really did differ on very fundamental points ? "

" Then I should await the first dissolution of parliament, to advise you to canvass for some other borough, or to stand for a county."

" I have, then, no objection whatever to accept your offer, my lord marquis, and to become a moral barrier in favor of equal rights and privileges as member for Helkington."

———

Marsden Park was a superb place in its own style ; a style strongly contrasted to Woolton Court. It had the fine old timber of ages, a luxuriance of smaller foliage, a limpid winding river, and all that modern art could desire and supply in conservatories, orangeries, aviaries, fish-ponds, labyrinths, bridges, temples,

and hermitages ; but ——. This objective monosyl-
lable had presented itself to our hero, as, on the first
evening of his arrival, turning his admiring gaze
from the rich groups of oak, beech, and lime-trees,
he looked around the whole visible domain. It was a
dead flat. "The moon had climbed the highest hill ;"
directly her beams fell beyond the raised flower-beds
on the lawn ; but, then, — what flower-beds ! and
what a lawn !

"Do you love Marsden or Rockley best ?" demanded Lord Stanmore of Lady Violet, as they
stood together after breakfast in the conservatory,
the day following his most peaceful, non-contested
election to the borough of Helkington.

"Papa has given me Rockley," said she, "because I cannot inherit Marsden. This old place is
strictly entailed on the male heirs, and, therefore,
has remained to the Chamberlaynes ever since the
first grant of the lands. I was born at Marsden ; I
have passed almost all my life here, and yet it must
pass from me. It is very profitable to live in a place
that must pass from you."

"Why ? "

"Because it is a type constantly before you of *all*
earthly possessions, and all earthly —— "

"Why do you hesitate ? All earthly what ? "

"All earthly affections, that are not fit to be eternal. This I have been long taught by Dr. Rollings,
our chaplain."

11

".He has an apt pupil; but all *your* affections, Lady Violet, are fit to be eternal. Woe be to him who would dare to engage them only for time. But you have not yet told me which place you love the best."

" I love both."

" That is not an answer."

" Both places have remembrances."   .

" Very true. Who do you remember in connection with Rockley?"

" I remember the dear Duchess of Peterworth; she is my godmother. Did you know that?"

" No, indeed, I did not. That accounts for the sort of authority with which she made me the happiest of men. She made it impossible that I should be totally forgotten in the many remembrances of Rockley. But for her, perhaps, I should have become but as a ripple of the Lake of Windermere, broken and lost in the succeeding wave."

" Oh, no," said Violet, at length, believing her companion to be very much in earnest; " I do not remember you because the duchess wishes it, although I love and respect her very much. I have my own individual being. Every one's soul is an independent creation of God, with its own faculties, and feelings, and preferences. This soul of mine must love God supremely, and then ——"

" And then *me*."

" If you really wish it."

"*If* I wish it.   Oh! Violet can you doubt me? This place of your birth may pass from you, but Woolton Court and the heart of its owner shall honor and adore you."

"Oh, that is too French!" cried she; "do not use that word to a poor mortal.   I prefer you to any one I have ever seen; but I cannot interest and occupy your heart yet, I am so young.   I try to find out the things you like, and I learn them.   I have learned to draw for some time, and now I wish to paint; for I see you love paintings.   But above all, I try to profit by all the wise and learned things I constantly hear from papa and his friends; for papa says you have one of the most intelligent minds he ever met with.   He did not say this to please me. He said it in a low voice to the present prime minister, and I was tuning my harp; but I heard it. And now you are to enter parliament, and influence the multitude to all that is great and good.   I shall read all your speeches; and, above all, I shall like to hear your first speech.   If you outlive the Earl of Charleton, and speak in the house of lords, I shall always go into the peeress' box to listen.   I admire eloquence and argument.   I was very much interested the other night in hearing papa and Sir Henry Moorland on the respective merits of diplomacy and war.   But why were you so silent?"

"Because, sweetest Violet, like you, I am very young.   I am often encouraged by my superiors in age and wisdom to give my opinion on various points, and I *then*, being so invited, give it freely.   But I cannot venture to decide weighty matters that involve responsibility, and pronounce on a theory without experience."

" If you would never willingly talk to any woman until she is five-and-twenty," said Violet, " it will be almost eleven years before my conversation can have any charms for you; and oh! what a long while that appears.   What a pity to be so young."

Large tears stood in her eyes, and then overflowed, all the more because Lord Stanmore, in his usual style, as he said, of a prince in a fairy tale, had dropped on one knee, and was alternately looking up at those brimful eyes and covering her hands with kisses.

" I feel so jealous, so painfully jealous of every one who is older than myself, and then such scruples about being jealous; and then to look forward to eleven long years of jealous scruples."

The tears now rained on the hands, and were kissed away, and the question asked —

" When did I say such nonsense? "

" You said it only two days ago."

" And the lady to whom I said it was, of course, past the age of five-and-twenty? "

" Yes, she was."

" Then, sweetest Violet, I think I may rise from my knees."

"Pray rise, my lord, and never think such a posture required by me, however you make me suffer."

"I make you suffer; my angel — my seraph! How?"

"You told Miss Tolman last night that her rich contralto notes would mingle with your dreams."

"What next?"

"And you kissed Lady Mary Pulteney's hand when she gave you one of the photographs of the late Duke of Wellington."

"What more?"

"When we all go to London, I shall still be too young to be presented. I shall be far less likely to see you. You will be conversing with and dreaming of those intellectual and well-stored minds, and deep rich voices, neither of which I yet possess. I will endeavor during these eleven long years——"

"Lady Violet," said Lord Stanmore, very gently, yet very gravely, "so long as you see on this hand the ring of our betrothal, be convinced that I cherish in deep affection, ardent admiration, and fondest hope, all that is promised me by that pledge. When your father placed me at liberty to consider the engagement as merely a frolic of the warm heart and lively imagination of the Duchess of Peterworth, I obtained his consent to consider the betrothal as binding on myself, though I left you free. I have hoped, from beholding on your hand the same pledge, that your affection and respect for the marquis had induced

11*

you to listen favorably to my wishes through him. I am but too much flattered by the favorable opinion you have of me; I feel still more touched by your artless fears of having rivals in this heart. Fear nothing from that vague, general admiration of your sex, which in the country that reared me is more demonstrative than in England. As my future wife, I love you alone. Your wonderful humility is such that, perhaps, even a little authority on my part may please instead of displease you. Is it so?"

Her brightened countenance said "Yes," and he continued.

"You have justly imagined that I shall prefer to find in my wife an intelligent and cultivated mind, in preference to a proficiency in superficial accomplishments; but in you, I hope, all these qualities will be blended. I do not wish an overwise and learned wife. It will refresh me more — if, indeed, I am to launch forth into public life — to find, on my return home, a companion who can recreate my mind and please my fancy by those unspeakable graces which are natural to you. From the heated debate or prosy speech of my fellow-men, I—young, gay, impetuous, as I am — shall enjoy, after such constraint, to laugh and play a little with my young wife. After a great deal of ponderous sense, there is nothing better than a little good nonsense."

"Ah!" cried Lady Violet, "there you are, like papa, but he also says that for nine persons who can talk good sense, the tenth only can talk good non-sense. Uncle Claud can, and makes papa laugh till he cries ' stop, Claude; now stop.' If you remain here when the other guests are gone, you may hear a fine skirmish of good-natured wit between papa, uncle Claud, aunt Clara, and the Duchess of Peter-worth, at the card table : I enjoy it all ; I appreciate it all ; but if I have wit, it is of a graver sort. I think that if ever I have the happiness to welcome you home from what papa calls over-tension of mind in public life, that you will be the one to talk the good nonsense, and I to laugh."

" That will do admirably well," said Lord Stan-more, " and that happy time will arrive, please God, in two years, for you are past fourteen, and your father exacts no longer delay than that you shall have attained the age of my mother at the epoch of her marriage with my father. She was sixteen, and my father three-and-twenty ; exactly the age I shall be in that happy year. Ah, Violet, my treasure," cried he again, seizing her hand, " do not shrink from me when I praise you ; you are far more fitted to give me lessons in virtue and conduct than I you. You, who have given me, after God, your first and pure affections ; trust me, the desire of my heart is to merit them through life."

CHAPTER XVI.

A PAINFUL DISCOVERY.

THE remainder of Lord Stanmore's visit at Marsden Park was occupied with preparations for the public career that now lay before him; and by the excitement of a threatened change of ministry, which, after various endeavors to form a better cabinet under a different chief, was reinstated, with some partial modifications. The Marquis of Seaham became minister for foreign affairs, and his previous office for the colonies was filled by the Marquis of Penzance, who had, till then, held the woods and forests. Lord Seaham had been mostly in London, or at a villa he had purchased at Richmond, but which could not be termed, like the one on Windermere, "Holiday Cottage"—transfers and assumptions of office always involving additional labor. It now became doubtful whether Lord Claud Chamberlayne, instead of returning to Munich, would not be sent to Vienna, as an important step towards becoming one day ambassador. In the midst of these various plans of public and private interest, Lord Stanmore and Lady Violet had one more long and private conversation, the evening before his departure from Marsden to join the marquis in London. All guests had departed save the Moorlands, Lord Claud, and our hero; and on the evening in question, the former trio were seated together in deep private discourse near the fire, while at the further end of the room, sheltered by the musical instruments, sat Lord Stanmore and Lady Violet, making some final arrangements, among the rest, a correspondence while in London, to be conducted under the names of "Arthur" and "Violet," an immediate renewal of the betrothal, by each taking off the ring of the other, kissing it, and replacing it on the loved hand; a promise of miniatures from the skilful hand of the most eminent artist of the day, the which last arrangement led, most unexpectedly, from joy to sorrow, in the following manner: —

. "I have already shown you the miniatures of my parents," said Lord Stanmore, "and I have seen several portraits of your father, dear Violet; but, to my surprise, I can nowhere discover any portrait, or even sketch, of your mother, the late Marchioness of Seaham. This surprises me the more, as Lady Clara has taken pains to leave no vacuum in your family line of pictures. Is there any portrait of her — of your mother? However badly executed, it would be interesting, and we could have it copied by some skilful artist. Can you remember her?"

A long pause, then the words, scarcely audible —

"I was only three years old when she left me."

"When she left you for a better world," added Lord Stanmore. "But the duchess led me to think that you were in the slight mourning preparatory to resuming colors, when I first saw you at the Lake of Windermere, a few months ago."

"I was nearly thirteen years old when she died," said Violet.

"Where did she die?"

"In Italy."

"Ah, she was taken to Italy for her health and there died. But who were with her of the family?"

"No one," said Violet, weeping; "they could not. She had obtained leave to enter the strict branch of the Franciscan Order called the 'Entombed Alive'—*Le Sepolte Vive*."

"Who gave leave?"

"Papa gave leave, and then the Pope."

A sudden light flashed on the mind of Lord Stanmore. He felt inexpressibly shocked, and could only say:

"Oh, my poor Violet!"

"Uncle Claud will tell you," whispered she; "he was very kind to poor mamma. I shall see you to-morrow before you go, if not, we shall meet in London next week; and I have requested Dr. Rollings for to-morrow's mass to be for you, Arthur.

As Lady Violet passed the still consulting trio to bid good-night, she bent to her uncle's car the entreaty that he would "explain about poor mamma to

Lord Stanmore." Lord Claud immediately complied, and found our hero with his hands clasped over his face in a state of the most painful emotion.

"My dear Stanmore," said Lord Claud, "I trust that this cruel family blot and affliction will cause no change in your sentiments towards our angelic Violet. It is not as if she had been educated by a frail mother. She was only three years old when that unfortunate mother left her,—an abandonment of duty that poor Lady Seaham expiated by the most heartfelt and severe penance. I am ready to reply to any questions."

"Thank you, Lord Claud. My first question is, —Why was I never told this history?"

"I may safely reply that there has been no intention, on our part, to keep you in ignorance of a thing so publicly known that it has been taken for granted you were aware of it."

"Who was the seducer?"

"Lord Edwin Fitzjames, brother to the present Marquis of Penzance."

"Is he alive?"

"He is."

"The wretch! Oh! if I ever meet him!"

"My dear Stanmore, he has been met by one whom he has far more grievously injured than you, or any man. He was shown last year into a room where my brother was waiting to speak to the first lord of the treasury. These two men, the injurer and the injured, stood opposite each other as if struck motionless. At length, Lord Edwin sank on his knees and said, ' she is dead. Let me die forgiven?' My brother said, ' you are forgiven,' and fell back fainting into the chair, from which he had started up. He had an illness of three weeks ; but that heroic act will send him a happy death and favorable judgment, when that supreme hour shall arrive."

" Yes, yes, it was heroic, — too heroic. But the marquis was already injured. And you, Lord Claud, you have known all this so many years that you are accustomed to it. With him, and with you all, the guilt, the blot is irretrievable ; you cannot escape from it."

" Good heavens ! Lord Stanmore, escape from us if you wish it," cried Lord Claud. " Clara, will you come here ?"

Lady Clara immediately arose, but Sir Henry detained her first, saying in his usual tone of voice :

" Is he worth all this ?" Then adding loudly to Lord Stanmore, " come my young viscount the world has hitherto smiled a little too softly on you ; some humiliation and adversity will do you no harm."

" Mon Dieu," cried Arthur, suddenly leaping from his seat and clenching his hands, while he continued, rapidly in French, " is this the man to be taunting me with being a spoiled boy, who has caused the one great adversity of my life, and who continues selfishly to occupy the whole time and attention of her who used to be the 'light,' the real 'Clara' of her house.

"What is all that?" inquired the general, of Lady Clara.

"Oh!" replied she, "do permit me to soothe him; the blood is going to his head. He is speaking in delirium ——"

"Well, I hope so. But go to him, for God forbid that any one from want of care or skill should have a stroke."

"My cousin, Arthur," said she, gently approaching him with her handkerchief steeped in eau de cologne, "sit down here, and let me lay this across your forehead. If we could have prevented this shock to you, we would have done so. God has permitted it; we must permit it. There now; is it not refreshingly cold?"

Lord Stanmore did not reply but by kissing the ministering hands; at length he said:

"It was *you* wished it."

"Exactly so," replied she, "I take the whole responsibility on myself. I did wish it, and I do wish it. Violet has been my child, my pupil, my congenial companion, the object of my tender solicitude and affection. I wish to make her happy by confiding her to your warm and generous heart. To-morrow, my brother Claud and I will edify you by a recital of the penitent years of our lovely and unfortunate sister-in-law. Her fault having been public, her penance became so; and the expiation has been deemed sufficient in the sight of her erring fellow-mortals. No shadow can fall on her innocent child. Do you feel better?"

"If he does *not*," said the general, feeling for the bell-handle, " he must be bled moderately; and if he *is* better, we should all go to repose, for it is past eleven o'clock."

"Of course, I feel better," said Arthur, in a low voice, to the brother and sister. " Thank you, Lord Claud, for bearing with me so patiently. And you, Lady Clara, what can I say to you?"

"Just what you have said, that you really feel better. A good night will restore you."

During the excitement in the room below, the young Violet, perfectly unconscious, in her inexperience of life, that her mother's fault could react on herself, after a few tender tears to that mother's memory, and the accustomed prayers for the repose of her soul, fell asleep amid thoughts of pleasantness and peace.

CHAPTER XVII.

By the first of February the London residences
were occupied by those who were to conduct England
with honor, and in strict alliance with France, through
the approaching war in the Crimea; and the quaint
old drawing-room in Downing Street now heard repeated the names, since become historical, of the royal
and military heroes of that gallant and victorious, yet
chequered campaign.

The short Easter holidays were passed by the family of the Marquis of Seaham at Richmond, whither
he went from St. James's Square as often as possible.
It had been an agreement, before the marriage of
Lady Clara Chamberlayne to Sir Henry Moorland,
that she should never cease to be mistress of her
brother's house until one of three events should
occur: the second marriage of the marquis, the sufficiently matured age of the Lady Violet, or the
marriage and residence in England of the younger
brother, Lord Claud Chamberlayne.

After Easter the parliamentary season commenced
in earnest. Richmond was relinquished in favor of

James's Square, the hereditary residence of the Marquis of Seaham. The Duke of Peterworth and family were in the same square, with the exception of the dowager duchess, who occupied the mansion always assigned to the widows of that ducal house, in Stanhope Street, Mayfair.

The London residence of the Earls of Charleton had been sold to satisfy the creditors more than fifty years before, and a house had been bought to supply the loss in Carlton Gardens, to which the earl came soon after Easter week, at the earnest entreaty of the Marquis of Seaham, that the venerable nobleman might be presented without delay by himself and the Duke of Peterworth to the house of lords. Lord Charleton, who had been rather indisposed, would have postponed this public presentation for a few days, but his friend became so nervously irritable at the bare mention of delay, that the earl yielded, and was warmly greeted by his peers on the 20th April, 1854.

On their return from the house all three dined together, not at either of their homes, but at the Clarendon hotel, at the earnest request of the marquis, that no interruption might occur to the confidential and important topic he had to lay before his two friends. During the dinner, of which he scarcely partook, he became so abstracted, that on the duke asking him whether he patronized the South African wines, he replied :

" I patronize such a complication of villany ! No, duke."

At which the duke, highly amused by this reply, at cross purposes, observed to Lord Charleton that they had better postpone any reference to the most noble marquis, until the privacy he sought for was more complete. This was soon effected by the withdrawal of the waiters, when the marquis, still absorbed by his one subject, exclaimed :

" Yes ; I repeat it, — complication of villany ! All this came to my knowledge during the last month I was in office for the colonies ; not that I was made officially acquainted with the ultimate view this colonial personage had in coming to England, but I was applied to, as the head of the colonial department, to befriend and patronize this Mr. Gerard Woolton. Lord Charleton, are you aware that you have such a relative, — a grandson of your precious uncle Gilbert, consequently a first cousin, once removed, to yourself, and, in the same way, second cousin to Stanmore. Are you aware of his existence ? "

" Of his existence, yes ; but of little further. Is he not contented to be one of the richest planters in Jamaica ? "

" It appears not. He is getting up a formidable attack against the existence of a far better man than himself : not by means of poniard, pistol, or poisoned bowl, but by decision of the supreme court,

12*

that there exists no such person as Viscount Stanmore?"

"His exertions are useless," observed Lord Charleton; "every formality was fulfilled, every document
most carefully preserved relating to the birth of my
grandson."

"He does not pretend to deny the birth. He
found, as you state, that documents existed too
powerful to enable him to call in question the birth;
but he pretends to have in his possession the still
more powerful document of the death."

"The death!" exclaimed both auditors.

"Yes; he pretends that the nurse's infant that
died at Dieppe, in Normandy, was, in truth, the
little Arthur Dieudonné Bryce Woolton, Viscount
Stanmore; and that, consequently, he, Gerard
Woolton, is heir presumptive to the title and estates
of the Earls of Charleton."

"Something more than mere assertion would be
required for him to obtain even a patient hearing,"
said Lord Charleton, quietly.

"Can you remember the nurse?"

"Yes, perfectly well. It is only twenty-one years
and a few months since I first saw her at Dover.
Madame de Courtrai had met with her at Calais
while awaiting the vessel to cross over to her daughter."

"Can you also remember her child?"

"Yes; I remember the infant. He was seven

weeks older than my grandson, and might then have passed for his elder twin-brother, so great was the resemblance. A resemblance to be accounted for in the accidental likeness of the two young mothers."

" Mr. Gerard Woolton asserts that the Comtesse de Courtrai took advantage of this likeness between the two infants to substitute the living child of the nurse for your dead heir, after a most mysterious visit that the two ladies paid to the sea-side, *without the nurse*. What imprudent things women will do! Have you any recollection of this circumstance? for, on its truth rests the main *hinge* of Mr. Woolton's accusations. He has now in London this former nurse, once Sophie Bauvin, now Madame Pierre Boule, married a second time to a hotel-keeper at Versailles. He has either convinced or highly bribed this woman to be a terribly powerful witness in his favor. Have you any notes, memoranda, or letters that could be produced to nullify those accusations?"

" I have kept all the letters of my daughter-in-law," said Lord Charleton. " I will refer to the date of her residence at Versailles; for it must have been thence that the excursion was made to the sea-side."

" Are these letters in England?"

" They are. But, my dear marquis, do not permit this attack to annoy you. All will be explained, and set at rest."

" Well, I hope so; but this Gerard Woolton is a

clever man, and not scrupulous about bribes. There is a man brought over from Versailles who, it seems, lived as lady's footman with your daughter-in-law and her family, and accompanied the ladies to Dieppe; also a woman who was lady's maid at the time, and of this fatal party. They pretend, and of course will swear, to have overheard various sentences which will be all in favor of Mr. Woolton's assertion, that the child who died was the little heir."

"What were the overheard sentences?"

"'Oh, mamma! that I should have lived to see this hour of woe.' 'Calm yourself, my child, — leave it all to me, — I will arrange it all. Oh! I can never face Sophie again, or let her see the child.' There are several more such sentences; but at this moment I can remember only these. I have seen a list of them, for the use of the advocate on their side. However, they cannot refuse in court for their witnesses to answer the interrogatories of the counsel for the defence, and he may probably insist on receiving all these expressions as the natural outpouring of a delicate and wounded honor, at having taken the child from its mother, to share in the benefit of the sea-air, and having then lost it. The sentences will quite bear this interpretation, as well as the other point I now remember, — the inconsolable weeping of Lady Stanmore over the dead child, and refusing to look even at the living one, until reproved by her mother."

" All that you have hitherto mentioned," observed the duke, " will bear the best interpretation."

. " And all perfectly in keeping with the generous and impetuous character of my daughter-in-law," added Lord Charleton. " The least likely person I ever knew to lend herself to any deception ; besides she was so young! When we had returned from Dover, and I consented to remain a few weeks at Versailles, I used to watch with pleasure the natural effect of time in restoring to Celeste the playfulness of her character. She and the peasant wet-nurse would play at hide and seek with the two infants, and I have occasionally been interrupted in my writing or reading with, ' Oh ! permettez papa,' and one or other little bundle placed on my knees, or behind me in my chair, as a temporary hiding place. Ah ! my poor little Celeste."

" I conclude," said the duke, " that you will secure the first counsel on your side, and also look after a few useful swearers. The medical man, for instance, at Versailles, who recommended this trip to the sea, and still better, the medical practitioner at Dieppe."

" Your grace is right," said Lord Charleton ; " I will send my own trusty valet, Julien, a native of France, to both those places, with written directions for himself alone."

" Yes, for himself alone," observed the marquis ; " that is wise. We must at present seem to be doing nothing ; above all, do not let anything transpire to

Stanmore; he is to make his maiden speech on or about the 28th, 'On the importance of Peace with France.' He chose that from a variety of subjects I offered him. He will come off brilliantly."

"And solidly," added the duke. "Let us drink to his success, and then I will tell you my own experience of good swearing on the part of faithful servants." After a short pause, he resumed — "My step-mother, whom I call 'mother,' — for I have always felt her to be such, — was also, indeed, primarily my effective friend during a most trying twelvemonth of my younger life. She became my father's second wife when I was three years old; my sisters were then aged four, seven, and nine. Poor Augusta died unmarried; she was the youngest. The present duchess dowager was first cousin to my father, and in case of my death, the whole affair would go to her own brother, Lord Dartfort, and to his son. I mention this to show that flesh and blood did not move her fidelity to me. My own mother had declared, on her death-bed, in presence of this cousin, and of several female servants, that I was *not* the son of the duke, her husband." Lord Charleton gave a suppressed cry of horror. "Well, my lord, the hired nurse reported this death-bed declaration. It was not to be denied. Five persons heard it; the nurse more than once. I alone never knew the report. Lord Dartfort made no move. All seemed to die off, when my father's death induced the Dartfort family to begin a private amicable arrangement. I was then twelve years old. I was taking a lesson in painting, when the lawyer, on the Dartfort side, broke the news to me. I felt so stunned and bewildered, that I went on painting. My master had retired; the lawyer, after saying some civil things, also withdrew. My step-mother came to me, and exclaimed — 'Oh! George, are you caring more for your painting than for all that is hanging over you?' I replied — 'No, mamma, but I shall still go on painting; for if I am duke, it will always be an agreeable pastime, and if I am no duke, I will be an artist.' This private arbitration was closed in my favor, owing to the irreproachable life of my mother, to her having always retained about her person the same female servants, who could vouch for every hour of her married life, and from the zeal and intelligence of the present duchess, in giving the best solution to the extraordinary turn of the delirium under which my mother had pronounced such a decree against me. Among the prayer-books constantly on the sick-bed, the present dowager had found a little book of fairy tales that must have been left by one of the children at a visit from the nursery. In this collection there was a tale of a prince, brought up by a certain duke as his son, the which prince, assisted by a fairy, goes in the end to reign over his own principality, having married the daughter of the duke. In my mother's mind I had become identified with the prince of the story. My wise step-mother had kept this book locked up with a memorandum of several things uttered by my mother; amongst the rest, 'Does he not look like a prince?' These were produced by her, and obtained the sentence in my favor."

" These investigations, to clear the innocent are most deeply interesting," observed Lord Charleton. " Well done, Emma."

" So much so," continued the duke, " that I have sat up whole nights reading the collections of 'Proofs of Innocence,' after circumstantial evidence had gone against the victims of a false suspicion. As I had nearly been one of those victims myself, I felt bound to give all the support in my power in the upper house to do away altogether with capital punishment, which was then a question before parliament. These collections had been made in support of the question, and were most powerful in aiding the good cause; I will now do all in my power for young Stanmore."

" Thank you, my lord duke, for this promise, and for your personal narrative. My own first proceedings must be to send to Woolton Court for my private letters, and to dispatch my faithful Julien to France."

CHAPTER XVIII.

A SYREN.

THE unconscious Arthur was enjoying himself extremely during the early part of the London season, among the friends of the Duchess of Peterworth and of the Chamberlayne family, who had become his. He particularly liked the youngest daughter, or rather step-daughter, of the duchess, the Lady Emily Whynne, and accepted with pleasure an invitation to her house, on the night following the revelations made to Lord Charleton. The ball of Lady Emily's was preceded by a dinner at the Duchess of Peterworth's, consisting of those young persons who are likely to enjoy that species of festivity. One or two mammas, or grandmammas, completed the staff of chaperons. All the young couples started for the ball, fully engaged among themselves, and our hero, involved in happiness three deep. These triple engagements did not prevent him, however, from becoming extremely interested in a certain young person, who, first as vis-à-vis, then placed at the side next him in the quadrilles, recalled to him most forcibly the sunny south. Perhaps she was in him

13

reminded of the same; for certain glances, quickly withdrawn, assured him that she had remarked him. At the conclusion of his previous engagements he resolved to wait for no introduction, but to follow the customs of France; so, crossing over to the southern beauty, he demanded, in French, the honor of her hand for the next dance.. The unknown looked pleased, and accepted his hand. The dance concluded, they remained occupied by each other, and rapidly exchanging in perfect French the questions and replies pertaining to the antecedents of the interesting young foreigner.

" But I ought not to be called a *foreigner* in England," said she, " for by law, the colonies have the same rights in every respect as the mother country. I am a native of Jamaica; my family was originally English, and of the ancient nobility; my mother is French, of the Island of Cuba, and therefore partly Spanish; I have been brought up at a Sacré Cœur, in Paris, and have returned there during the last year, for certain reasons."

" So this is your first visit to England: I hope it will be a long one."

" That depends on the good success of my father's cause. He is in England to expose a most wicked plot to deprive him of his rightful inheritance in this country; and as I am the eldest of his daughters and his heiress, he wishes me to be on the spot."

"Really? Then we must wish his cause to be slow and sure, that we may detain you the longer."

"You must yourself be attached to the French embassy," observed she, "as you make use of the word 'detain' me with reference to England; for, you are not English: you belong to dear France, surely?"

"Ah! you love France!" cried he. "Your mother is French; so was mine. One always loves one's mother's country. There is, then, a tie between us, mademoiselle, that can never be forgotten."

"Hortense," said a middle-aged, fine-looking man, tapping the young lady on the shoulder. She turned to be introduced to a new partner, and at the same instant the Duchess of Peterworth whispered to Lord Stanmore—

"My lord, you must ask Miss Whynne to dance, were it only out of compliment to me; and promise me not to sail off to the island of Cuba, or Jamaica, till I have given you a word or two of warning."

"I shall be beyond anything flattered to have the felicity of dancing with Miss Whynne," said our hero; "but with respect to my sailing off to the West Indies, I have no wish to raise the anchor you have cast for me here," and he kissed the well-known ring.

"Well, well," said the duchess, smiling, "begone now to your new partner."

The following day two equestrians were slowly

pursuing the usual round of Hyde-park, their grooms having discreetly dropped behind, beyond listening distance.

"Yes," said one of these gentlemen, "everything progresses most favorably. I had already ascertained that, although the line has never wanted a male heir, and therefore no countess in her own right appears since the first creation of Henry the Fifth, yet there is nothing in the wording of the original grant to exclude females; and yesterday I received the assurance of Lord Pomfret that he will support my petition to the utmost in the highest quarter."

"You are still in the prime of life yourself," observed the other gentleman, "and to be anxious about the claim of your successor may seem premature. However, I believe neither the Queen nor the Lords will interest themselves for a revived or disputed title, unless there be direct heirs."

"That is exactly it," said the first speaker. "The Queen's drawing-room is to be on the twenty-fifth, and the Marchioness of Penzance has promised to introduce my daughter. I flatter myself Hortense will produce an effect; for Lady Penzance will endeavor to interest her Majesty in the story before the presentation, so that my beautiful daughter will appear, with quite dramatic effect, as the injured heroine. Now, Lord Claud, let me thank you for your support and kindness on my first arrival. I feel it all the more because of the coldness of the

Marquis of Seaham. But one must have patience. He requires proof, as in a court of law, that there is no such person existing as the Viscount Stanmore, and he shall have it before many weeks are over."

"My brother is faithful to tenacity in his friendships," returned Lord Claud, "and has from the first taken the warmest interest in Lord Stanmore, as I must still call him until the decision of the court. Still, the love of truth has ever been one of my brother's greatest characteristics; and, though he will be immensely pained, he will withdraw all opposition sooner than oppose the truth."

"The Court of Scotland, and other friends of the supposed Duke of York, must have been greatly pained in the same way," observed the father of Hortense, "but withdrew their support when he was proved an impostor."

"But now, after all," said Lord Claud, "when the historian can investigate unrestrainedly and publish boldly, without caring to please the Tudors, it has become more than a doubtful point whether there existed any impostor, — whether the name of Perkin Warbeck was not fabricated to sustain the usurpation of Henry the Seventh, and the young king, Richard the Fourth, as basely murdered, by his execution at the age of twenty, as if he had been really smothered as a child."

"Oh, my lord?" cried Mr. Gerard Woolton, with darkened brow, "spare me these historical researches; though I own to having first quoted the victim, — for thus I consider Perkin Warbeck, — of a prodigious imposture."

"The same as that of Monsieur Léon Bauvin, as Viscount Stanmore?" added Lord Claud.

"How well you have remembered the name of this young man!"

"Yes, I prefer the modern history that passes before my eyes, and sounds in my ears;—I prefer to lay hold of living witnesses, and listen to the fireside story: it was in this way I first caught glimpses of the plot against the succession of the younger branch of my family, and resolved to pursue and expose it."

As these words passed his lips, a gleam of sunshine illumined the vindictive countenance of the West Indian, and expanded into a radiant smile. It was fully, and still more beautifully, returned by the centre person of a group of equestrians, — a girl in the full bloom of tropical beauty. Hortense Woolton was riding under the protection of the Spanish ambassador, and followed or surrounded, as it might please her caprice, by an increasing train of subordinate personages. The father was recognized by all, and after an exchange of smiling bows with the ambassador, took his place on the other side of the star of the day, — the enchantress of one brief London spring.

At that very hour, driving round the park *téte-a-téte*,

and so engrossed in conversation that they could only return, mechanically, the salutes of those who passed them, were the dowager Duchess of Peterworth and her most congenial step-daughter, Lady Emily Whynne.

"Now, then, my love," said the duchess, "I do begin to understand more distinctly this attempt of the younger branch of the Wooltons to dispossess Lord Stanmore of his birthright. Keep neutral, Emily, my dear child,—keep neutral. I rejoice that it is your sister, not you, who is to present Miss Woolton on the twenty-fifth, and to previously interest the Queen in her position; because Charlotte, being lady in waiting, does not become so much involved in a private act of friendship by so doing. You perceive, I do not ask you to feel, as I do, the whole corruption of the proceeding: I ask only neutrality, for the sake of family peace, as Colonel Whynne is in favor of the younger branch. But, now, tell me more minutely and consecutively, the account given by this infamous——, well, God forgive me! this important witness, who was once in the service of the Countess de Courtrai, maternal grandmother to Lord Stanmore, then lived with a family who took her to the isle of Cuba, where she passed to the service of Mrs. Gerard Woolton, at that time on a visit to her parents from Jamaica. Now, for the actual legend of the two baby boys."

"She states," said Lady Emily, "that when in

the service of the Countess de Courtrai, at Versailles, more than twenty years ago, she accompanied that lady and her daughter, the young widow, Lady Stanmore, to the sea-side, owing to the dangerous state of health of the little viscount. That the fever increased from the journey; that before the ladies sent for the medical practitioner of the place, they consulted together about changing the clothes of the two babies, and that Madame de Courtrai said, ' not yet, for he may recover;' that the medical man never saw, or knew there was more than one infant in the house, till after the death of the little lord; that he paid his little patient every attention possible, but happened not to be present at his death; that as this woman had to supply, in some measure, for the nurse's inattention to the healthy child, she watched all that was going on; and further states, that when the medical gentleman came to make the attestation of the death, he was astonished to be given the name of Léon Bauvin, and said: ' Why, ladies, I. was sent for to attend the infant child of Lady Stanmore. Madame, is not this your child?' The younger lady was weeping over the dead child, and could only sob out, ' Ah, yes.' But the countess said, ' My dear, your grief makes you talk quite foolishly. Lucille, take our little Arthur into the drawing-room, where Monsieur shall see him.' Lucille then went to fetch the nurse's child, that had been dressed by Madame de Courtrai, and when the doctor saw him, he started,

and cried, ' It seems the same ! oh, what a likeness ! ' "

" Why did they leave the wet-nurse behind, and
yet take her child to the sea-side ? " demanded the
duchess.

" Lucille always persists she does not know, and
the colonel says it is the worst point in the case," replied Lady Emily. " Oh ! mamma, is Lord Charleton feeling so secure that he is doing nothing for his
grandson ? Do persuade him to exert himself."

" I will, my dear child ; I shall see him to-night
at a private collection of choice paintings. He is to
show me one especial small picture that he thinks a
gem, almost hidden in a corner. I can speak quite
confidentially in that corner. I will entreat him to
get witnesses, and letters, and proofs of all kinds.
I well know the value of such things."

" Yes, indeed, mamma ; and George gratefully
remembers it all. He says he shall always believe
well for the termination of a cause, if you persevere
in it. He has already asked me, in this case, what
does D. D. think of it ? "

" But here, unfortunately," observed the duchess,
" we can only, in reply to all these bold assertions,
invoke the spirits of the departed. The mother and
daughter thus calumniated are both dead. There
must have been some perfectly good reason for not
taking the nurse,—for separating both children from
her,—most probably some infectious disorder ; but

this woman, her fellow-servant at the time, pretends not to know why she was left behind. This Lucille has been gained over to tell that one fact and no more. How true it is that 'facts are not truth.'"

While a certain circle in the London world of high life was occupied most intently with a painful mystery, that in a few weeks was to be set at rest by a private arbitration; the day arrived for the maiden speech in the House of Commons by the young Viscount Stanmore. The place for lady auditors was filled to personal inconvenience by his real friends, his doubtful friends, and those who wished to say they had heard the man who had become the chief topic of the day. Amongst the first of these, were the faithful friends of his mountain-home, the ladies Clara Moorland and Violet Chamberlayne, who were escorted to their seats by Lord Claud, with the promise to fetch them, when required, from his own allotted station in the diplomatic section. The young orator had already perceived his grandfather and the Marquis of Seaham, planted where they could see as well as hear him. From the excitement that had occurred during the previous fortnight between the two nations, both noblemen were rejoicing that Arthur had chosen for his subject the importance of peace with France. Their presence far from alarming, reassured him. He felt but one drawback; it was the conviction that, directly he became animated and warmed by his subject, a slight French cadence, more than accent, became confirmed. But as a foreign cadence is far better than constraint, Arthur resolved to forget the sound in the sense; and, in fact, gave the listening house so much solid sense, that the marquis, at first delighted, began to fear that he would prove only solid, and, in the end, heavy. The silent attention of the house, however, continued, and Lord Stanmore rising, at length, to the impassioned eloquence of which both himself and subject were capable, bore all hearts and votes in sympathy with his ardent desire, that the two noble and gifted nations of France and England, disdaining all petty jealousies, should unite in generous emulation for "Glory to God and peace to men of good-will!" The applause given was unanimous, heartfelt, and continuous. Congratulations to the venerable Earl of Charleton followed the sensation caused by the young orator, and were renewed later in the upper house, to which Lord Charleton and the Marquis of Seaham had then hastened. All clouds over the prospects of his beloved Arthur had dispersed to the view of the happy grandfather, and were forgotten for the next few hours by Lord Seaham. They lowered and blackened, however, more and more, as they approached to discharge the final thunder-bolt.

CHAPTER XIX.

FIDELITY IN ADVERSITY.

" Violet," said Lord Claud, in a few days after
the maiden speech of Lord Stanmore, " will you
lend me your pretty emerald ring for a few hours?"

" Certainly, dear uncle. I am so glad you admire
it. I am sure you will take care of it,—the greatest
care of it. You will return it to me this evening,
will you not?"

" I can promise to take the greatest care of it;
but as to returning it to you this very evening, I had
better not promise."

Violet, who had nearly withdrawn the ring, now
replaced it, saying :

" If you wish to order a similar ring, uncle, I will
execute the commission for you. Any experienced
jeweller can make one resembling this, by merely
looking at it. He will not require to keep it by
him."

" But I am not sure that I wish a fac-simile," said
Lord Claud. " Let me look at the setting."

She gave it into his hand, and while he appeared
to examine the setting, she watched the expression

of his countenance.   At length, to her astonishment, she perceived the tears in his eyes, and exclaimed,—
· "Oh! uncle Claud, you are unhappy; you who are generally so joyous.   It is something about the ring you are going to order.   You wish to make a farewell present to some one you love, because you are going back to Munich.   But, dear uncle, now that papa is minister for foreign affairs, you will soon be an ambassador, and you can marry this lady.   Is she the Countess Hortense?"

"Good heavens!" cried Lord Claud, extremely agitated, "what can you know of Hortense?"

"Ever since we have been in town this year," replied Violet, "I have heard the ladies of the French embassy talk of 'la belle Hortense,' and now this last week Lady Emily Whynne and the Marchioness of Penzance, who call to take me out driving, talking together in a mysterious way of 'la Hortense;' and they say, uncle, that you are fascinated by her."

" Every one is fascinated by her," said Lord Claud.

" Yes," continued Violet, " the marchioness has presented this beautiful Hortense at court, and told her sister that the sensation produced was unprece- dented."

" Ah, yes, of course; it could not be otherwise. But, Violet, my dearest girl, this beautiful Hortense is likely to cause you great unhappiness.   She is—"

" Oh, uncle, I understand.   You have taken off my ring.   Lord Stanmore has engaged himself to

14

this beautiful Hortense; and you love her. This is very wrong of him. I saw the ring he took from me glittering on his hand that day in the House of Commons. He caused a great sensation. Papa says it was the best maiden-speech he ever heard; and I was so proud to be betrothed to so fine an orator. Oh, how wrong of him to wear his ring, and·yet engage himself to another!"

While Violet bent her head on her hands, Lord Claud slipped the ring into his waistcoat-pocket, and said:

"Perhap, it would be easier for me to leave you under your present impression, my dear Violet; but truth is best. In the first place, Hortense is not engaged to any one. Secondly, she is not yet a countess, but claims, after her father, to be presumptive heiress to the earldom, — must I say it? — of Charleton."

"How can that be?" said Violet; "I do not understand."

"It has been discovered," continued Lord Claud, "that, without any fault on his part, the young man we have hitherto known as Lord Stanmore, has, in reality, no claim to that or any other title."

"When I first knew him," said Violet, "he was called Mr. Arthur Bryce. I liked him very much. It will make very little difference. I shall retain my own title, as my aunt does. I shall be Lady Violet Bryce. You may give me back my ring, uncle.".

"Dearest Violet, if it were as you suppose, all might still be arranged. But he is no relation whatever to his hitherto supposed grandfather. He is neither Bryce nor Woolton. He cannot claim even the baptismal names of Arthur Philip Dieudonné. He was changed at nurse, as it is commonly called. But in his case, the treacherous act was not by the nurse, his mother, but by the Countess de Courtrai, the maternal grandmother of the real little viscount, who, at his death, to prevent the grief of her daughter and the earl, and keep up her daughter's consequence, continued to have it believed that the nurse's child had died, — the likeness between the infants facilitating the deceit. The young man's real name is Léon Bauvin. He is the son of a simple soldier."

"But he is very good and very clever, and is faithful to me," said Violet, raising her head. "He is very graceful and accomplished and handsome. What does it signify that his name is Léon? I like the name."

"And could you bear the name of Bauvin?"

"Why not? Give me back my ring."

"Sweet Violet," said Lord Claud, "I will place the ring, this evening, in the hands of your father. Let his authority alone induce you now to wear it. You were not betrothed to Léon Bauvin."

Nearly at the very hour of that day, our hero received from the venerable earl the same announcement, with some modifications. Lord Charleton remained unshaken in the belief that he spoke with his own flesh and blood; and that bribes and perjury were about to produce a false sentence against his beloved grandson. This belief greatly mitigated the horror of the announcement. Arthur,—we will still thus term him,—felt also his spirit roused and his intellect quickened to defend the wounded honor of his mother and grandmother; and he listened eagerly to all that his grandfather and the marquis had prepared for the defence. The next surprise was, to find in the father of the captivating Hortense the rival to his claims; and to hear that the first legal authority had given his opinion that the family had far better settle their opposing claims by the marriage of the young people.

"Does mademoiselle know of this legal advice?" demanded Arthur, smiling.

"She does," replied Lord Charleton; "and told her father that had you been really cousins, the affair could easily have been thus settled; but that never would she marry the son of a peasant."

Just then a few hurried lines from the Marquis of Seaham were placed before Lord Charleton, to the intent, that the most pressing business had occupied him, and would occupy him till late at night; but that he had secured a private dinner, to which he invited his two friends, at seven o'clock.

Lord Charleton had a friend to dine with him; but Arthur was punctual to the time appointed. Towards the close of dinner, before the usual time for the servants to retire, the marquis desired the dumb waiter to be placed by him, and to be left with Lord Stanmore. A short pause followed the departure of the domestics, when the marquis said, with emotion:

"Stanmore, this may be the last time I thus address you."

"Good heavens! marquis, do you too, then, think so badly of my cause?"

"I think," replied Lord Seaham, "we have not yet done enough to frustrate the false swearing of the three witnesses from France. But this is what I have effected: I have engaged the active and practical assistance of the French government; so that the police, being made acquainted with the object of your grandfather's valet Julien's visit to Versailles and elsewhere, will aid him to the utmost, and they have already discovered the *conciérge* who lived with the Count and Countess de Courtrai. This has been useful. The old man remembers perfectly well that the nurse had a violent fever, which turned to typhus, and that all the family dispersed. Of course, her own child was removed with the rest."

"But this is admirable news," observed Arthur. "Why are you discouraged, my lord?"

"Yes, this is good; but still not enough to counterbalance the assertion of that woman, the lady's maid, that she actually watched Madame de Courtrai take the coarse linen chemise off the little Léon

14*

Bauvin, and place the fine cambric and lace on him, saying, 'none but the best henceforth for the little Arthur Dieudonné.' The woman was then called by madame, who put the infant into her arms, telling her to dress him directly in the clothes laid ready, and to take him into the drawing-room, to the medical gentleman."

There was here another pause : the marquis then added,

"You are, perhaps, not aware that, when once the sentence is given by arbitration, it is just as powerful as if, in an open criminal court, the judge pulled on his black cap against you. A few friends may still surround you, and call you Lord Stanmore ; but in the first new edition of the peerage, instead of Arthur Philip Dieudonné, &c., Viscount Stanmore, heir apparent, will be Gerard Woolton, Esq., heir presumptive ; and the doors of the royal palaces are closed against you as Viscount Stanmore, there being no such person in existence. However," continued the marquis, "if we look thus at the worst, it is that, being prepared, we may receive adversity with a manly spirit, and pursue the best path open to us. Lord Charleton, with his usual decision of character, has already written, and made legal, a new will, in which he leaves you, as Léon Bauvin, the whole of his immense fortune, and the re-purchased estate of Woolton Court, with the obligation of resuming the names of Bryce, Woolton, and of naming your eldest son Arthur Philip. Thus," continued his lordship, "if you are pronounced to be Monsieur Léon Bauvin, a native of France, you can be naturalized in England, or trust to me for getting you into the French embassy, where your own abilities and industry will raise you to an eminence. perhaps equal, if not superior to what you might have obtained as hereditary peer."

At these words of encouragement Arthur ventured to say :

" And Lady Violet ? "

" You are both very young," replied the father; " and while there is youth there is hope."

The following evening Arthur, charged with the commission to search through his mother's correspondence with his grandfather, and, accompanied by his own valet, Mr. Temple, was drawing near to the descent in the valley of Woolton Court. He had started early in the morning, and felt extremely fatigued. Yet this lassitude was overcome by painful excitement, as the pitch of the mountain was passed, and he approached the domain won back through years of toil, and still to be his by the faithful love of his grandfather.

" Heaven wills to show me the nothingness of accidental position," thought he. " I was first here as Arthur Bryce, heir of the rich merchant of Marseilles ; secondly as Viscount Stanmore, the future Earl of Charleton ; and now, to be probably declared

Léon Bauvin, the peasant soldier's son.   Well, be it so.   My soul, with all its powers and its faith in a better world, remains to me."

He entered Woolton Court, and while the valet and other domestics were occupied for his comforts on this unexpected arrival, he passed through the lonely echoing halls to the library.   There were already in his short experience many sweet memories attached to that and the other rooms.   While waiting for lights, he passed through the suite of drawing-rooms to the one where still stood, but in a sheltered corner, the harp of Lady Violet.   He partially removed the case, and gazed on the wreath of emblematic flowers that, in the short notice of three weeks, had been so beautifully executed on the white enamel.   A pang of tender remorse struck his heart, as he remembered its waywardness on the evening of her first performance.   He turned to the window : but the obscurity was becoming too confirmed, and he returned through the rooms, guided by the lights in the distant library.   There he found the refreshment he had ordered : after which, remembering the all-important motive for his presence at Woolton Court, he took a taper, and, mounting the stairs, proceeded to the once mysterious quarter of the nocturnal music, and entered the private sitting-room of the Earl of Charleton.   He came provided with the proper keys, and the papers and letters were all kept with such regularity, that Arthur easily found the packet of his mother's letters; that is, the correspondence of the late Lady Stanmore, during her residence at Versailles. As the earl had given him full permission to read what he pleased, Arthur passed the next hour in the perusal of these artless and interesting effusions of a young mother's love; but at length some passages, in the present state of his feelings, became too acutely painful: he rushed from them, and, hastily locking the door, fled to the chapel. Just at the entrance he rushed against the chaplain; but, instead of apologizing, he seized his hand, and dragged him before that point of the Stations of the Passion, where the soldiery are despoiling the Saviour of his garments.

"There!" cried he. "That is what they are doing to me. But I can bear all except to know that I was not *her* son!"

The utter astonishment of the reverend chaplain was succeeded by the deepest sympathy, as by degrees the whole story and its doubtful result were unfolded to him.

"But these letters," suggested he, "surely they will convince the impartial arbitrators that only a fond mother could have written them?"

"We must hope so," sighed Arthur. "I have come here for them alone. I am glad to have met you, reverend sir. You will now remember me before the altar."

"I always do so," replied he. "I have daily

remembered you before God, as one young and prosperous; praying that the world's smiles may not lead you to forget Him. I will now pray that its frowns may not drive you to murmur and upbraid Him."

Although Woolton Court and all its dependencies were still to be his, Arthur felt that when he next looked on each part, it might be under such circumstances of humiliation, of deprivation, of loss of confidence in his own identity, that he felt comfort in the holy presence and influence of his reverend companion.

They talked long and earnestly together, and with such good effect that our young hero, on retiring to rest, felt the soothing effects of resignation on even the physical nerves, and fell into slumbers long and deep.

CHAPTER XX.

THE ARBITRATION.

On Arthur's return to London he was agreeably struck with the happy look of his grandfather. Was it merely the affectionate feeling that the one he most loved was again beside him, or did the arrival of the letters reassure his hopes? Arthur could not determine the point, and began to question his lordship on the confidence he still felt in the issue of the arbitration; but Lord Charleton, placing his finger on his lips, said that more than strong hope would be premature, and our hero became for the next hour absorbed in a letter from Lady Clara Moorland.

"My dear cousin,—I risk what may appear superfluous to the sympathy of our friendship, a renewed assurance of that which you must claim through life, fidelity in my regard for you, which no accident can diminish. Should the arbitration deprive you of your title and position as head of your long line, the wise precaution of Lord Charleton in creating a new branch to his house in your person, and your accession to the family property by purchase, keeps you among the landed gentry who are, for the most part, younger branches of the nobility, or sufficiently ancient to be termed the untitled aristocracy. I am too much of an artist not to agree with your grandfather, that there exists between you certain family characteristics that are unmistakable to one who can distinguish between modelling and coloring. Therefore, you will ever be the 'Arthur Bryce' of our first meeting to your faithful friend and cousin,

CLARA MOORLAND."

This was the first time she had ever traced a line to him. His adversity had caused them to flow thus gracefully from her generous heart. Lady Clara had not requested any information, direct from himself, of the result of the arbitration; but as he folded up her first letter and placed it near his heart, he felt that, should the decree be adverse, he could reveal it the sooner to her.

On the important day our hero was not required to be present. The investigation of whether he was the future Earl of Charleton or Léon Bauvin could not be assisted by a witness who, at the date in question, was ten months old. The present earl, accompanied by his two most anxious friends, the Marquis of Seaham and the Duke of Peterworth, arrived at the appointed room in Somerset House, just after Mr. Gerard Woolton and his party, among whom were Colonel Whynne and the two eldest sons of the Marquis of Penzance. The witnesses for the plaintiff first recounted their several experiences of the

artful substitution of one infant for the other by the
Countess de Courtrai, in which the daughter, if not
active, was a passive participator. The counsel for
the defence then read the letters of the accused passive participator. They produced a marked effect,
but were soon nullified by the assertion of the chief
witness — the former lady's maid — that the young
Lady Stanmore, at the time of her infant's death,
was so bewildered with grief, that her mother could
persuade her to anything, and actually did induce
her to believe that she had had a brain fever, the
effect of which remained to make her mistake one
child for the other. Thus, the letters being written
by an innocently deceived person, instead of a participator in the plot, rendered them insufficient to
overthrow the testimony of the three former servants,
that on the 9th of February, 1833, at the town of
Dieppe, in Normandy, at the turn of the morning,
died Arthur Philip Dieudonné Bryce Woolton, Viscount Stanmore, aged ten months; and that a false
certificate was written by his maternal grandmother,
and sent to the authorities by the man-servant, one
of the present witnesses, mentioning the death in her
house, by fever, of Léon Bauvin, foster-brother of
her grandson, son of Jules Bauvin, soldier of the
regiment of Zouaves in Algiers, and of Sophie Mus-
cat, his wife, aged eleven months. The chief witness, Lucille Brontel, former lady's maid, further
deposed that she watched Madame de Courtrai take

the coarse linen off the little living child, and place on him the fine cambric and lace, saying, 'Nothing henceforth but what is choicest and best for the little Arthur Dieudonné.' To this last statement, however, the counsel for defence begged to remind the arbitrators that they just heard mentioned, in the letters of Lady Stanmore, that during the raging fever of the little Léon, he was given the softer linen of his foster-brother, which might, very probably, have left the infant viscount with no resources but to be supplied with the coarser wardrobe of the little peasant. There was now a pause. One of the arbitrators then said:

"Has the defendant anything to produce that can overbalance this strong circumstantial evidence?"

The Earl of Charleton, then arose and said:

"My lords and gentlemen, you have heard in the defence of the accusation brought against the Countess de Courtrai, that the nurse of her grandchild and mine was seized with a dangerous and contagious fever, from which, leaving her under efficient care, the whole family fled, the two ladies and their servants bearing with them to the sea-side, not only their own precious infant, but also the little child of the nurse, who soon became the chief object of their tender care and painful anxiety. You have heard passages in the letters, which give the opinion of the medical man at Dieppe, that one child having caught the fever, while the other escaped, was to be accounted for by the circumstance, that the nurse's infant always slept with its mother: the little viscount always in the room of his own mother, Lady Stanmore, in a little crib, close to her bed. Both infants were partially weaned. These circumstances, my lords and gentlemen, although to be duly considered, you have not deemed sufficient to outweigh the preponderating evidence given on the side of the plaintiff. I have been prepared for this, because, extraneous of the knowledge I possess of the character of Madame de Courtrai, they would not have sufficiently satisfied my own mind. I have, therefore, had recourse to anatomical science, to place beyond a doubt that the child interred in the cemetery at Dieppe was not my grandson. Much has been said of the likeness between the two infants; but, with the exception of the eyes, it was more likeness of age and coloring, than of feature and form. I could never have mistaken them beyond an instant. I had perceived each month certain characteristics to develop more strongly, which would, in after life, have rendered easy their immediate recognition. I, therefore, invited the visit of our eminent surgeon and publisher on anatomy, Sir Bentley Burder, and to meet him, one of the most celebrated artists for the *Illustrated News*, Mr. Otway; of whom I had been told that he could, at a glance, retain and place accurately on paper, every characteristic of a form and face. These two gentlemen met three weeks ago at my house in Carlton Gardens, and were introduced to my grandson, Viscount Stanmore. Mr. Otway made a full-length sketch of Lord Stanmore, and then, under the minute direction of Sir Bentley, a careful anatomical drawing of the face and of the hand. This letter was to me especially valuable as a test. Through the interest of my friend, the Marquis of Seaham, now minister for foreign affairs, I obtained the permission of the French government to exhume the skeleton of the infant in the cemetery at Dieppe. Two English surgeons, selected for their profound anatomical knowledge by Sir Bentley Burder, and the chief surgeon of Dieppe, made their observations together, and also the following attestation, to which they have affixed their names; and which Mr. Caldwell, one of two English surgeons, now present, will read aloud:

" We, the undersigned, charged with the secret confidential commission from the Earl of Charleton, and, under the protection of the English and French governments, arrived in Dieppe on the 3d of May, 1854. We proceeded, by appointment, to the house of the Sous-Préfect, where the police officers, having previously arranged everything, accompanied us to the chapel of the cemetery. Monsieur Foulet, the chief surgeon, and his assistant, had already arrived. Some formularies were gone through, to prove that the skeleton before us was the child buried on the 9th of February, 1833, as Léon Bauvin. We then proceeded to the anatomical examination of the face and hands, as follows : the head, a well-formed, full oval, the orbit of the eye large, the cheek-bones high, the lower jaw-bone short and square, the hand thick and strong, the bones perfect, the wrist large.

(Signed,)   WILLIAM CALDWELL,
               THOMAS HENRY NEEDHAM,
               ANTOINE FOULET."

The one then present of the three surgeons, read the following testimony of Sir Bentley Burder, on the anatomical examination of the head and hand of Viscount Stanmore :

" The head, a well-formed long oval, the eyes large, the nose Grecian, the cheek-bones small, the lower jaw-bone delicate, and rather long and narrow, the hand long and slender, the wrist small.

(Signed,)   BENTLEY BURDER."

Mr. Caldwell then came forward, and mentioned that the written testimony of Sir Bentley had not been shown to either himself or Mr. Needham, previous to their journey ; and was then further proceeding to point out the peculiarities distinct in the two formations, when Sir Bentley, in evident haste and excitement, entered the room ; and, after having bowed right and left, and all round, took the sign from Mr. Caldwell, that his presence was opportune, all preliminaries having been duly despatched.

15*

CHAPTER XXI.

Sir Bentley then commenced :

" My lords and gentlemen present, in addition to
the testimonial just read, I have to mention some
particulars relating to the visit paid last month to the
Earl of Charleton, when the examination was made
of the head and hand of Viscount Stanmore. The
gentleman artist who accompanied me was so much
struck with the resemblance in profile of the grandfather and grandson, that, while he was awaiting his
instructions, he drew, for his own amusement, the
two profiles, side by side, and wrote beneath, 'twenty and sixty.' Lord Charleton, on seeing it, said,
' add eleven years to the sixty, sir, and your sketch
is wonderfully correct.' His lordship then made to
us both the same comment you have heard of the
likeness in eyes and general coloring between Lord
Stanmore, when an infant, and his little foster-
brother : each being, in these respects, like his
mother ; but that there were marked characteristics
of form and expression belonging to his father's race
in Lord Stanmore, which time had, as he expected,

more fully developed: but which, even from his birth, were, to Lord Charleton, distinguishable from those of the other child. I noted, in my pocket-book, precisely as Lord Charleton enumerated to me, these hereditary characteristics, and I now draw them forth for the first time, to compare them with those just made by our scientific gentlemen on the little skeleton at Dieppe: first mentioning, that on parting, the earl risked these remarkable words: 'Should the gentlemen whom you have selected testify that, in the infant skeleton at Dieppe, they have found the head a longer oval, the cheek-bones smaller, the chin more pointed, and the hand and foot more slender than those of Lord Stanmore, I may then begin to doubt.'"

Sir Bentley now, taking from Mr. Caldwell the paper signed by the three surgical anatomists, proceeded to compare the structure of the two infants: first informing the arbitrators and the rest of the select assembly, that the circumstance of one of these infants having grown up to manhood, threw no difficulty in the way of the experienced anatomist. The two papers were handed round to all who had any responsibility in the utterance of their judgment; after which Sir Bentley thus resumed:

" Seeing, therefore, my lords and gentlemen, that, by the test of art and science, the little skeleton at Dieppe bears no resemblance to the Earl of Charleton, while, on the contrary, the young gentleman, called Viscount Stanmore, does bear the very facial lines of that nobleman, and the slender family hand and foot, we, scientific men, enter our protest against the sentence sought to be pronounced, that the two infants were changed."

Lord Charleton then requested to put some questions to the three former servants of Madame de Courtrai, which was granted; and, with visible reluctance, they stood at length before him. His lordship first spoke to the nurse, saying, in French :

" My good Sophie, I recognize you perfectly well. I remember you as a warm-hearted, industrious, and faithful creature; also as very fond of play when work was over,—another good feature in a character. The only thing I cannot satisfactorily make out in the part you are given now to play, is, your character of witness. A witness is a person who has seen something; and the meaning is stretched to a person who has heard something. Now, the scene of this supposed plot, to change your living child into my dead grandson, was the seacoast town of Dieppe, where you never were. Consequently, as you could neither see nor hear from Versailles what was passing at Dieppe, at what part of the history do you start forth as witness?"

Here Lucille, the lady's maid, reminded her thus :

" When the ladies came back."

" Oh ! yes," said Sophie. " When the ladies came back, my lord, I saw that the live child they brought back was my child."

"Now, listen, Sophie, and you, my lords and gentlemen, to a few short extracts from the letters already referred to : — 'The worst is now over, dear papa, of all our late affliction, — the announcement to poor Sophie that her little Léon was really dead ; for, of course she had been prepared for the event by being informed that the child had already caught the disease from her, and carried the seeds of it to Dieppe, to the great danger of us all. Mamma saved me, as she had promised, the agony of telling her the worst. When she had relieved herself by tears, I went to her with the beautiful locks I had cut off at the commencement of the fever ; also with a miniature I had painted of him surrounded by clouds, to show he had become an angel. She knows not which to prize the most — the hair or the likeness. At length I ventured to fetch our little Arthur, telling her she should always look on herself as his other mother. She almost devoured him with kisses, but then began to weep again ; and showed her grief in a way so poetical, that I must relate it : — She caught up the locks of hair I had brought, and, placing them on Arthur's head, bent her lips on them, that she might, while embracing Arthur, kiss what was left of her own Léon. Do not be afraid, — they were well purified. I see that Léon's hair is much darker than Arthur's, which seems to become more chestnut.' Now, Sophie, this is nature, — this is truth," observed Lord Charleton, as he folded the letter.

" What have you done with those relics of your little angel ? "

" I used to wear them, my lord; but you know I was advised to make a second marriage, so now I wear only the hair."

" And your present husband is such a kind, good man, he does not object to your wearing the hair ? "

" Oh, my lord, no."

" Well, my good Sophie, then let no other man deprive you of this consolation to a mother's love. Léon was your first-born, and he will come to meet you with other angels in the purity of love and truth, provided you duly prepare yourself for that hour by avoiding all subterfuge and deceit, and the entanglement of other people's falsehoods."

Some pencil words on a leaf from Lord Seaham's pocket-book were then placed in Lord Charleton's hands :

" The duke is dying to vindicate Madame de C— ; but I tell him that is most probably to be the winding up. Your valet, Julien, is also gasping to say something to that lady's maid of hell — that Lucille."

The reply to this announcement was to request that Mr. Julien, valet to the Earl of Charleton, might come forward as witness, and also put some questions to Madlle. Lucille, whom he knew. This being granted, Julien, with great alacrity, came forward, and, after the proper ceremonial bows, commenced as follows : —

"I humbly beg leave of this august company to mention some things to the credit of those virtuous and noble persons whom I have known while in the service of the Earl of Charleton, my best of earthly lords and masters. In the first place, I wish to do away with the impression that Lord Charleton and Madame la Comtesse de Courtrai were so wilfully determined to have an heir to the title, that they would have risked displeasing God by deceiving man. They were both sincerely pious, and often prepared for the possible loss of the little viscount, by counting up the various childish maladies he had to pass through. I remember, on one occasion I brought him in my arms to his grandfather and grandmother; and on madame's saying, — 'Ah, we must not make idols,' Lord Charleton replied, — 'Madame, what determination do you think I have made in the event of losing this child?' 'I cannot think,' said she. 'Why, to marry,' said my lord. 'Yes, madame, to marry again. I am but little past fifty, and am not an ugly man.'"

A general smile passed over the countenances of that grave assembly, with the exception of Julien, who now proceeded to accost his old acquaintance, Mademoiselle Lucille Brontel.

"Bon jour, Mademoiselle Lucille! You perceive that you are the only witness to be really interrogated, exposed, and punished; for this simple-hearted Sophie, notwithstanding your wicked prompting, soon agreed to the truthful statement of her young lady, that she had recognized and gratefully accepted the hair and picture of her child.   We shall hear no more of her as a witness; and as for my old acquaintance, Joseph, I cannot make out that he distinguished himself in any way at Dieppe, but in running for the doctor, and at length to give notice for the interment.   That he filled up his time most usefully between those two acts, I cannot doubt; but still there remain but these two incidents, to swear to which he has been brought from France and lodged for some weeks in London.   Let us commence with his fetching the doctor to the sick child of Lady Stanmore.   Did Joseph ever take a message accurately during the four years we served together in the two families of Lord Charleton and Monsieur le Comte de Courtrai?   And if about for once to start off with the correct message, were you not, mademoiselle, perfectly capable of suggesting to him that the doctor would come more readily if he thought the real child, instead of the adopted child of milady were his future patient.   Ah, mademoiselle, how often have I heard your worthy mistress say to you, — 'The truth, Lucille, the truth;' and our young lady, with more vivacity, — ' Come, mam'selle, I am wearied of all this duplicity; let me know the plain truth.'   To proceed to the second event of Joseph's stay at Dieppe, he being the bearer of the written announcement from Madame de Cour-

trai to the authorities, of the death, from fever, of
Léon Bauvin, aged eleven months, you have now
heard, with every one else that, by the testimony of
the most learned and impartial witnesses of London,
Madame la Comtesse wrote the simple truth. So
now, mademoiselle, take this advice from me, — for,
once we had a little kindness for each other, — take
this advice, to repent on the spot, of your breaking
God's command, ' Thou shalt not bear false witness.'
Become a great penitent on the spot, mademoiselle,
or you will become none at all. I know you well;
here, now, down on your knees, — that's it, — precisely. May God be praised !"

And, to the astonishment of all, Mademoiselle
Lucille Brontel fell on her knees, and, with clasped
hands and streaming eyes, followed the dictation of
Monsieur Julien in a most complete refutation of all
the calumnies she had uttered and sworn to ; while he
promised, on the part of God and those especial saints
of his and her devotion, pardon and protection, and
grace of perseverance : also, on the part of the noble
Lords Charleton and Stanmore pardon and protection.

The Marquis of Seaham now arose, saying :

" As when things have arrived at a crisis nothing
can be added, I have merely to suggest that a vote
of thanks be passed to the most noble and learned
arbitrators, who, having nothing left on which to
arbitrate, may be glad to breathe an air more pure,
and finally eat their dinners."

CHAPTER XXII.

SOME HAPPY DAYS.

"Let us all go back to one house," cried the Duke of Peterworth. "Let us all dine together, and talk it well over. Where shall it be?"

"Oh! at Lord Charleton's, decidedly," observed the Marquis of Seaham. "He must wish to see Lord Stanmore; and we deserve to be present at the meeting."

"Very true, my dear faithful friends," said Lord Charleton. "Let us have the enjoyment of an unconstrained dinner of us four only: giving God thanks, and then, as the duke says, talking it all well over."

As Lord Charleton turned from the heated room to his carriage, he perceived Sir Bentley Burder waiting for his, whom he took warmly by the hand.

"Your time, Sir Bentley, is more precious than mine: fix your own day to meet Lord Stanmore at dinner in Carlton Gardens."

"I think, my lord, I can name Sunday."

"Be it so, then. Shall it be seven or eight?"

"Either, my lord, will be equally convenient. I feel much gratified."

"It is *I*, Sir Bentley, who am the man deeply obliged."

So all the carriages rolled away; three of them, however, keeping in the same direction, and depositing their several lords in the entry of Lord Charleton's house, in Carlton Gardens.

"Is Lord Stanmore within?" was the first inquiry.

"Yes, my lord; came in about half an hour since; is in your lordship's own study below."

The three friends entered together, and Lord Stanmore, who had risen from his chair, stood silently awaiting the announcement that he was henceforth nobody, according to the laws of the country, and dependent solely on the faithful love of Lord Charleton.

"My dearest boy," said the earl, "what do you expect?"

"The constancy of your parental affection," returned he calmly, but very gravely, "and the friendship of the duke and marquis."

"And all you ever had or expected besides, Arthur," said Lord Charleton, placing a hand on each shoulder of our hero. "The arbitration is favorable—or rather has been anticipated, and rendered unnecessary, by the preponderating weight of evidence on our side, that you, and no other, are the true Arthur Philip Dieudonné Bryce Woolton, Viscount Stanmore, and future Earl of Charleton."

"Which last title may God long avert," said the

duke, smiling, and shaking Lord Stanmore warmly by the hand.

The marquis could not speak: so great a rush of feeling — of tender feeling — overcame him, that, detaining Arthur's hand within his, he seated himself by the table, on which he leaned, while Lord Charleton and the duke related the most important parts of the day's proceedings. The next half hour found the little party dispersed in the various dressing-rooms, attended by valets with all the luxuries of a renewed toilet. The marquis had sealed with an envelope the precious ring that had lain in the obscurity of his waistcoat-pocket so many days, and directing it to the Lady Violet Chamberlayne, sent it by one of his own footmen, whom he had detained. Beneath the address he wrote " Laudate Dominum." Having thus tenderly cared for the feelings of his young daughter, the marquis stretched himself on a chaise longue, until the summons to dinner; but, instead of falling asleep, refreshed his mind by an investigation of that of his temporary valet, Monsieur Julien, who had respectfully attended his lordship's toilet.

Julien had confided Mademoiselle Lucille Brontel to the care of long-known and respected friends, *en route* from Somerset House to Carlton Gardens, and had reached home in time to attend on his lord's guests. Finding that Mr. Temple had already shown the duke his room, Julien devoted himself to the marquis.

" Well, Julien," said Lord Seaham, " let me a little into your secrets. Having made this wonderful conversion of Mademoiselle Lucille, are you going to marry her?"

" Oh! no, my lord marquis," replied Julien, very gravely. " I wish her to become the foundress of a new Order in the Church — an order of penitents — of those who have offended by the tongue."

"Ha!" exclaimed the marquis; " a large community, Julien. No fear of want of members, but difficult to keep the peace."

" Not only difficult, my lord marquis, but impossible without good rules, and obedience to those rules."

" A great deal of silence, Julien?"

" Yes, my lord, a great deal of silence, but not total. The tongue is not to become a dead member, but a well-regulated and useful one, making reparation for the past."

" Why, Julien, you are a wonderful man. I am considering whether I ought to look for wings to your shoulders or a cloven foot."

" Neither, my lord marquis; there has never been anything wonderful in me. But a great many things have passed under my observation. I have been, from a boy, observing and thoughtful. God has led me particularly to remark and regret the sins committed by the tongue — sins confined to no class of society, pervading all ranks."

16*

"But, Julien, is it not a pity to confine this reformation to a cloister. Can you not extend the reform over all classes by means of associations, confraternities, third orders?"

"Yes, my lord marquis; that is my wish, that is my hope. If your lordship were not so harassed with foreign business, I might be encouraged to submit the rules to you for your enlightened observations."

"Are they drawn up?"

"They are, my lord. Those for the convent, and those for the world. I can take the latter to St. James'-square, when the London parliamentary season is over, and your lordship is starting for the country."

"Why, what a patient man you are, Monsieur Julien: like your good earl, with his thirty years at Marseilles. The parliament may not be released till August, and we are now only at the end of May."

"That is but a little interval, my lord, for me who have been wishing to have a reparation made to God since I was quite a lad. It seems to me, that when God wills a new service to be performed for Him, He throws in the path of him or her, who is to be the humble instrument, so many striking circumstances in that particular line of service, that, at length, the mind becomes quite ardent to have something effected; and, at length, in God's own good time, the moment comes for every detail to appear clear — the moment for action."

The dinner was then announced; the marquis wrote in his pocket-book—"Julien, valet to Lord C.—new Order—penitents—evil tongues—rules—confraternities—speak to the duchess of P.—August." In the leaf preceding, had been written—"Murat—Naples—Warn the A. at B.—write to A. at V."

The marquis was passing through the door-way, when Julien, who had opened it for him, said:

"One moment, my lord; I must detain you to mention that I am not the originator, even on earth, of this Order of the Holy Tongue. There is one who has felt called by God to institute it, but desires to remain hidden. This person drew up all the rules, and requested me to become the agent in London and Paris, just when I was travelling to bring proof of the evil tongues against Madame de Courtrai. I had, as I tell you, my lord marquis, been inspired since my youth to desire such an association, and that was just the moment to fire my zeal. The coincidence was very remarkable; but you see I was not really the first institutor. The truth above all things, my lord, when it injures no one."

With still greater regard for Julien, Lord Seaham descended to the cheerful little dinner-party; the conversation being, at first, kept up chiefly by himself and the duke; for Lord Charleton and his grandson seemed more disposed to listen in the tranquil sense of peace after the storm. A couple of hours had passed thus pleasantly, when the duties of the State were again thrust on Lord Seaham, by the arrival of his carriage, containing his most confidential secretary, Mr. Pemble. Lord Charleton offered his private study, which was accepted; but the conference did not end, as the marquis had hoped, in being left at liberty to accompany the duke to Stanhope-street, and carry the good news to the dowager duchess. The two carriages rolled off, the one to Mayfair, the other to Downing-street, while the two owners of the mansion entered their domestic chapel.

Nearly the whole of the following day was spent by Arthur with the family of the marquis in St. James'-square, and principally with his faithful Violet. Calm happy hours these, enhanced by the details which Lord Claud had enabled the marquis to give of her immovable constancy. Lord Stanmore also saw Lady Clara, and gratefully acknowledged the precious letter that, as a relic, he still wore. Both aunt and niece found traces of the adversity that would fain have claimed him. Violet observed, with tearful emotion, that his spirit seemed subdued; but Clara, remembering the almost prophetic adjuration of Sir Henry Moorland, at Marsden Park, silently prayed that the good effects of the past trial might endure to the end.

On the 1st of June, the grandsire and his heir, remembered, as a duty to early friendship, a long-announced matineé champêtre in the grounds of a certain

Mrs. Colville, whom Lord Charleton had known and esteemed during his long residence abroad. She had returned rich to England, a few years before the re-purchase of Woolton Court, and had bought a lovely place on the banks of the Thames, at Chelsea. Shy, proud, and diffident of her own power to inspire or retain the friendship of others, she had shunned making any claim to that of "Mr. Bryce, of Marseilles," suddenly made known to her by a mutual acquaintance as the Earl of Charleton. They met; however, accidentally in London; and so much real regard was evinced by his lordship in the mutual pleasure of meeting, that Mrs. Colville ventured to request the honor of his company at the "fête champêtre, with pretty little Arthur, if the Easter holydays were not over."

Lord Charleton promised for himself, and conditionally for "pretty Arthur," now six feet high. He now reminded our hero of the day, and requested him, as a favor to himself, not to accept any other engagement.

Dear England was kind enough to smile her best on that summer day, amid the walks and grottoes, and rockwork, and waterfalls, and views of the river, and sudden turns and surprises, with aviaries and water-fowl, and garland arches, and a Welch harper, around whom amateur villagers danced most merrily. It was consistent with Mrs. Colville's timidity that she preferred to the regular breakfast tables in the banquet style, refreshments awaiting her guests at every turn, temptingly arranged, and offered by Damons and Delias of most approved Arcadian descent. After paying their respects in true cordiality to their hostess, Lord Charleton wandered here and there with the being he most loved on earth, in perfect enjoyment of his society and appreciation of the scene around them : Arthur appeared to be in a sympathetic mood.

"How delightful it is to know no one here?" exclaimed he. "I think I enjoy this festive scene more than anything presented to me as pleasure, since our arrival in London."

At length they stopped at a vista commanding the river, not far from which appeared a little empty bower.

"Let us enter there," said Lord Charleton; "the view must be the same as from this spot."

They turned to enter, but another and unperceived shady little walk led to the same unoccupied arbor, to which advanced, at the same moment, a middle-aged gentleman and a young lady, apparently his daughter. Both parties drew back, bowing politely; then each protested they were not fatigued, and begged not to prevent the others from entering, till at length the stranger addressed Lord Charleton by his title, who, looking more directly at the former, recognized Mr. Gerard Woolton, while Lord Stanmore, who had been watching the averted head of the young lady, now ventured to claim a fair cousin in his partner at Lady Emily Whynne's ball. Lord Charleton, surprised and gratified at being thus sought by relations he had feared would continue estranged, if not antagonist, gave both father and daughter an affectionate and joyful greeting.

"There is really not sufficient room for four persons," at length observed Hortense to Arthur; "we are too young to be tired. Let us walk to the cascade, and hear the band. They have finished their monotonous repetitions for the dances, and are now commencing strains worth hearing."

With a graceful farewell to Lord Charleton, the beautiful girl led the way, and our hero followed, leaving the plaintiff and defendant of an anxious cause in the bonds, apparently, of a fast cementing friendship.

CHAPTER XXIII.

VERY EQUIVOCAL PROOFS OF FRIENDSHIP.

The youthful couple proceeded, arm in arm, to the spot where the instruments of harmony invited them; our hero feeling and professing that the charge of so newly-found and lovely a cousin, would make any cascade, and any music, seem perfect to his senses. The agreeable lassitude he had felt after the mental tension of the preceding days, was now succeeded by an animation and enthusiasm that was not lost on his companion. From an embarrassed and even pained expression, near the bower, her countenance became the sunny dial of their first meeting; yet she was, for her, very silent. Was she quite engrossed by the music, or had she on her mind something difficult to be confided? Arthur at length became aware that such must be the case; he first rallied, then entreated, and finally drew forth the words:

" The chief arbitrator still says the same thing."

" The chief arbitrator," echoed our hero, greatly amazed. " Is it possible that your father has left you uninformed of the result of the examination ? "

" There was no result," said Hortense. " The arbitration has not been given.   All yet remains suspended; and it is for that reason I mention to you, for your own sake, that there is a way to effect a private compromise. Why do you force me to say this? Why cannot you understand me?"

" I do, — I do understand you; and Oh! Hortense, when this suggestion was first made, had you then replied less proudly, the proposed union between us would have caused the most terrific struggle in my heart, for you fascinated me as you have many others; but even then I was betrothed, and now — "

" Yes; you were insulted by my reply," interrupted she.   " But remember that I fully believed what I said; and I said the truth so far, that if you were not Lord Stanmore, you were the son of a peasant, — of a common soldier."

" But even had it been so, the secret would have been kept. I had received the education of a nobleman; I had the tastes, the feelings, the habits of one : all this my friends of the nobility fully recognized and appreciated ; they promised me fidelity, and would have kept it."

" But for all that you would have been base-born."

" No, Miss Woolton; no one born in lawful wedlock is base-born. Besides, I cannot feel that honest lowly station is base, or that I need have blushed for the brave young soldier who fell for his country on the sands of Africa."

"Who you are," said Hortense, "is not yet decided. You are risking more than you are aware of by stifling the feeling you have for me under this foolish resentment. Let us return to the arbor, where our two natural guardians sit, and declare ourselves plighted to each other. All will then go smoothly for the future Earl and Countess of Charleton. If not, you will bitterly repent this sullen anger for a few rash words. My father never will look upon you but as a peasant changeling."

"He is welcome to his thoughts," returned Lord Stanmore; "but now listen to me,—you, his daughter, whom I do love and admire with the pride of a relative. I have no sullen anger, or anger of any sort against you. On the contrary, I feel most grateful for the benevolent and cousinly wish to sacrifice yourself to the general peace and welfare of the family. I am not so blind as to suppose that *you* would be otherwise than a victim, were I to act as you propose: and other ties bind *me*. The Lady Violet Chamberlayne, daughter of the Marquis of Seaham, whose young heart had, with her father's approbation, been given me some months before this late discussion, has remained constant to a betrothal that did not rigorously bind her. It has been in vain to represent to her, in detail, that the accidents of my life were changed. *I* was the same, she pleaded.

She has remained heroically firm to me.   I am hers forever!"

A short pause followed.   Hortense Woolton then said, in a solemn manner:

" Remember, I have warned you."

" You do not seriously mean," said Lord Stanmore, " that your father, in the first rage of disappointed ambition, would attempt my life?"

" Not, perhaps, your life," she returned, in the same solemn tone; " but in youth and health and prosperity there are things still more precious than life.   However, I have warned you.   Let us go down nearer the river; my father talked of boating from these grounds.   We can all return together."

As Miss Woolton arose from where she had been seated, she placed, as a signal, her delicate handkerchief on the end of her parasol, and waved it high above her head.   One of the hired attendants immediately informed her, respectfully, that servants in livery were not permitted to enter the gardens; but that he would immediately go to one entrance, and send to the other to secure her carriage.   Miss Woolton took the man a little aside to explain to him the return by the river; and immediately, as if having awaited an opportunity to speak in confidence, the voice of his own valet, Mr. Temple, in very bad French, commenced, thus translated:

" My lord, I beg of you not to turn round to me, or seem to hear or know me in the least.   No one knows my person in these gardens, therefore I can warn you. There is a plot, my lord, to get you down the river to the docks, and put you on board one of the Jamaica merchant vessels, with some false story against you, as a runaway. That young lady meant no good by the signal of her handkerchief on the parasol. Oh, pray do not turn towards me, my lord! If you wish to give any orders, call my little dog, and talk seemingly to him, if you please, my lord."

"Or rather as *you* please, my good friend," replied Lord Stanmore. "Here Cherry! Cherry!" and the little dog ran capering to the summons: "where is my grandfather, pretty Cherry?"

"My lord is gone home," said Temple, "having had a false message from his grandson, that he had suddenly felt ill, and had borrowed Mrs. Colville's carriage to return to Carlton Gardens."

Lord Stanmore continued to play with the dog, while he ruminated thus:

"So, the kidnapping to Jamaica, and the imprisonment in that island, was the worse than death, of which that extraordinary girl has warned me. But how inconsistent in her, to first warn, and then betray me? Is it revenge against me for my fidelity to Violet, or ambition that can endure no longer the one obstacle to her personal elevation? Who can tell! Does she herself know her own heart? Has she one?"

In the midst of these unanswerable questions, a note was placed in his hand:

"We are all waiting for you. I was obliged to leave you to take the man for orders to papa. We are all going in the boat as far as Whitehall Stairs, and to sup in Carlton Gardens. Follow the bearer of this.   HORTENSE."

"Ha! syren," thought Lord Stanmore, "I will not let you know that I have unmasked you. Present my compliments to Mr. and Miss Woolton, and that I regret I must renounce the pleasure of the water-party, having to pay my respects to Mrs. Colville before I leave her hospitable grounds."

"Mrs. Colville is gone down to the water, sir, to see the party off. I'll show you the way—the nearest way, sir. Oh, here is Mrs. Colville, and here are all the water-party. It's to be the original time, I suppose, and then all her own guests being gone, Mrs. Colville will go in the pleasure-boat, and sup at the Earl of Charleton's in Carlton Garden."

"Oh, that is the original plan, is it? Made while Lord Charleton was here this morning?"

"Yes, sir, precisely."

Lord Stanmore, as if still playing with the dog, moved from the man to the other side of his valet, Temple, saying in French:

"Come, Cherry, hide yourself in the crowd; but call the real Cherry away from me, for fear he should be lost; and in a few minutes come forward, as if

17*

just arrived with letters for me of great importance from the town I represent in parliament; I will then say more. Better make some change in your dress," he added, as he returned to the hired attendant, still caressing and playing with the little dog, who remained very contentedly with him till whistled for by Mr. Temple, who had strolled to a thick group of persons. These were complacently and loyally listening to the national anthem, while a well-dressed file of company were moving from the grounds; and by passing between our hero and the machinators, called "the water-party," gave him a few minutes longer to form his plan of escape. He felt convinced that the man still standing near him, and many, if not all the occasional attendants out of livery, were in the pay of Mr. Gerard Woolton, and that even good Mrs. Colville had been made to believe the original story of the changeling and the generosity of Mr. Woolton, in wishing to hush all further investigation, by the marriage of the young people. With this perfect confidence in her elder guest, words would be useless from himself, whom she still called "Mr. Arthur," and, probably, was induced by Mr. Woolton to consider a wilful boy. He had no confidence that the so-called "police in plain clothes," were really such, and felt himself to be already virtually a prisoner. A few minutes more, and his plan of action was determined; and with it all his courage and self-possession.

The band passed with the few lingering guests, and the water-party, headed by Mrs. Colville, on the arm of Mr. Woolton, crossed the chief walk, to which Lord Stanmore, with perfect self-possession, had advanced to meet them.

"I think, said that lady, " that where we now are is as pretty a spot as any to remain quietly in — just our own little snug party — till six o'clock, the hour for our boat."

All, of course, assented; the "all" consisting, besides Mr. Woolton, his daughter, and Lord Stanmore, of Mrs. Colville's niece, an extremely pretty girl, and two partners of the late Mr. Colville, who looked alternately at the queenly Hortense and the gentle shepherdess, Maria Colville, then at each other, mutually said " humph," and recommenced their scrutinizing comparison; while Mr. Woolton held Mrs. Colville in discourse respecting the splendid offers he had refused for Hortense; and that young lady, surprised and piqued by the self-possessed and dignified attentions of Lord Stanmore, seemed determined to probe his inmost soul.

Thus had passed half an hour, when, advancing rapidly from the principal entrance, appeared the valet, Temple, closely buttoned to the throat, very genteelly equipped, and holding, as most precious, a long, official-looking packet of letters. The young man, on reaching the seated group, bowed to all; then said respectfully to Lord Stanmore:

"I believe I have the honor to address the new member for Helkington, in Cheshire, Viscount Stanmore?"

"I am he," replied Lord Stanmore. "May I inquire the motive of this visit?"

"My name, my lord, is Temple; perhaps you may remember me at the town-hall at Helkington. I have brought some important letters and papers, which require an answer."

"Ha!—Temple. Oh! yes, I remember perfectly. Permit me, Mrs. Colville, for a few instants."

And Lord Stanmore, taking the packet from Temple, stood with him opening the papers quite in sight, but out of hearing, to prepare their counterplot.

"Temple," said Lord Stanmore, "I can fix my mind but on one mode of escaping, without quarelling, or having to accept or refuse a duel, from this most cunning and bitter enemy. There is no time left to combat my plan, and my reasons for it. You must simply aid me in my hour of peril, as I will reward you when once more at rest. You must get a common boat, and fee the men well. You will make them place a white flag at the helm. Your only care is to watch the pleasure-boat, which will start from the steps of this garden at six o'clock. You must keep a little in advance. At the moment this pleasure-boat will pass the hospital, you will see me throw myself overboard, and sink. I shall dive and float with the stream, under water, while the pleasure-boat will, of course, be stopped. Directly you perceive my head above water, stop your boat. I shall soon arrive at the side. Before committing myself to the water, I shall row a little with the boatmen, which will give me the opportunity to throw off my coat, and ' loosen all ties,' " added he, smiling for the first time.

Poor Mr. Temple, who had turned very pale at the words " throw myself overboard, and sink," now responded to the smile.

Lord Stanmore opened another letter, and said :

" I must not omit one very important direction. It is, that you must pay some other boatman to keep near you, and to hoist the white flag in his boat directly you shall have lowered it in yours, which must be the instant I have my hand on the side of your boat to enter it. This is done to mislead our pursuers, should they distinguish my form issuing from the cold bosom of Father Thames. I think, Mr. Temple," added his lordship, in a louder tone, as he returned to the water-party, " that for the present we have done all that can be effected by mere arrangement. We shall soon, I hope, meet to thank Heaven for our success."

Before Lord Stanmore and Mr. Temple bowed and parted, the former whispered,—

" Temple, have you a rosary ? "

" Yes ; and have you, my lord, a medal ? "

" Yes ; that will be one of the ' ties ' *not* to be loosened, — au revoir ! "

"I think," said Mrs. Colville, "you must have received some good news, Mr. Arthur, you look in such high spirits. It is a great thing to get into parliament so young."

"It strikes me I saw that young man in the gardens earlier in the day," observed Mr. Woolton.

.But conjectures on that topic were interrupted by the arrival of refreshments in a neighboring summer-house, whither the little party repaired, as a final act, before going on the water. Mrs. Colville had possessed sufficient penetration to see that the interview with that Mr. Temple had produced an exhilarating effect on "Mr. Arthur." In truth, the excitement was beginning to be too apparent, and was conquered only by painful thought regarding Hortense. He could no longer hope that her warning had been more than a threat. This afflicted him. He longed to find in her some generosity of heart; but the interval in which to prove it was becoming very contracted. They had already descended the steps of the summer-house. Mr. Woolton presented his arm to Mrs. Colville. Lord Stanmore had the privilege of supporting his fair cousin; and Miss Colville followed, with the two partners of her late uncle.

"Hortense must believe that I am, on entering this fatal boat, to bid adieu to all that life holds dear; yet she prevents me not. Oh! blessed betrothal to another, that has saved me from this heartless worldling. She would have married me to have become Countess of Charleton; but prefers to be so eventually in her own right: and, therefore, after a few vague warnings and threats, becomes an accomplice in this scene of kidnapping me to Jamaica!"

Thus ran the undercurrent of Lord Stanmore's thoughts, while the upper flow was all hilarity and compliments to the object of them, as they seated themselves in the graceful little pleasure-boat, and pushed out from the garden bank.

"I believe we are ordered for the West Injee docks," half observed and half demanded the senior boatmen.

"Oh! my goodness," cried Mrs. Colville, laughing. "Pray, come and rectify this mistake, Mr. Woolton. We are going to Whitehall Stairs, my good man."

"Very likely, marm; but that does n't prevent both."

"True, true," said Mr. Woolton, with a ghastly smile; "but pull away now, my men. 'T will be time enough to think of other excursions when we have managed the stairs."

He then placed himself so that the men only could see his countenance, and a few low words were uttered on both sides. Still Hortense spoke, not to prevent, but to deceive, in bewitching prattle.

In the mean time, Mr. Temple had secured the little boat of rescue, with two strong rowers, and a white flag at the helm. At six o'clock he entered it, and a few minutes after the men were resting on their oars, within hail of Chèlsea Hospital. There were several pleasure-boats advancing from the west at the same time. Mr. Temple had hoped to recognize the white sleeves when Lord Stanmore should cast off his coat to row; but the rowers in each of the boats looked alike. "Five of these boats were approaching, two were passing the hospital, when, like a flash, the white vest and sleeves from the second in advance showed on the edge, and a tall form was lost to sight in the waters. A piercing shriek followed from that same boat, — a shriek of wild remorse !

As Lord Stanmore had foreseen, the pleasure-boat stopped : so did the others less in advance, as soon as they had arrived sufficiently near to offer assistance; while the one ahead turned back. In the mean time our hero swam under water with the current so swiftly that while Mr. Temple was gazing on the part near those boats, the head of the fugitive swimmer had drawn near to the friendly bark, and the stout rowers, seizing the raised arm, assisted him in. Lord Stanmore embraced his faithful servant, — both exclaimed : "Thank God!" while the latter immediately lowered the white flag, and handed it to the men of the next boat, who fixed it high at their helm.

"Now, cried Lord Stanmore, addressing his own

immediate rowers; "now row, my men, for the very nearest stairs, however steep and unfashionable they may be. We will clamber up. In the mean time, give me an oar, for a dripping man must keep in action."

They soon arrived at some safe but uncommemorated steps, which, happily, proved not far from a cab-stand, and, taking the first within hail, made the best of their way, not to Carlton Gardens, but to the Marquis of Seaham's, in St. James'-square.

18

CHAPTER XXIV.

MR. TEMPLE had taken the precaution to purchase, at a ready-made warehouse, a large wrapping woollen cloak and a hat; therefore, on arriving in St. James'-square, Lord Stanmore was sufficiently clad to present himself to those who knew him, and to retire to a dressing-room until Temple, who had detained the cab, should proceed to Carlton Gardens, and send him a complete suit, with linen, by Monsieur Julien, if possible. Temple himself was to remain there, and relate the whole proceedings to the earl, who would, therefore, know many things of which his grandson was still ignorant,—the chief of these being, how Temple had become acquainted with the plot against the freedom of Lord Stanmore. The latter had suspected the truth, that Julien's influence over Mademoiselle Lucille Brontel had frustrated the machinations in which she was to have borne a part, and have reaped the bad reward. He did not, however, make either inquiry or comment during the drive from the river; and was now, as he reposed in a warm bed, at leisure to reflect on the whole of that remarkable day, — resolving to keep silence, and to induce others to keep it, on the painful part enacted by his kindred. This feeling had developed into a principle by the arrival of Julien with the materials for a renewed toilet, and he informed that faithful domestic of the resolution he had made, to divulge to no one but the Marquis of Seaham, whose self-invited guest he was, the extraordinary events of the day.

"Mr. Woolton and his daughter," said Lord Stanmore, "are acting under the influence of a stronger temptation than the mere earldom of Charleton; they are endeavoring to secure that as a step to something greater. What that elevation may be, I cannot divine; but I am convinced, that all the powers of mind and heart of Miss Woolton are bent towards the attainment of something hidden and unknown to us. Having said this to you, Julien, which I shall repeat to the marquis alone, I shall say no more, even to those who have my confidence. Let no revenge sully my tongue."

"Oh, my lord!" cried Julien, "I am edified beyond expression. Your lordship is, indeed, fit to become the first knight of the Holy Tongue. I have the power to do this; I mean that, having already inscribed the names of fifty associates, I am eligible to be a knight, which honor can be transferred, and I beg to name your lordship."

"It is now my turn to be edified," said Lord

Stanmore; "for you are renouncing what you have justly earned."

"But an heroic silence like yours, my lord, is far beyond the mere trouble of collecting fifty associates; besides, in the world, knights are noble, which I am not."

"But this order of the Holy Tongue is the nobility of heaven," returned Lord Stanmore. "However, my good Julien, as I well know that the first desire of your heart is to found this confraternity, and that your zeal will soon collect fifty more members, I will accept to be your first knight, and will ask Lady Violet to be the first canoness."

The entrance of the marquis, to greet his guests, here arrested the conversation.

At that hour, the venerable Earl of Charleton was hearing the narrative, from his grandson's faithful and intelligent valet, of the second attempt, made by a desperate ambition, on the personality of his heir.

Although related in the manner the least calculated to excite the alarm of the aged nobleman, the mere facts could not but make the heart to suffer, and the head to ponder long and painfully; yet, in the midst of this mental suffering, arose a twofold thanksgiving: first, for the preservation of his grandson; secondly, for the courage and prudence of his whole plan of escape; the last, but not least, being his choice of St. James'-square, instead of Carlton Gardens, in case the rescue had been perceived on the river.

"Did ever the patience of heaven witness so cool and noble-looking a rogue!" at length escaped from the self-control of Mr. Temple. "I should not be surprised if to-morrow morning he came as your heir-presumptive, my lord, to offer you his heart-felt condolence, to tell you the river had been dragged without success, and to inquire whether you or himself should officiate as chief mourner."

Temple, in predicting this, was a true prophet. All happened exactly to the letter, yet all around looked so little like a tragedy of real life. And where was Hortense, and what her feelings? The evening of the scene on the river, after the real horror and remorse for having caused the suicide, as she thought, of the obstacle to her ambition, followed the complacent sense of the advantages of so sudden and self-inflicted a removal. At her request, she was taken by her father to the house of Colonel Whynne, in Belgrave-square, being the nearest to the river belonging to a friend. There, more than ever, the heroine of an admiring and excited group, Hortense related the despair of Léon Bauvin, and the fatal act which left her father heir to his just claims. Colonel Whynne had been present at the complete refutation of this story of the change of infants, at the arbitration in Somerset House; but the heat of the room had made him drowsy, and the

18*

assurance afterwards of Mr. Woolton, that the united testimony of the surgeons was a discovered piece of rascality, made him confess himself unable to follow the right clue.

"I shall be happy to wish you joy, my dear sir," said the gallant soldier; "when it all comes to a fortunate conclusion; but I confess myself totally unable to discover the truth. I am no lawyer."

Hortense was removed the following morning to the house, in Lower Brook-street, that her father had taken for the season; and the following letter was written in the quiet of her temporary home, at the time Mr. Woolton, according to Temple's conjecture, was proceeding to visit his supposed bereaved relative, the Earl of Charleton :—

"To his Serene Highness Prince Ernest Walfenshreidenfel, to the care of Field-Marshal Von Pillinsgrennen, Baden,—In my last letter I informed your highness that I was about compelled, by obedience to the wishes of my father, to espouse the dying Earl of Charleton. I would have proved a faithful and tender nurse the few weeks he might have lingered; but fate has decreed to remove him to another world; therefore, my father and myself, having now the rank required by the formalities of the German courts, your highness has only to place the proper announcement of your wishes in the hands of the chamberlain, Von Haufmans, and to claim the promise made by your august brother, that, once a countess in my own right, the marriage should receive his sanction. Let me then be insulted no more by the offer of the left hand in marriage to Hortense Woolton, who though noble, was without title. I never have consented — I never will consent, to our union, but with the free right hand, giving me the title of serene highness, the ermine, the equerry, the ladies-in-waiting, the guard of honor. Your last letter was too full of those passionate but vague expressions, which I have before told you, suit neither my birth, my character, nor the trust I have placed in the truth and perseverance of your love. But I will not close this letter, my too dearly loved Ernest, &c."

Then followed lines from the heart. The letter was sealed and despatched, by previous permission, to one of the secretaries of the Prussian ambassador; in whose bag it departed from London, at the very hour in which with rage and despair distorting every feature, Gerard Woolton re-entered his house, and informed his daughter that Lord Stanmore was alive and well; that the discovery of their plan to decoy him on the river to the docks, and thence to Jamaica, had been announced to him in the gardens at Chelsea. That he dived and swam to a boat prepared for him, and had passed the night at the Marquis of Seaham's, in St. James'-square.

If great part of the torments of the eternally-condemned consist in mutual upbraiding and recrimination; there are scenes on earth which, in sad horror, give a foretaste of those worse, because hopeless, halls of anguish. Such as these occupied the following two hours in Brook-street, during which some discoveries were taking place in Belgrave-square, by Lady Emily Whynne, that tended to close — politely close — that house to both father and daughter. Lady Emily, on receiving Miss Woolton on the previous evening, had arranged that her eldest daughter, Georgina, should resign her room to her young friend, and sleep in a smaller one adjacent. This was effected, though half the night was passed, not in sleep, but in most unprofitable discourse. One confidence made that night was the now hoped-for marriage of Hortense to the youngest brother of a reigning duke in Germany; and the rough copy of the letter, just described, was then dictated by one and written in pencil by the other to Prince Ernest, which, on the departure of Hortense to her own house, had been accidentally left on the toilet table. This paper, in a handwriting which Lady Emily perceived to be that of her own daughter, was brought to her by the maid servants, who were restoring the room to its usual use; and Lady Emily Whynne, puzzled and shocked, read it over with Colonel Whynne, till, at length, their hearts were inexpressibly relieved to find that the tissue of falsehoods, and the secret engagement to the foreign prince, were to be traced, not to their own child, but to their late guest.

" Well, poor girl," observed the colonel, " we must keep her secret now we have read it. How like the pencilling looks to Georgina's? Thank God *she* has no secrets; at least, I hope not; for they involve, by degrees, such falsehoods and deceit."

The colonel rang the bell.

" Is Miss Whynne within ? "

" I will inquire, sir."

" Tell her I desire to see her immediately," and in a few instants the lovely Georgina appeared.

" Tell me," said her father, " whether during this enthusiastic friendship with Miss Woolton, you have ever seen or known anything that you would be ashamed to tell your parents ? "

" Never but once, papa."

" I shall not betray you, Georgina; tell me of that once ? "

" Hortense once told me, papa, that she knew a beautiful girl, who was going to marry a man that she did not love, merely because his rank would enable her afterwards to marry the man she did love, and who was too far above her in her present position. She laughed at my not understanding how the first marriage could help her to the second, and told me that this beautiful girl had been taught to manage poisons so skilfully, that it would not be long before she was a widow. I was so filled with horror, papa, that I did not recover my esteem for Hortense until she assured me that she only spoke in that light manner about it to try my disposition.   This is not quite all, papa."

Here the colonel started to his feet, Lady Emily seized the open letter, and poor Georgina burst into tears.

"Yes," cried Lady Emily, "here is the clue to them,—to all this hitherto incomprehensible part in the letter, ' I would have proved a tender nurse during the few weeks he would have lingered.'"

"This must have been planned at the moment Mr. Woolton lost the cause by arbitration, and for a second time thought of the alliance between Lord Stanmore and his cousin; and this fine young nobleman would have been given gentle doses of arsenic, or some other poison, by his tender bride, that would have left her, just as she says, *in a few weeks*, a widow, heiress to the Earl of Charleton, and consequently, it seems, by some promise of the reigning Duke of Wolfenshriedenfel, eligible to become the wife of his youngest brother!"

"Yes, mamma, the precedent has been given now some time in the smaller German courts, by the marriage of Princess Mary of Baden to our Scotch duke."

"There is a great deal still very inexplicable," observed Lady Emily, pondering.   "The duchess would probe the affair far better than I."

"Oh! mamma," cried Georgina, "private papers ought to be respected.   I cannot help feeling some surprise that you and papa have read the confidential letter of a guest under your roof to a perfect stranger. And grandmamma is not disposed favorably to Hortense. She would have become her enemy directly."

"I must first reply, my dear child, to your feelings of consternation at my having read this rough copy of a letter. The handwriting is not that of Hortense till just the close. Great as the likeness is between your style and hers, I know them apart. She must have dictated the letter, and you handled the pencil."

"You are right, mamma. Hortense was so excited and fatigued with the shock of seeing Lord Stanmore throw himself into the water, that she could only dictate."

"Then, my dear Georgina, all surprise on your part ought to cease. A mother has a paper brought her by her servant, in her young daughter's handwriting, and her eyes rest on these words : 'your last letter,' &c. Ah! thank God that this dangerous friendship has not proved fatal; and that no correspondence of my own child, secret from her parents, has been revealed by this paper. Having read this most extraordinary document, in which to approach nearer to the rank exacted by the reigning duke, Hortense calls Lord Stanmore the Earl of Charleton; I shall certainly place it in the hands of my mother, that she may warn her old friend, the real earl, that *his* days are also, doubtless, menaced, notwithstanding his advanced age."

"For my part," said Colonel Whynne, turning round from the window, "I do not believe that Lord Stanmore has either committed suicide, or that he is dead by accident. I will call on Lord Claud Chamberlayne on my way to the club, and I shall then know the truth. In the mean time, Miss Whynne, you will please to remain by the side of your mother, or grandmother: and if any letter or message should come from her would-be-serene highness, you will know of it solely through them. I permit no intercourse whatever between you two girls: the one wicked, and the other weak. Why, even her own father is not safe, if to be less than a countess in her own right is insufficient for her ambitious schemes. Remember, I am peremptory!"

While poor Georgina, who well knew her father's firmness, sank weeping in a chair, the parents discussed, in a low voice, the advantages and difficulties of leaving town before the end of the season for the Baths of Lucca, ostensibly for the sake of Leonora, the youngest of their two daughters.

CHAPTER XXV.

ABOUT three weeks after the events of the last chapter, the Earl of Charleton was seated with the Duchess of Peterworth in a little third drawing-room, in her house in Stanhope-street. This was not the first visit paid to his old friend; but their previous meeting had been shared with others. Now, it seemed that their conversation had been not only confidential, but of personal interest to both; for, after a pause, the earl said:

" Do not upbraid yourself, Emma, for fear you should upbraid Divine Providence. We each have had a mission from God; to fulfil which, we were to act apart. You have been the instrument to preserve the dukedom to your stepson, as he has related the circumstance to me. I was to toil in exile, to regain a lost inheritance."

" I ought to have shared that exile with you!" cried the duchess. " I should have made a very good poor man's wife. How wonderful that I took for granted we were to part. I expected you to return, or, at least, to write. I heard you were at Caen, and then that you had married. My cousin, Helena, the late duchess, had been dead only a few weeks. I was with her when she expired; and remained at Polhill Towers with the children, until the duke returned. The morning I left the old place, he said he hoped that when he next fetched me to Polhill, it would be forever. That I was the only stepmother he would ever place over his children; and that he trusted I would forgive his speaking thus early, as it was quite confidential between us; and I was returning to my brother's place, where other claimants to my favor would surely present themselves.

"My dear duke," said I, "you have had your first-love; I have had mine. You have lost yours by death; I have lost mine by his marriage to another. If at the end of the proper term of mourning, you will speak to my brother on the subject of your present wishes, I would do my best to make you and the dear children happy. After the year's mourning, the duke came to Eagle Crag, and we were publicly engaged. Six months after, I became Duchess of Peterworth, happy in making others happy; but the heart that dared no longer be yours, and which the good duke and his children occupied, but could not fill, that heart, — can I venture on this seeming boasting? — that heart was raised to God! I passed scatheless through the fiery ordeal of the world's witcheries and temptations, by His grace alone: but I called in aid, to strengthen me, all those inferior instruments and subordinate motives, which, in the whirl of seductive pleasures, will sometimes strike more forcibly and practically, than sublime and abstract truths. One of these was, when *he* returns, God grant he may respect me." Lord Charleton raised the unresting hand to his lips, and the duchess continued : " My other safeguard was, to have one or other of the children always with me. In school-room hours I borrowed from the nursery ; but when those were over, I made Charlotte and Emily my willing companions. After they were in their early beds, and the more dangerous world began its evening amusements, I had the choice of these alternatives : to win the duke to be my protector abroad, to remain with him at home, or to be accompanied by Mrs. Crawley. Do you remember her at Eagle Crag, as my governess ?"

" I do ; and that on leaving the position of governess, she remained your confidential friend."

" Yes ; Mrs. Crawley consented to act as companion to her former pupil during the gay London season, still retaining her own modest home in Chapel-street. Thanks to her presence, I was saved the reputation, I might have gained, of the willing enchantress of the day."

" I have heard of you," said Lord Charleton, " at that period of your London celebrity. You created the same sensation that now surrounds Miss Woolton. I sometimes, when at Caen, entertained a few of my countrymen; and on one of these occasions, was gratified to find the undeviating rectitude of your life, acknowledged by the very beings who would fain have tarnished it. One nobleman, notoriously your admirer, terminated his enthusiastic encomiums, by lowering his voice to scandal pitch, and avowing that he had heard, from authority he could not dispute, that you were actually,—although you had the exquisite tact and taste not to make it evident, — but it was a fact——that you were pious!"

The duchess smiled, and continued:

"With respect to my position as stepmother, I was favored; for the relations of the first wife are generally those to inspire suspicion, if not dislike, of the second wife, in the ductile minds of the children; but in any case, the first duchess and myself had the same relations, who were delighted that the children of their dear Helena should fall to my inheritance. Still there was a precaution to take; it was with the governesses and the old confidential servants, especially the head of the nursery. All this was happily arranged, and having once determined to live for others, not for myself; remembering, also, that without the spirit of sacrifice, — of daily sacrifice, — to the characters, habits, and infirmities of others, there is no carriage of the Cross, consequently no security that one is on the straight and narrow road; I prayed for perseverance, and God granted it. So here am I, a respectable old duchess of sixty-three, who has made no heart ache but her own, here below, and is looking forward to the wonderful time, or rather the wonderful eternity of all things prosperous, all things harmonious; no partings, but the security that those we love are ours forever."

"And that reunion of faithful hearts has commenced, even here, with you and me, Emma," said Lord Charleton; "since here we are, after nearly fifty years' separation, seated side by side, with the same faith, and the same glorious hopes before us."

"Yes," replied the duchess; "it is nearly fifty years ago since, in the most inconceivable manner, we two broken-hearted lovers parted forever; when, had we thoroughly sounded each other's generosity and power of sacrifice, we need never have parted. You would not invite me to share the painful exile before you, and I misunderstood your delicacy for a tacit avowal that the step would be impossible."

"Had God intended your mission on earth to have been with me," said Lord Charleton, "He would have inspired us both differently. It is true, I dared not request so great a sacrifice from one on whom the world smiled so lavishly."

"What did you do with all the little keepsakes?" interrupted the duchess.

"On the eve of my marriage, I gave them, sealed up, into the hands of my confessor at Caen; with directions to his successor to preserve the packet until called for by the Earl of Charleton. On my return through that city, to England, I received back the packet; and its contents are in my private desk, which never leaves me. Why should I entertain any scruple respecting them? If second marriages are permitted by the church, why not still more the pure union of two hearts that adversity and other ties had parted, but are now re-united in the fine sunset glow of their evening days. Why should I scruple to love you now, Emma, just as if you had been with me during those fifty years? And what has become of a certain number of little trifles, valued because of the donor, once in the private safe-keeping of the Honorable Emma Sedley?"

"They are buried," replied the duchess; "they are in the vault at Eagles Crag. When I go there in the autumn, I will have the little coffer brought up from its long entombment."

"In the mean time," said Lord Charleton, "let us make an exchange of presents, in remembrance of this, to me, most interesting conversation; and permit me to request that the choice you make, may be guided by the lines I now repeat from Cowper's address to Mrs. Unwin:

> 'Thy silver locks, once auburn bright,
> Are still more lovely in my sight
> Than golden beams of Orient light —
> My Mary.'"

"It shall be so," said the duchess. "This day

week, should jewellers prove true, ' the silver lock' shall be sent to you."

" And the bearer must await a similar little packet from me, bearing the date of to-day, June 22d, 1854," added Lord Charleton, rising to depart.

" Stay for ten minutes longer," said the duchess; " although the subject on which I have to speak, will, assuredly, drop bitterness into the cup of joy."

" Then I will not hear it, Emma, even from your lips.   It will give me an excellent reason for calling on you again in a few days."

" Oh, a few days hence may be too late.   Come to-morrow."

" Well, then, be it to-morrow.   But do not let that, or any other subject, mar the joy of to-day, — a day of renewal of youth to me.   I am going to ride into the country."

" Oh, Charleton !" cried she, " I must speak these few words : your life is in danger.   Do not ride in lonely places.   Two grooms are better than one; let them be armed; but, above all, do not dine out to-day at any new house."

" I have a few friends at home to-day," said his lordship, smiling; " and before there will be a question of dining to-morrow, your grace will have given me all the details of this bitter drop."

CHAPTER XXVI.

DISCUSSIONS ON PRACTICAL MORALITY.

" A FASHIONABLE three months in this largest
capital of Europe, affords unlimited opportunity for
ignoring the Ten Commandments, and cultivating
the seven deadly sins. I am about to give you a
proof of this sentiment, my lord,"·said the duchess
on the following day, " by producing a document,
placed in my hands by Colonel Whynne and his
wife, which I must render more intelligible by a
short and authentic preface." Her grace then recounted the impression on Miss Woolton's mind, that
Lord Stanmore had perished in the water; and that,
unable to bear a longer removal than to Belgrave-
square, she had passed the night in dictating to her
bosom friend, Georgina Whynne, the letter to his
Serene Highness Prince Ernest Wolfenschriedenfel.
Lord Charleton attentively listened, and as attentively
perused the " brouillon." At length he drew forth
his pocket-book, and produced a letter from Mr.
Gerard Woolton, which he handed to the duchess,
saying :

" The two letters appear to have a hidden link between them."

The letter ran thus : —

" MY DEAR LORD, — The youthful frolic of Lord Stanmore, in diving into the water from our pleasure-boat, has, strange to say, been so maliciously interpreted by a gossipping world, ever craving for excitement, that it has become not only a matter of respectful and affectionate feeling, but one of imperative necessity, for the preservation of our moral standing in the world, that both elder and younger branches of the house of Woolton should prove to be on friendly terms with each other. To effect this, I have arranged for a large dinner-party, at my house in Brook-street, which I trust will be graced by your presence and that of Lord Stanmore. Our mutual friends, Lord Claud Chamberlayne and Colonel Whynne and family, will decline all other engagements, to be present at this happy family reunion, assuring me that, from the knowledge they have of your character, you will not refuse this most earnest invitation. Leaving, therefore, your lordship to fix your own day,

" I am, with sincere esteem,

" Your lordship's humble servant and cousin,

" GERARD PHILIP WOOLTON.

" Lower Brook-street, Grosvenor-square,
June 22d, 1854."

The duchess having perused this letter, exclaimed :
" What can you do?"

"I can do this," replied Lord Charleton, showing the copy of his reply, which was as follows : —

"My dear Sir,—Your kind proposal of a family dinner, in the company of mutual friends, meets with my warmest approval ; but as *I* am the head of the Wooltons, the first meeting ought to be at *my* house, to which I will invite all those mutual friends, who have judged so kindly of me.   Permit me, therefore, to name Tuesday the 28th of June, for welcoming yourself and Miss Woolton to Carlton Gardens ; and believe me, &c."

"This admirably postpones the evil day," observed the duchess.   "Nothing can be better.   The dinner, however, in Lower Brook-street is only deferred. You, are, I am aware, determined not to expose and disgrace your kindred, and we must trust that some event will occur to render your presence there gracefully impossible.   In the mean time, your safety and that of Lord Stanmore is not exposed ; for, a hoped-for banquet of deadly viands is prepared for you both, and father and daughter are biding their time with a determination worthy a better cause. Alas ! poor Hortense : the Evil One is fascinating her, as she fascinates others.   This attainment of something unexpectedly brilliant, and just possible to her ambition, is the bait that has won her."

At this instant Colonel and Lady Emily Whynne were announced, and shortly after Lord Claud Chamberlayne.   The short interval before his arrival had been passed in interchange of kind inquiries, and in some arrangement between the duchess and Lady Emily, respecting flower-stands in the balcony; but the previous and painful topic that had occupied the private thoughts of all, had taken full possession of the mind of Lord Claud; so much so, that he had scarcely paid his brief respects to her grace, than he commenced with:

"What is a man's duty when a friend is virtually convicted of being a rascal? I should like to have that point cleared up, before I leave London for Vienna. Come, duchess, get Lord Charleton to pronounce; or, if he will not, arrange this difficult matter yourself. Your grace has not only a good head, but has made practical morality your especial study, for which this wicked London ought to be most particularly obliged to you."

The duchess turned to Lord Charleton, who said:

"I suppose that, in the difficult case of a conscientious struggle, between moral rectitude and fidelity to friendship, the decision would greatly depend on the repentance of the erring friend. Let us imagine some cases. Let us suppose a case doubtful as to perfect integrity, on the part of a banker who fails; of the perfect courage and disinterested action of a captain who loses a vessel; of a general who loses a battle, or capitulates a fort; of an ambassador who concludes a disadvantageous treaty; we will suppose in one of these cases, a strong painful doubt in the mind of a hitherto friend, of the strict integrity of the man who has held the high trust. Does that man, suspected, but still prosperous, surrounded by flatterers, and at ease with himself, require no moral support from his former friend — that friend may very well withdraw; but should it, on the contrary, be found that his withdrawal turns the scales against the suspected man, then, I feel, that the friend should return to his side. Remember, that we are supposing a case of suspicion, not conviction. In a case of conviction of guilt, I repeat, that the repentance of the erring man should bring back his friend."

"There are some minds, unfortunately, that never, humanly speaking, can repent," observed Lord Claud. "The state of their conscience is so warped, so false, that they cannot see the truth. They seem so honest in their false view of things, that they become quite respectable. You begin by lamenting their infatuation, and you end by thinking what good things they can say! What, after all, if they should be right? These persons are particularly prone to assist Divine Providence in adjusting society. They like to have the power over their social chess-board, to move, or even remove, the pieces to win their game. The conquerors of old did so; and great, more than good, men have done so in more modern times. If one or two persons mar an earnestly-desired and desirable adjustment of things, these persons are to be removed. Does not the mind become, at length, quite confused?"

"Not if we consult the Divine Mind," replied Lord Charleton. "None but the Creative Hand must touch the social chess-board. It is good, after listening to the sophistries of those who would fain bewilder more honest minds, to take up the simple rudiments of the Christian faith, in a child's catechism; and after listening to theories of general good, ultimate benefit, choice of the lesser evil, impediments removed, a too prolonged or inopportune life abridged, &c., to read the Ten Commandments and the Sermon on the Mount. We Christians have no excuse in letting our minds become bewildered, while we possess these simple and accessible tests of truth. In pagan times, the most heroic virtue was that which involved the greatest personal sacrifice. Brutus, therefore, might stab his friend. But, however we might personally suffer and our country gain, we have been told, 'Thou shalt not kill'—thou shalt not, from the most heroic spirit of self-sacrifice, send a soul from time into eternity."

"We are advancing very gradually, discreetly, and diplomatically to the point," observed the duchess: "the suspicion, if not conviction, that the minds of two of our acquaintances require a return to first principles."

"In fact," cried Colonel Whynne, "we want to know whether a man and his daughter, natives of Jamaica, are to come to England from Germany, expressly to kill two men who stand in the way of that particular adjustment of society, in a petty German court, which they deem advisable; and, whether, from politeness, we are to take no effectual remedies against them, but let them help Divine Providence to abridge the too-prolonged life of the Earl of Charleton, and the inopportune life of Viscount Stanmore, in order that this immense good, — this ultimate benefit may be given to Europe and all creation, in the elevation of a young witch called Hortense Woolton, to be her serene highness, right-handed wife of the fourth son of the late reigning Duke of Wolfenschriedenfel. No, my dear friends; your tender sensibilities do not suit a plain soldier. I will now relate my morning call this very day, in Lower Brook-street, before meeting my wife, by appointment, here in Stanhope-street. My visit was in reply to an invitation to dinner, on whatever day the Earl of Charleton should name for an all but public meeting, on friendly terms, of the two branches of the Wooltons in the sympathizing company of mutual friends. Mr. Woolton was alone, and hoped my answer would be as practically friendly as all my conduct towards him had been since his arrival in England. I told him that to dine, or permit the Earl of Charleton to dine in his house, must depend on the explanation he could give me of a certain paper, left by his daughter at my house. Now see the guilt of the man! — He thought I meant a paper containing a powder; for he first turned pale as death, then, exerting himself, laughed and said: ' Oh ! it 's only a powder to be dissolved in a certain acid for cementing glass and fine china.   Do not let the children get at it, however : for the inventor warned me it was a subtle poison.   I hope no harm has been done?   It was careless of Hortense to leave it.'   I asked, in my turn, what a young lady could possibly require of a powder to mend china, or of a subtle poison at a country fête, at a distance from her own home.   To which he replied that, were it not that I had given hospitality to his daughter, he would ask me how I dared make such a remark.   I then told him that the paper in question contained no powder whatever : that it was the rough draught of a letter dictated by his daughter, and written by mine.   That the circumstance of the handwriting being that of her own child had induced Lady Emily to retain the original ; but that I laid the exact copy before him.   I think nothing of the agitation of his countenance as he perused it.   On the contrary, an innocent father would have showed more horror.   At length he recovered himself and again laughed, saying, " Oh, come — this betrays itself to be a complete history to mystify Miss Whynne.   This is a school-girl's frolic.   No truth in it from beginning to end.   I am sorry it has so frightened you all — you sober English !   But I will, if you will permit me, keep this production to show Hortense : and I will reprimand her well.   Tell your sweet Georgina to teach a little of her steadiness to my wild puss.' "

" Well !" cried Lord Claud, his countenance radiant with hope; "perhaps he is quite right. Perhaps it is merely a girl's frolic after all. It is by far the most charitable view to take. Hortense is a genius —full of wit and spirit; just a creature to love a little mischief with her more sedate friend."

"Lord Claud, you are in love—you are bewitched. Now, do not be angry. We are all confidential friends here," said Colonel Whynne. "Would to God I could think with you. Remember that this so-called 'girl's frolic' took place during the night following Lord Stanmore's plunge into the river. She believed he was drowned; she was too excited, too nervous to steady her hand. She could only dictate."

" Suppose we all drive together into the country," interposed the duchess; " and as we have fully discussed one dinner-party, let us accomplish another in the rural shades of the Marquis of Seaham's villa, at Richmond. Come, Lord Claud, you and I will perform the honors, as your brother has often invited me to do."

After a little hesitation, and a note or two despatched to promise a return for later engagements, the little party — heated and nervous by painful topics — resolved to cast aside care for a while; accordingly they drove in the two carriages, already at the door, to the proposed pleasant bowers at Richmond.

CHAPTER XXVII.

A MORTUARY CHAMBER.

The dinner-party of the elder to the younger branch of the house of Woolton took place as appointed on the 28th of June, at the residence of the Earl of Charleton, in Carlton Gardens. The mansion was well adapted for an entertainment; and arches of colored lamps and evergreens, produced the words of "Welcome" and "Hortense," with great effect. The dinner, being one of state, was of long duration; and a band of music filled the pauses of the conversation. This was succeeded by a select party of professional vocalists in the drawing-rooms, who were invited to remain for the crowning entertainment, a lottery of prizes.

Still, as the Duchess of Peterworth had observed, this dinner and evening festivity were but palliatives. There was the dinner, *par excellence*, in Lower Brook-street, threatening the lives of one party and the damnation of the other. Accordingly, in the following first week of July, embossed cards appeared for a dinner at the house of Mr. Gerard Woolton, on the 20th instant, in honor of the Earl of Charleton, the head of the family, and others of similar elegance for Viscount Stanmore, in the handwriting of Hortense.

This wonderful girl had so well contrived, during the dinner and succeeding hours in Carlton Gardens, to interest, delight, and even inspire, with confidence, both grandfather and grandson, that on their consulting together on the prudence of venturing to accept the invitation to Brook-street, on the 20th of July, each found the other disposed to risk the visit, as not deserving the fears of any reasonable man. The Marquis of Seaham was not on visiting terms, but Lord Claud had accepted the invitation sent him.

" I think the chain armor I sent you, Stanmore, need not be thrown off that day," observed the marquis ; " and remember that tobacco is an antidote to arsenic ! "

It so happened that a small party of intimate friends of Colonel and Lady Emily Whynne met at their dinner-table in Belgrave-square, on the day previous to the proposed entertainment in Lower Brook-street : the Duke and dowager Duchess of Peterworth, Lord Claud Chamberlayne, the Marchioness of Penzance, and her younger son and daughter, Lord Albert and Lady Charlotte Fitzjames, who, with the fair Georgina Whynne, made a pleasant number for general conversation. Georgina was happy to have Lord Claud on one side, while her cousin, Lord Albert, was on the other beside her at table; for, both being ardent admirers and chivalrous defenders of the much-discussed Hortense Woolton, still, as ever, her idol; she was assisted in bringing back the subject, however it might wander, to the one theme of her daily thoughts,—her nightly dreams. Perhaps the supposed persecution of her father in forbidding further intercourse, and, in the family circle, further mention of the beautiful West Indian, might have heightened the delight with which, on this day, she fearlessly indulged in the prohibited topic.

"Quite a mental possession," sighed Lady Emily, at length, to the duke, at her right hand.

"Never mind, Emily," returned he, "Georgina looks so unconsciously beautiful, while raving nonsense about her friend, that I am obliged to forgive her."

This was at the close of dinner; the servants had retired, the little subdued movements of eating sweetmeats and drinking choice wines had also ceased, the softest sound could be heard, and Lord Claud looked and smiled his full assent to the uncle's defence of his niece. A few instants later, the butler entered, and whispered to his master that the confidential valet of the Earl of Charleton wished to speak to him.

"It is something very serious, sir," added the man. "It is better for you to be prepared. It is something very shocking!"

" Come, Bookham," said the colonel, " I see you know all about it. I prefer hearing the bad news here among my friends. The earl himself is quite safe, as he sends the message. Bring in the valet."

Monsieur Julien entered, and bowed in silence to the whole company; then stood near the colonel, who, fearing for Lord Stanmore, began to feel agitated.

" Who is the object of this bad news, Julien?"

" Miss Woolton, colonel."

" Miss Woolton! Oh, my God! who has she been poisoning?"

" Herself, sir!"

A wild shriek from poor Georgina, a low groan from Lord Claud, and an entreaty like a command from the duchess, to relate particulars, followed simultaneously. Julien, who had expected to be thus called on, commenced as follows:

" Last week a packet came from the Foreign Office, to Miss Woolton, the contents of which appeared to agitate and distress her, almost to madness. The letter which is supposed to have most affected her, is in German. Mr. Woolton, the day before yesterday, found from Miss Woolton's maid, that she had not been able to gain admittance to her young lady's room. It was then late in the afternoon, and Mr. Woolton became alarmed. He had the door opened, and directly he saw his daughter, he sent for medical assistance. The nearest doctor came,

and found that the young lady had been dead some
hours. Mr. Woolton then asked for a pair of scis-
sors, and making the maid undo the hair, cut from
the roots a long tress. He next kissed her on the
forehead, and said to the maid : ' Lucille has turned
traitress. All now rests with you and your husband.
Let Jerome find my lawyer directly, and have all
things done, as befits my eldest daughter and heiress.
I shall leave two letters in Mr. Childer's hands : one
to guide your proceedings, the other for the Earl of
Charleton.' The maid cried, ' What, sir, are you
leaving us before your daughter is buried ? ' He replied, ' All is contained in my letter to Lord Charleton.' Yesterday he left London forever. My lord
received this letter last night, and immediately desired to have a visit from Sir Bentley Burder, who
was fortunately at home, and came directly to Carlton Gardens. He took me in his carriage to Brook-
street, and into the death-chamber, which the two
confidential servants had fitted up with the greatest
solemnity, although they were both convinced that
their young lady's death had been an act of suicide.
In her jewel-box was a small case containing poisons
in powders, indorsed, in her own handwriting, thus :
' slow ' — ' immediate ' — ' leaves a sediment ' — ' no
sediment.' This case was placed out of its usual
corner in the jewel-box, as if it had been used.
When Sir Bentley Burder entered the death-room,
he stood in grave silence at the foot of the bier ;

then spoke these important words : — ' This is no case of poison.' We all stood in respectful astonishment. Then one servant pointed out the poisons in the little case ; another recounted the disappointment conveyed in the letter from Germany : but Sir Bentley, who had moved to the head of the bier, said, on closely examining the countenance, ' My opinion to the jury is, that this young lady has died by sudden cessation of the action of the heart.' Sir Bentley left this opinion in writing for the foreman of the jury. They met this morning, and their verdict was, — ' Died by the visitation of God ! ' ".

" Ah ! good old language, good old truth," exclaimed the Duchess of Peterworth. " It is exactly as the verdict worded it : ' Died by the visitation of God ! ' Did God, in His eternal councils, foresee that a further prolongation of life would only add to her resistance to grace ! — did He so care for the living, that He cut the thread of her guilty young life, before she could be fatally successful ! — did she ever approach the tribunal of penance ! Ah ! good old language, good old truth : ' Died by the visitation of God ! ' —— "

" Oh ! how cruel," exclaimed Georgina Whynne, starting from the stupor of grief which had succeeded her cry of anguish. " Hortense, — my Hortense, — has died of a broken heart ! Oh ! take me to her, Lord Claud. Let me see once more the broken-hearted girl, lying there alone, — desolate, — in her

cold beauty. No! I will not go with grandmamma;
I will go only with you, Lord Claud."

"Is the thing possible?" asked Lord Claud of
Julien.

"Quite, my lord," replied he. "There has been
a mistake in the length of the coffin, or the body has
extended since death: for another has to be made,
and the young lady still lies on the bier."

"Where?"

"In the back drawing-room of the house in Lower
Brook-street."

"Oh! my dearest aunt," cried Georgina to Lady
Penzance; "you, who introduced Hortense, in all
her beauty and bright hopes, to the Queen and Court
of England, take me now to her. I cannot, I suppose, go alone with Lord Claud at night. He is too
young, perhaps —— "

There was a pause. The marchioness trembled
with nervous terror: at length she said:

"My dear child, if your uncle will take care of
me, and Lord Claud of you, and Monsieur Julien
can admit us quietly, for your sake, — as we may
hope the soul is not lost, — I will go."

"Oh! bless my soul, Charlotte," cried the duke,
"I never thought of intruding on the dead in this
unheard-of way. I suppose there is no altar, or
religious rite going on, to warrant the entrance of
strangers."

"Oh! uncle, dear uncle, we are not strangers.

This was the first house in London Hortense was ever in ; and my aunt came to fetch her to St. James', in all her gayety and beauty, the delight of all hearts. You, uncle duke, were then, like all the rest. Do not refuse this last respect to the one I have so loved. You will come, I know."

The good-natured duke turned round to look at the countenances of the rest of the party ; but no one seemed so much in earnest to prevent, as Georgina to persuade him ; and at length, the duke's carriage being announced, the four departed in awe and silence for the chamber of death.

CHAPTER XXVIII.

STILL THE MORTUARY CHAMBER.

THE customs of her mother's Isle of Cuba, had been followed in laying out the remains of Hortense Woolton; for the two confidential servants were natives of that island. The court-robe in which she had been presented, in all the brilliancy of her wonderful beauty, as the future Countess of Charleton, in her own right, and affianced princess of the ducal throne of Wolfenschriedenfel; this robe now arrayed the sternly majestic corpse. A small diadem of brilliants was fixed high across the forehead, and corresponding ornaments were profusely scattered over the whole person. The friends, who had so enthusiastically followed at her chariot-wheels in life, now stole into the death-room, in respectful sorrow. Julien relit some more of the many tapers that had burned alternately around the bier, and the arrangement then truly deserved the term, to " lie in state."

The two ladies of the group knelt, and commenced the psalm *De profundis*, — " From the depths I have cried unto Thee, O Lord !" Lord Claud, much agitated, attempted to join them, while the duke remained perfectly silent, with his eyes, that had been fixed on Hortense, now turned as fixedly on a solitary figure standing near him, in comparative shadow; — it was Lord Stanmore. The duke grasped his hand, and led him aside.

" Can you pray?"

" I am in doubt," was the reply, " whether "———

" Exactly so," interrupted the duke; " whether our prayers may not increase her sufferings. I have such an internal conviction they will do so, that I cannot utter a word. I firmly believe that the wicked soul of that proudly handsome corpse, is now one of the queens of Lucifer, the fallen angel. She is in a larger court than that of Wolfenschriedenfel."

" Oh, stop, duke!" said Lord Stanmore; " we dare not pronounce. Remember, she did not commit suicide : she died suddenly of the heart disease."

" And the case of poisons," whispered the duke; " all labelled to send others scientifically and prudently out of her path of ambition. You cannot reason upon that, Stanmore. Come into the next room with me, and leave poor Georgina to torment her lost friend, by prayers worse than unavailing. Now, tell me," continued he, when in the front drawing-room, with the folding-doors closed, " what has her father requested of Lord Charleton, in the letter I have heard of ?"

" Mr. Woolton," replied Lord Stanmore, " has written, that if the best medical authority can pronounce that his daughter did not commit suicide, he makes it the last request, with which he shall ever trouble the head of his family, that Hortense may lie in the vaults of her ancestors."

"And what has the earl decided?"

"He has consented."

"I thought so — I feared so. Now, Stanmore, we both know that souls wander about where their bodies lie, — good souls as well as bad ones, — and therefore we cry, ' Eternal rest give unto them, O Lord !' and God hears that cry. But just see in what you are going to involve yourselves, with a restless, wandering soul that cannot be prayed for, and whose one especial line of damnation was to raise herself, at the cost of all living obstacles — yourself in particular. I know of your engagement to the Marquis of Seaham's charming daughter ; and that you are to be married in two years : may God bless that marriage. Now, some things have fallen curiously in my way through life, which prove of use as warnings. I have one of these to mention to you in Lord Charleton's presence. Have you your carriage here?"

"I have."

The duke rang the bell, and Julien entered.

" Tell the ladies to make use of my carriage back to Belgrave-square, and then send it to Carlton Gardens. I am going with Lord Stanmore."

Julien re-entered the death-room in time to assist Lord Claud and the Marchioness of Penzance, in gently compelling the nearly-fainting Georgina to quit the body of her friend. Julien advancing, unexpectedly, covered the face of the corpse; and Georgina's two protectors bore her from the room. After assisting the aunt and niece into the carriage, Lord Claud said to the footman, accompanied by a *douceur :*

"Request the coachman to drive very slowly."

This was complied with, to the surprise and regret of Lady Penzance, who, wearied with the painful emotions of the evening, wished to lay her head on her pillow; but she soon rallied her spirits, when Lord Claud explained, that he desired to speak to Miss Whynne in the sole presence of her ladyship, whose kind influence he hoped to obtain.

"The only event that has saddened our two families," said he, "the early mutual affection that existed between Lord Edwin Fitzjames and my poor sister-in-law — a prepossession of heart never, alas ! confided to my brother — has made me resolve not to marry any one whose first affections have been won by another man. I think, I perceive in the enthusiastic attachment of Miss Whynne for her young friend, that no other absorbing affection has gained her heart. I can promise her, on my part, the devoted fidelity of my life."

"My dear Georgina," said Lady Penzance, "there is no one who would make you more happy than Lord Claud."

"Most true," replied Georgina; "for Lord Claud and you are the only two who have remained faithful to my beloved Hortense."

"But perhaps," said her ladyship, smiling, "you may feel a little jealous that he admired her so much?"

"Who? I jealous of such a superior being? Oh, never! But how can he think of me?"

"To that question, my dear Lord Claud," said the marchioness, "you must yourself reply."

His lordship did reply; and so much to the satisfaction of all parties, that on the arrival in Belgrave-square an immediate reference to the parents, through the favorable medium of Lady Penzance, was resolved on for that night, to be followed by a visit to those parents by Lord Claud on the following morning.

In the mean time, the Duke of Peterworth and Lord Stanmore drove rapidly, and almost in silence, to Carlton Gardens. They entered the earl's private sitting-room, and found him well, and, as usual, calm and benignant, but with the traces of sorrow on his countenance. The duke spoke at once on the purport of his untimely visit; for it was past eleven o'clock.

"My dear lord," said he, "you have faith — stronger faith than I have; for you have more grace. I believe you to be a living saint; but I find you have consented to a proposition I do not think saintly at all. You have weakly acceded to the request of Mr. Woolton, that his daughter shall be in the vaults at Woolton Court, among all those who have died in a state of grace, fortified by the last sacraments, and eligible to the benefits of the Holy Sacrifice, offered daily in the chapel above — she who has died in mortal sin, with the evidence of her murderous ambition left in the case of labelled poisons. And now, before I speak further on the subject of your vaults, let me ask you whether it has not struck you, that if she had intended to die, by poison or otherwise, she would have taken the precaution to burn the contents of that case? and God has cut her off in her sins, leaving proof of them, that those who happily have survived her iniquity might take warning. I do not believe that she died of a broken heart; for I question that she had any heart to break. If this Prince Ernest Wolfenschriedenfel has jilted her, and married another, she might be cast down for an hour or so, but she never destroyed her little case of poisons, and one or the other powder would have been emptied into whatever solution she thought best, at a reconciliation banquet at the court of Wolfenschriedenfel. She would have killed the new wife, and married Prince Ernest, if her life had not been cut off. She has, I repeat it, died in mortal sin; and you are going to permit her lost soul to wander through the halls and corridors of Woolton Court, to the horror and danger of your innocent successors. You have taken very proper measures to clear your hereditary mansion from the unjust stigma of being haunted by the lost soul of your uncle; and now you are going to permit a really lost soul, not only to haunt the place herself, but also introduce her masters, the demons."

Lord Charleton rested his head on his hand, and replied no further than by passing to the duke, with his disengaged hand, the letter he had received from Mr. Woolton.

"Of course it is very eloquent and pathetic, and he leaves England and all Europe as a heart-stricken man," said the duke, "but I cannot read it. Stanmore, will you ring, and order some lemonade, I am so feverish and excited."

In a short time Julien, followed by another domestic, introduced not only lemonade, but ices, to the heated indignation of the duke, who at length read the letter, and was arrested only by the latter part, which was perfectly new to him.

"My dear Stanmore, do read this part aloud to me, slowly and distinctly, if Lord Charleton will permit."

The paragraph ran thus: — "The early womanhood of Hortense has been wasted and deluded by one of those foolish prophecies which girls love to hear, from the gipsy tribe. It was foretold to her that she would 'blaze as a beacon, shooting high and seen from afar.' Great admiration has followed her; and had she been content with high nobility, she might now be alive in health and honor; but that prophecy, to which she attached one special meaning, deceived her."

"I am surprised," observed the duke, "that this prophecy has not been fulfilled in some way; for the devil is cunning, and generally contrives that, in some startling way, his agents shall have told the coming fact. But let me now proceed to relate the history I promised, Stanmore; it is of a man who persisted in remaining in a haunted house, with his wife and children, because he had it rent-free. I had the account from the only survivor, whose truth and intelligence were beyond suspicion. From avarice and incredulity this man persisted, till two infant children were successively strangled in their cradles. The father and mother then always placed the surviving infant between them at night, in their bed; but one morning they missed the child, and, found him dead beneath the bed, having been *spirited away* during its parents' sleep. In agony of late repentance, the bereaved couple left the accursed place, and were blessed with another child, who, in middle age, entered my service. Yes, in a place haunted by lost souls the devil has power."

"My dear duke," replied Lord Charleton, "I feel the full force of all your reasonings; I feel, still more, the full force of your friendship: I will think the subject over. Will you dine here to-morrow?"

"I will," replied the duke; "but your invitation is

a good hint that it is now near one o'clock by your timepiece, which I suppose to be infallible. May your decision, when we next meet, be for the peace of your noble and virtuous house."

The Duke of Peterworth could not fulfil his engagement until the day following the one proposed. In the interval, the officials charged with the order to transport the body of the late Miss Woolton to within one stage of Woolton Court, were proceeding to their destination, charged also with a letter that the head undertaker was to deliver to the Rev. Chaplain of the mansion. On the decision of that ecclesiastic was to rest the responsibility of admitting the corpse to the vaults of the family chapel, or of performing the funeral service in the village cemetery, above mentioned, and giving orders for a plain stone slab, with the simple name engraved of "Hortense." Neither of these arrangements were destined to take effect. The coffin, on arriving at this village, had to be placed in a sort of mortuary chamber, formed from a large room connected with the inn for the service of all public assemblies. A few tapers were lit, and the door locked. In the night the villagers were alarmed, but aroused too late, the people of the inn and the undertakers, by a " blaze like a beacon, shooting high and seen from afar," rising from the room in which had lain the corpse of Hortense Woolton. The inn was untouched; that mortuary chamber and all it contained was alone consumed.

This literal fulfilment, in its physical sense, of the

gipsy's bad knowledge of the fate that awaited Hortense Woolton, was conveyed to Lord Charleton in a letter from his domestic chaplain, who wrote from the village inn, by an express train.

"How wonderful! Oh, my God!" exclaimed the earl, as he closed the paper and clasped his hands.

"What is wonderful?" demanded, in the same breath, the Duke of Peterworth and the dowager duchess, who, with Lord Stanmore, were at the dinner-table.

Monsieur Julien motioned to the domestics, who were just retiring, to hasten their exit, and said softly:

"The intelligence has already arrived at the police office. The chief undertaker hopes, my lord, you will not prosecute."

"What!" cried the duchess, "is that hypocritical Mr. Woolton machinating again?"

"No," said Lord Charleton, "but the corpse of his daughter has been totally consumed by fire!"

"Ha!" exclaimed the duke; "she was to blaze like a beacon? D. D., you did not know that a soothsayer had prophesied to Miss Woolton, that she was to 'blaze like a beacon, shooting high and seen from afar.' When I heard this, the night before last, I was struck by the word 'blaze' instead of 'shine,' coupled with a beacon. Now I trace the full meaning. But is it not a thing worthy of note that what these wicked soothsayers prognosticate does come true?"

CHAPTER XXIX.

FAMILY SORROWS AND SYMPATHIES.

Lord Claud Chamberlayne had engaged Lady
Clara to be present at the announcement to their
brother, the Marquis of Seaham, of his intended
marriage. He felt for the marquis, and sympathized
in all the mingled tenderness and bitterness which the
marriage of his only brother would recall to his heart.
The first evening that promised an uninterrupted family conversation was watched for and secured; the
brothers were alone after dinner, when Lord Claud
prefaced his announcement by requesting the marquis
to finish his wine, and join their sister in the drawing-
room.

"I have invited Clara to be there to-night," added
he, "without Sir Henry, because Hugh — I — have
something to say to you both, alone."

"As I happen, Claud, to know your political prospects even better than yourself," returned the marquis, "I suppose this very particular announcement
must be your marriage." Then rising from the table
and leading to the drawing-room, he saluted Lady
Clara with his usual affection, and turning to his

brother, said : " Well, Claud, to dispense with preliminaries, who is the fair lady ?"

" Miss Whynne," replied Lord Claud.

A pause ensued.

"My dear Hugh," resumed he, "there is no
blood relationship between Miss Whynne and the
elder —— "

" Fitzjameses," added the marquis, in a hollow
voice.

Lady Clara looked tenderly at her elder brother.

" No," continued the marquis; " I am aware of
that ; but remember, Claud, that during my life not
one that bears the name can enter here, the London
family mansion, nor Marsden Park ; yet, the young
generation are Miss Whynne's first cousins. I am
ready to meet your wishes in any purchase you may
wish to make of a new residence. You are my
heir."

" I hope not," said Lord Claud, warmly taking
the extended hand. " There are not so many years
between us, that I must necessarily outlive you.
With respect to the purchase of any additional residence, that is quite unnecessary. I am, thanks to
you, going to a splendid one in Vienna ; one that
will be my home for some years, should the two
courts remain on amicable terms. Georgina will
desire nothing better."

" I saw Miss Whynne in her grandmother's carriage the other day," said the marquis, recovering

himself. "She is a very lovely girl: and as she does not think you too old, I must not think her too young. I would, however, advise a good, steady lady-companion; not only for the public receptions in Vienna, but also for the hours of your forced absence from her, to attend to public affairs."

The countenance of the elder brother was again overshadowed, and Lady Clara rising, passed her arm through his; then beckoning Lord Claud, did the same with him, singing:

> "This is the way
> We used to play,
> The live-long day!"

"We had better think of the future than of the past, Clara," said the marquis.

"But our childhood, dear Hugh," continued Lady Clara, "was very happy. First Communions, serving Mass and Benediction, gathering and forming nosegays and garlands for the month of Mary, and all the other joys of Catholic children in country life. Oh! dearest Hugh and Claud, there are ties,—those early ties of brotherhood,—that, because they are the earliest, cling the closest round the heart. Still, the future is far better than the past; for the future extends throughout eternity,—an eternity of happy meetings. Claud with his ever-loved Georgina; I with one who will have regained a perfect vision; and you with a saint made perfect in suffering."

22

"Ha! Clara, you have never spoken so openly before," said the marquis. "Do not continue,—I cannot bear it."

But Lady Clara saw that his heart seemed more in peace.

Lord Claud now intimated that he had promised to visit the Whynnes, after he should have communicated to his brother the projected marriage. So the trio parted: Lord Claud to Belgrave-square, Lady Clara to read to her blind husband the landing in the Crimea, and the marquis to a house where he had long found a hidden consolation, not yet disclosed to the reader, and in which more, even, than in the society of his sister, might be discovered the reply to an oft-repeated question, "Why the Marquis of Seaham did not marry again?" This balm of a sympathy, with which no other could compete, was with the younger Duchess of Peterworth. She was a great invalid, and consequently always at home in the evening. Her indisposition had been chiefly caused by painful emotion, acting on a delicate frame, when scarcely recovered from her first confinement. The then agitation of her mind had so injured the nerves of the head, that she continued deaf for nearly two years; and even now, though partially recovered, could only hear distinctly those voices to which she was accustomed. This infirmity of deafness,—which, more than any other, invites or drives the afflicted person to seek, apart from his fellow-beings, employment, solace, and entertainment,—was not the only motive that had induced Anna, Duchess of Peterworth, to live secluded in the midst of all that rank, beauty, and affluence could offer. She was the victim, like the marquis, of a family dishonor, of a public excitement. This latter trial had passed away, leaving its sting, while the anguish of the former had been mitigated by the true repentance of the erring one. The younger Duchess of Peterworth was sister to the late Marchioness of Seaham. The " young duchess," as she was still called in the circle of relations, generally occupied a third drawing-room, that she had fitted up since her bereavement, partly as an oratory, leaving, however, sufficient space for all that an invalid required of sofa, easy-chairs, and different sized tables. Her grace was seated in her favorite chair, with a book-stand, and tapers just lighted, when the marquis entered.

" I expected you to-night," said she ; " but not so soon. The duke told me there would be no House of Lords. · He is gone to see Lady Emily. Quite a mysterious invitation came this morning."

" Then you do not yet know the approaching marriage of Miss Whynne ? "

" No, indeed. To whom is she going to be married ? "

" To my brother."

The duchess was silent. She saw, precisely as the marquis, the too near approach by this marriage of the obnoxious family of Fitzjames, — the family of the seducer of her sister.

" Ah ! " cried she, at length, " what sorrows are now revived ! These are the thorns of the bridal roses."

" You do not know either, but you shall hear it from good authority," said the marquis, " that Claud is to go to Vienna as ambassador."

" That is a great mitigation of the painful alliance," observed the duchess. " I may now begin to rejoice in the happiness of your brother, whom I so much esteem, and in that of my husband's young niece, Georgina ; but, I have something to show you, nay, more, something to give you, — if it produce the effect on you that it does on me of tender resignation."

The marquis took from the hand of her grace a large morocco picture-case, and held it while she applied a key to the patent lock, saying :

" Anna, I am quite aware of what this picture-frame must contain ; and I thank you, as you well know, for this and all your share in the painful past ; but it is more than probable I may never wish to possess this miniature. I conclude it to be the one you spoke of some months ago, as of a copy you wished to possess from the one painted by Sir Charles Ross at the marriage. You then thought of having the costume changed to that of St. Mary Magdalen. Have you kept to that idea ? "

"There was a subsequent idea that I thought still better," replied the duchess, "and to which I have faithfully adhered; it was to represent *our* holy penitent in the actual garb in which she obtained not only pardon, but rich graces from God, the costume of that strict branch of the Franciscan Order which she embraced, — the 'Entombed Alive.'"

The marquis suddenly opened the case; his sister-in-law, from delicacy, turned away, and took up a book, of which she comprehended and distinguished nothing; her heart beat, and she felt faint; but how intrude her sorrows on one still deeper stricken? A long silence ensued, broken at length by the return of the Duke of Peterworth and his usual hearty "How are you, Anna?" After half an hour's converse on the proposed marriage, Lord Claud's appointment, the bad German spoken in Vienna, and other topics that ran lightly over a bleeding heart, the Marquis of Seaham departed, leaving the case: and the duchess fainted, as she often did, unperceived, recovering in the same unexacting manner.

CHAPTER XXX.

A FALSE AND FATAL SYSTEM IN LOVE AFFAIRS.

THE young duchess, although unable physically to support any new affliction, had no sooner risen on the following morning, than she resolved to try whether, among the papers in her possession of her late sister's private thoughts and prayers, she might not discover some sentence to soften the imbittered feeling in the mind of her brother-in-law, that he had never been loved. He had once said to her, — "If I could but be convinced that Ethel had loved me for one day, — nay, for one hour, I should have one spot of remembrance on which to dwell ; I should keep by me many tokens of affection that I now cast from me."

Two small boxes of manuscripts, at the request of the dying penitent, had been sent from Italy to her sister, the Duchess of Peterworth, and had reached their destination the previous year. The afflicted mourner had then felt more inclined to occupy herself, as we have seen, with the costume of a new picture, than trust herself to the perusal of those heart-rending papers ; but now, with a strong motive in view, she drew forth these records of the nine years of penance which the Marchioness of Seaham had voluntary undergone; and after reading several pages of the same holy spirit of compunction, humility, and fervent aspirations, she alighted on the following sentence:—" There is one, O my God! an injured one, whom I dare not name, who thinks, perchance, I never loved him. Oh, that I could make him know the truth; but I must offer that wish on the holocaust of my whole being."

The duchess sank on her knees in thanksgiving. She then carefully separated the page that contained these lines, but would not further isolate them from the preceding and subsequent sentences, for they were beautiful in sentiment and expression, and all in harmony with the heroic perseverance of that most penitent life. Her grace now felt strength to re-open the case of the rejected picture.

" Alas!" thought she, " when gazing on that wasted beauty, that garb of seclusion, those instruments of penance, that crucifix, the conviction of his mind remained unchanged, that in the sacrifice of all human love, the husband had cost not a pang." She remembered having once said to her brother-in-law, —" Ah! *do* compare our penitent Ethel to those of rank and beauty like her, and with more than her fault to expiate, who, with a coterie of distinguished followers, have their villa on the lake of Como, their palace at Florence, and who publish their poetry, their travels, and even their memoirs."

The marquis had replied:

"Do not think, Anna, that I undervalue the repentance of your sister. I have never doubted its sincerity or its perseverance; I have sent her my forgiveness; I even feel that, in justice, her great abandonment of duty was of less turpitude; because she had loved and been beloved before marriage, and fell from virtue for that one object of her heartfelt preference and constancy. I have been the unconscious and innocent instrument to separate two hearts that ought sooner to have known each other's sympathy. I knew and felt all this when I sent, through Monsignor Palmetto, my written pardon, with permission to enter the penitential order of her choice, and the control over whatever income she would name for benefactions to the convent and the poor around. Having done all this, Anna, be content that my marriage with Lady Ethel Haughton has given me her sister for my sister, her child for my child. I wish for no remembrance of herself personally. Let locks of hair, miniature portraits, letters, and all keepsakes, go from me forever."

This conversation had taken place during the life of the Marchioness of Seaham. Her sister had retained every word; and now, re-perusing the writing, she placed it between the leaves of a book of devotion, to await the next visit from her brother-in-law. Before many days had elapsed the conversation could be renewed under more favorable auspices; and the duchess, conquering the emotion and timidity, that were nearly subduing her physical force, said :

" Dear brother Marquis," — her early title for him — " had you read these lines before you opened the picture-case the other night, you would have accepted my present; but I had not myself then read them ; I have only just perused these consoling words : I have cut them from the manuscripts sent from Italy."

The marquis took the book, in which lay these treasured lines. He drew them forth, and perused them attentively. His sister-in-law was that evening employed in fancy needlework, to which she now devoted herself, as if all depended on the number of stitches effected before either again spoke. Half an hour passed — then an hour.

" These words *have* reached his heart," thought she, as the work proceeded calmly, when the marquis rose to depart. He pressed the hand of his sister-in-law in silence, and retired. The picture that had laid near him all the evening, was still left ; but the writing was gone. The pious duchess again rendered heartfelt thanks to heaven, that the dying wishes of her penitent sister had been fulfilled, and balm poured into the wounded heart of the husband.

As the history of the Marchioness of Seaham is not related merely as a romantic episode in the main narrative of this book, we will, preparatory to the deduction, introduce the reader to the comfortable end of a sofa, next to the equally comfortable arm-chair of the dowager Duchess of Peterworth; where, having excused herself from all late parties, she was seated at the especial work coeval with nationalities of the nineteenth century — that of crochet. The occupant of the sofa-end, and her sole companion, was Lord Stanmore. It would seem that both had been excited, if not angry; but people can be angry without sin: "Be ye angry, and sin not." However that may be, the old lady and the young lord had cooled; and, in the reaction, were disposed to do the most amiable things — the one to oblige the other. It was just in the phase of their good understanding, that Lord Stanmore said:

"I would rather hear from your grace, than from any other person, the real history of that unfortunate Lord Edwin Fitzjames: and when can I hope for such another opportunity? — you and I alone, in the fury of the London season! At what period of his life did you first know Lord Edwin?"

"It was at the marriage of his elder brother, the present Marquis of Penzance, to my eldest step-daughter, then Lady Charlotte Marlow. He was just two-and-twenty: very mild and pleasing; slender, and not tall, but with a classical head and face. We had privately thought of him for my dear Emily, who has since married Colonel Whynne; but no one could mistake the impression made on Lord Edwin by the freshly-beautiful and sportive young creature, just arrived from her convent-school, the Lady Ethel Haughton. She, and her younger sister, Lady Anna, were wards in Chancery, and placed under the care of the Countess of Silbrook, whom you have met at Marsden-park, and whom Lord Claud terms the Arachne of her epoch. She did not, however, at that time, concentrate herself on her web. She was very properly vigilant and observant, with a conscientious feeling of the responsibility of her charge. But, alas! when I look back on the innocently-gay young party that remained at Polhill Towers, after the bridal, how grieved I feel at my then want of experience! I limited my care of these young creatures to providing them with constant and profitable employment, or recreation, in the company of either Lady Silbrook or myself; also that they should duly attend to their religious duties. I clearly saw that the feeling was mutual between Lord Edwin Fitzjames and Lady Ethel Haughton; but, believing that Lady Silbrook was equally penetrating, as she was tenacious of her authority, I left their future happiness in her hands; too hopefully trusting, as was then my disposition. With my present convictions, I would not have acted thus. I would have written to the late marquis, Lord Edwin's father, for his consent; I would then have spoken to Lord Edwin; then to Ethel. I would not have permitted them to leave Polhill till Lady Silbrook had either consented, and won the Lord Chancellor to consent to their union;

or, they should have plainly understood they were not to think of each other. Each, especially Ethel, had strength of mind, strength of principle. In those early days to have been shown with certainty where lay her duty, would have been but common prudence, common humanity to that young creature, on the part of her elder friends. I let them depart, believing that Lady Silbrook would request the consent of the Lord Chancellor, and publish the engagement. Nothing was concluded. Lady Silbrook waited for Lord Edwin to speak, while he waited for more encouragement. Lady Silbrook, believing that the marriages made in heaven require no human assistance, left the young people to manage their own love affair, and never saw that this our English system is hateful and calamitous. Never did two young people meet under happier auspices; rank, fortune, youth, accomplishments, beauty, health, and first affections : surrounded by partial and affectionate relatives and friends. And why was all this marred? Why did no elder friend become the confidential deposit of the secret of each, and terminate a suspense caused by *over susceptibility on both sides?* Ah! false and fatal system! The London season of Lady Ethel's first introduction now arrived. She was presented at court, and graciously chosen for one of the maids of honor. This was almost immediately followed by the acquaintance of the Marquis of Seaham, and the sudden withdrawal of the attentions of Lord Edwin Fitzjames.

Lord Seaham in a few weeks proposed, through Lady Silbrook, followed by an appeal to Lady Ethel herself; which, after a short delay, she accepted. Her desire to have her sister living with her, in a home of her own, was one great motive for accepting and gratefully appreciating all that the Marquis of Seaham laid at her feet. She contrasted this open, earnest conduct with the apparent caprice and neglect of him she loved. In disappointed affection and wounded pride she resolved to forget her first love, and in a few months became Marchioness of Seaham. And where had been that first love? His home in London had been well known, since it was his father's hereditary mansion, in Grosvenor-square. Did Lady Silbrook ever invite that most afflicted young man to a private conference? Did she ever maternally assure him that, capricious as he might seem, she saw he had some secret withheld from her—some secret sorrow? —Did she not, on the contrary, constantly aggravate the indignant feeling of Ethel, by observing, ‘Very strange of Lord Edwin!’ ‘My dear Ethel, I hope you do not care for him,’ &c. At that time — that is, during the interval of the departure from Polhill Towers to the marriage of Lady Ethel Haughton, a period of ten months — Lord Edwin, the victim of a morbid sensibility, that has since found vent in poetry of rare beauty, fancied that, as a younger brother, he dared not venture to induce the celebrated ward of Chancery to share his comparatively humble lot. True, he was noble, he was titled; but the title was one of courtesy, and could not descend. This feeling increased when Lady Ethel Haughton became one of the maids of honor, and drove him frantically to the continent on her marriage with the Marquis of Seaham."

CHAPTER XXXI.

FURTHER ILLUSTRATIONS.

" Lady Anna Marlow, the younger sister of
the Marchioness of Seaham," continued the duchess,
" was married in the following year to my dear stepson, the Duke of Peterworth, from the Seaham's
country place, Marsden Park, in Cheshire. The love
of those two sisters for each other was the more remarkable and interesting, from the perfect innocence
with which they let it be perceived that the ' sister '
was the one idol paramount. This happily created
no jealousy on the part of the marquis. He loved
Anna as a sister, and the tie continues stronger than
ever, partly from this circumstance, that Anna was
still in her convent-school during the attentions of
Lord Edwin, and never even saw him. The only
lover she had ever known of her Ethel was the husband who welcomed herself, as a dear young sister,
to his house and heart. Here, again, I must make
my reflections, my regrets, my resolutions. While
the young marchioness had Anna with her at Marsden Park she was perfectly happy. The two young
creatures, with their studies and their pastimes, were

again in spirit in their convent-school. Therefore, when the younger left Marsden for a new home, the elder should have been surrounded by new occupations and other companions; for Ethel possessed a mind too thirsting — too energetic to be pacified by merely the heart's affections, although she doted on her child, Just at this time — truly an ' evil hour' — Lord Edwin was brought with other friends to Marsden, by the unsuspecting husband; for he had become acquainted with Lord Edwin as a poet, traveller, and author. In a still more evil hour was Lord Edwin betrayed into revealing to the still idolized Ethel, that he had acted an heroic part in keeping aloof, that he might not mar the brilliant future of the woman he adored. How fatally this now celebrated man broke through the reserve of former years, you already know. The flight to Italy; three short weeks of intoxicating love; nine years of self-imposed and appalling penance; the disgrace of two virtuous and noble families — a stigma——"

"Oh! yes. I understand but too well, duchess," interrupted Lord Stanmore; " a stigma on her child. You are now returning to our quarrel in the early part of my visit."

" Ah, not to quarrel," cried the duchess, while her eyes filled with tears, " but to agree, as good Catholics, that any criminal indulgence in human affections, — any departure from the straight and narrow way, involves a return so painful, that one stands in admiration of the extraordinary grace of God, and docile correspondence on the part of the repentant sinner. Now, look here."

The duchess had opened the picture-case already described, that had been lent to her that morning, and Lord Stanmore gazed on the once sportive and beautiful Ethel, — ' the Entombed Alive !' The duchess, perceiving him moved, thus again addressed him :

" Dear Lord Stanmore, I ought to have been your grandmother, therefore I feel and act as such. Let me recapitulate to you the wrong I feel done to two young persons, when the elder and more experienced friends gaze on their mutual affection, without giving aid or counsel of any beneficial nature, — nay, often proving worse than useless, by whispering comments of an irritating goading nature. It was cruel to permit those two young people to become the victims of their own morbid sensibilities, instead of betrothing them to each other, — to await, in peace and mutual esteem, their happy marriage."

" Certainly," said Lord Stanmore, abstractedly. He then added : " So you think that a first attachment can never be entirely overcome ?"

" I think," replied the duchess, " that a *permitted* and *mutual* attachment, is the marriage made in heaven. The only one that friends on earth ought to assist. I know your thoughts, my dear Stanmore ; I have read your young heart long ago. Thank God, that as it could be neither permitted nor mutual, your first earthly worship arose where it did."

" Where it does," said Lord Stanmore.

" Where it *did!*" cried the duchess, vehemently; " you wilful wicked boy! Are *you*, too, going to break God's commandments, and covet another man's wife?"

" No, duchess," replied he, " I covet not: that temptation has passed. She herself, by the blessing of God, has cured me. But I still may worship, as I have emulated, her immovable fidelity to her nuptial engagement. We are alone, duchess; I open my heart to you. I have often felt that, had Lady Clara been free, I could, perhaps, notwithstanding my youth, have created an interest in her heart. But heaven willed otherwise; and I now love her niece, my future wife, as truly and faithfully, as either could desire. Duty is the only true happiness."

" God bless you, my dear Stanmore," responded the duchess; " you now gladden my heart, and are more than ever my young hero."

The next few weeks were devoted to public business, principally with the Marquis of Seaham, Minister for Foreign Affairs, under whom our hero was soon to take office; but the marriage of Lord Claud Chamberlayne and Miss Whynne was the terminating event of that season to all those family connections who were not further detained by national affairs. During the preparations of milliners and jewellers, under the supreme decision of Lady Emily, the bride-elect was hurried each day by her father to view the historical parts of the great capital of England, lest the ambassador's wife, at Vienna, should betray ignorance of the city of her birth. The last of these sight-seeing days left but one intervening before the wedding. Lord Claud had, that evening, just entered the drawing-room in Belgrave-square, with his bridal offering of rare family jewels, given him by his brother, for the future Marchioness of Seaham. Georgina had not perceived his entrance, for she was bending an earnest face over a little manuscript book, wherein she was recording the chief points of interest viewed that day. After watching her a few moments, with a smile, Colonel Whynne said:

"I promised to remind you, Georgina, of whatever you may the most wish to remember."

"Yes, papa; thank you. I was just going to consult you about the two giants in Guild Hall; but now I remember them perfectly well, and have recorded them, Cock and Peacock."

When the merry laugh, at Georgina's expense, was over, and the due titles entered into the book, the jewels were produced, and accepted with artless pleasure. The really "happy pair" left England for

Vienna the last week in July, and all the wedding-party rushed from London; some to their own beautiful estates in green England, some to the sea-side, while others sought the German waters, or travelled elsewhere on the continent. Among the latter was Lord Stanmore, till Christmas; while his venerable grandsire returned to enjoy the calm solitudes of his cherished Woolton.

Thus passed the autumn of 1854, the chief event being the glorious first battle of the Crimea, — the victory of Alma. Then followed, after Christmas, a long parliamentary season, of which the movements and vicissitudes of our army in the East formed the principal public events. To be remembered also in the circles of our friends, as witnessing the flutter of the dove-like Anna, Duchess of Peterworth, because the Marquis of Seaham's family had taken for granted that the young Violet would be presented at court for the first time on her marriage.

"What will that marriage confer on my niece?" cried the duchess. "As the daughter of a marquis, she is of superior rank to Lord Stanmore. She will not be called Viscountess Stanmore, but Lady Violet Stanmore during the life of the Earl of Charleton. Her own family should present her. Her mother's sister has the first claim. Can any one venture to oppose the presentation of Lady Violet Chamberlayne, by her maternal aunt, the Duchess of Peterworth!"

Lady Violet's sixteenth birthday had but just occurred. Her aunt would admit no excuse for delay, either of the extreme youth of Violet, or of her own too delicate health. Although she had not appeared at court for many years, the duchess conquered all difficulties for the sake of her loved sister's memory, and, to the surprise of all her friends, returned home full of life and joy, claiming as her sole reward from Violet, that they should spend the rest of the day together. This last royal drawing-room terminated the London season. Again there was a flight to cool shades at home or aboad, and again was Lord Stanmore on the continent. His destination this year was the city of his early youth, Marseilles; for he resolved to reply in person to a letter received from a once favorite companion, requesting his attestation that, on a certain day, six years previously, the two young friends were together, at the house of a mutual acquaintance, at Marseilles. This attestation was important to nullify an attempt to criminate the young Étienne Belmont, as a boyish, and therefore unsuspected, political agent for the liberal party in Sicily.

Lord Stanmore, delighted to serve his early friend, to meet him in the scenes of their happy boyhood, and to revive some other pleasing memories, prolonged his visit some weeks on the shores of the Mediterranean; another few weeks, with distant relations of his mother, in the charming bowers of

Vaucleuse, brought our hero to the end of August, and to the fulfilment of an engagement to spend the first fortnight of September at Marsden Park. This visit would be the last before the return to claim his bride, and must be limited; for he had to pass on to Woolton Court, to give final orders for her reception. Journeying rapidly from Vaucleuse, Lord Stanmore found himself, on the morning of the 30th of August, on board the Boulogne steamer, with a rough but favorable wind, bearing swiftly towards England.

CHAPTER XXXII.

REGRET AND HOPE.

ONCE more the shores of France receded from the loving gaze of Lord Stanmore, and this time with an emotion for which he could not well account. Was it that events important to his happiness must occur before he could again course over her sunny plains? or was it a real preference for the land of his childhood and early youth? He could not resolve these questions; but the emotion, which he had believed unseen, had been watched with sympathy and interest by a countryman standing beside him, and leaning, like himself, on the side of the vessel. The stranger held a small note-book, and was apparently sufficiently inspired by the appearance or the sensibility of Lord Stanmore to deem him worthy of a line, in prose or verse, on the choice leaves of that little chronicler. The unknown was himself a person to be remarked and chronicled; and perchance he knew and dreaded his claims to observation; for large blue spectacles and a long scarf served to conceal his head and face, whenever the approach of English passengers placed his recognition in danger. At the moment, however,

when Lord Stanmore had attracted him, the unknown
had removed these guardians of his privacy, and he
looked out free o'er sky and sea. Then was displayed
a face that, in its noble and classic form, could not
be surpassed; yet on this faultless face were lines
ineffaceable, of woe.

Lord Stanmore, absorbed in thought, had, by degrees rested his form on the vessel, till his weight
preponderated towards the water, and the slightest
accident in the ship's course might throw him overboard. A moment like this approached; the weather
had not been propitious; it now became adverse;
the vessel lurched, and Lord Stanmore, balancing
on the edge, felt that he must take a forced leap into
the water, when an iron grasp brought him on his
feet, and a low, sweet voice uttered:

"Returning home, and yet so reckless of life!"

"Is England, in truth, my native land?" soliloquized, more than demanded, Lord Stanmore.

"Ah! you are English?" said the stranger;
"your speech and your regrets betray you."

"True," said our hero; "my regrets are in
France; my hopes are in England."

"You ought to thank God," said the stranger,
"that you *can* balance the one against the other,
and pronounce in favor of hope. But you are
young. You singularly interest me. Favor me by
telling me who you are?"

Lord Stanmore, with the frankness of youth, immediately responded to the request, without perceiving the additional pallor that overspread the countenance of the unknown, or hearing his low ejaculation :

"Oh, my God! how dost Thou pursue me!"

After a little pause, Lord Stanmore said :

"I thank you, not only for having saved me from a perilous leap into troubled waters, but also for reminding me of my hopes in England; for I have there, awaiting my return, a lovely and loving bride-elect."

"Yes," said the stranger; "the only child of the Marquis of Seaham."

"Who, then, are *you*," inquired Lord Stanmore, smiling, "who know so much of my happy prospects?"

"I cannot," replied the stranger, "reveal, as you have done, my identity; but as in speaking to Lord Stanmore I may claim the sympathy of a Catholic, I will confess myself to be a man who has greatly offended God; and if, indeed, I have saved you this day from great danger, I entreat, in return, that you will remember me before the altar, — especially before the domestic altar, — saying, 'God be merciful to *him* a sinner!'"

"We are told how that prayer was answered," observed Lord Stanmore. "Why do *you* not also weigh the balance between regret and hope, and choose the latter?"

24

"Because," replied the melancholy stranger, "although I have received sufficient grace to acknowledge and bewail my sin, I have not corresponded sufficiently to merit a practical and persevering line of conduct. I am but half a penitent; therefore, I need prayers. The prayers of your young bride-elect, would be most efficacious. I beseech you, recommend me to her prayers."

"I will do so with the greatest pleasure," said Lord Stanmore; "and to make the claim the more forcible, I will mention that you have this day saved me, not only from danger, but, probably, from death; for swimmer and diver though I be, I might, with such a sea as this, have been sucked under the vessel."

"Have you a miniature of your betrothed?" inquired the unknown. "I am something of an artist, and greatly admire the style of our modern painters."

Lord Stanmore, by the aid of a gold chain, drew forth from a recess near his heart, the morocco-case, and opened it to the gaze of his new friend, saying:

"It is very like; although I teazed the artist, till I wonder he had the patience to finish it. I wished that the eyes should meet mine, and yet give an expression that Lady Violet bestowed on heaven alone. She never fixedly looks on any one. I requested the artist to surprise and fix that look; and, I think, he has succeeded."

" Ah, yes," said the stranger, " heavenly, —
seraphic ! She will pray even for me : the heart
pertaining to such a countenance would pray, like
her Divine Model, for her greatest enemy. I thank
you, from the depths of a broken heart, Lord Stanmore, for this kind act."

The miniature was again concealed, and, after a
long pause, the next remark was on the favorable
change in the weather. The sea was calming, and
the stormy clouds heaping in gigantic masses on the
northern horizon, leaving the blue vault and the
meridian sun to be first praised and admired, then
condemned, as unbearable, by a now full assembly
of ladies from below. An awning was suspended,
during which process, our two friends being roused
to make way for poles and ropes, Lord Stanmore
perceived that the blue spectacles and long scarf had
been resumed. The conversation at length fell back
into the serious tone with which it had commenced,
and on the strangers again reverting to his misery in
having insufficient moral force to persevere in the
sublime penance of the saints, Lord Stanmore said :

" It may be presumptuous in one so much less
experienced to offer advice, therefore, I simply utter
what must often have occurred to yourself. Why
do you not entrench yourself by some religious engagement, of a nature to repair, by active good
works, instead of fasting, solitude, and prayer, those
faults of earlier life, which you so sincerely deplore?"

"Your suggestion is good," replied the unknown; "but I want the moral force to persevere in active good works. I am now returning from a fruitless trial of a novitiate in the south of France; yes, we have been fellow-travellers these three days."

"In what congregation were you?" asked Lord Stanmore.

The stranger immediately mentioned the title of the order, and Lord Stanmore exclaimed, with increased interest:

"Ah! indeed? I know those religious fathers very well. The present superior was my confessor for years. Where was your difficulty?

"In the edifying *precision* of their life. I should have felt the same in the army. I am a poet, and have the waywardness of one. I cannot endure the constraint of a life in community."

"You are a poet — an author!" exclaimed Lord Stanmore.

"I am," replied the stranger, "and, unfortunately, a favorite in the seductive circles of our modern Babylon. I told you that I was but half a penitent; yet could I but know in what manner to expiate my former life, I would become a penitent indeed."

"You are a poet," repeated Lord Stanmore, pondering. "Too probably your lines, like Lord Byron's, have hitherto been devoted to dangerously graphic descriptions of the loves of earth. Would it not be an acceptable sacrifice to lay your future poems at the foot of the altar?"

"Yes!" exclaimed the stranger. "At length I see my way; I thank you for it. I will henceforth write in expiation."

"It will be certainly far more in the usual and easy course of Divine Providence," continued Lord Stanmore, "that you devote to God the heavenly gift of poetry, than to place yourself in a life unsuited to all your former habits. What made you decide on an active congregation? Oh! I remember, it was because you shrank from the austerities of the old cloisters. But there are some, even of the most ancient, where there are no corporal macerations; because the silence and the solitude of their institute are considered by the Church surpassing austerities. In these cloisters you could welcome your holy muse, without danger of interruption from a frivolous world. My thoughts are more especially reverting to la Grande Chartreuse — to the Sons of St. Bruno — the Carthusians. You would have two small rooms and a little garden to yourself; access to a fine library; plenty of wood firing; your meals brought to you, and meat permitted to an Englishman. The sublimity of the scenes would bear your thoughts aloft, and your laborious hours would be devoted to your pen."

"Are you serious, Lord Stanmore?"

"I am so, indeed. I know the spot. After the classical tour made with my tutor, I visited, with an esteemed friend, the most celebrated monasteries of

France and Italy. Were *I* a poet, I would, with your feelings of compunction and dread of the world's further seductions, become a Carthusian monk. Will you not at least try? I will keep the secret that an unknown traveller, without landing from the shores of France, returned thither through Paris, Lyons, and Grenoble, to lead the only penitential life possible to him — that of calm seclusion, and the labors of the pen for God."

An hour later, the advice had practically prevailed. The luggage of the unknown had been transferred from the vessel just arrived at Folkestone, to that about to start for Boulogne; and Lord Stanmore, instead of proceeding by the express train to London, accompanied his new friend to the deck of the latter vessel, and some last words were exchanged thus:

"I have, to encourage me," said the unknown, "the example of the most heroic penance, that of a perfect martyr, in a form the most lovely and delicate of her sex — one, whose purgatory, self-inflicted, must have procured her an immediate admittance to the vision of her reconciled God."

"Will you not write to me?" said Lord Stanmore. "Will you not give me some account of your feelings amid the eternal snows? You can sign by whatever poetic name may suit you."

The stranger grasped Lord Stanmore's hand, while his eyes overflowed.

"*If* I persevere," said he, "angelic young man! you shall hear from me, and by the name I have disgraced. And now, Lord Stanmore, in return for holy advice, for which a saint in Heaven will bless you, let me venture to caution you, by the result of sad experience. You are about to espouse a young innocent creature, whose first earthly affections are yours. Happy man! Do not politely neglect her for the stirring arena of politics. Do not permit that the void of your absence shall be filled by male guests, whose tastes assimilate with hers in the sister arts. I have heard that Lady Violet Chamberlayne is an unusually fine performer on the harp, and sings most sweetly. Be more enthusiastic than any other man about these natural gifts or acquired talents. Above all, do not let poets hang around her, whispering adultation in her ear. *Be yourself the lover*, and your home will continue blessed. I suppose that Lady Violet has still retained her governess?"

"Yes," said Lord Stanmore; "Miss Campion is still with her."

"Then do prevail on that estimable lady to remain as companion. Occasional female visitors are not sufficient; neither are the most faithful servants. The beautiful young wife of a man forced from her by public affairs, should be protected by an elder female relative, or by the confidential instructress of her childhood."

"All that you have so wisely and kindly said,"

replied Lord Stanmore, " shall be entered to-night on the blank pages of my pocket-book; and shall be referred to in future years."

Some more last words, and the final grasp of hands was given.   Lord Stanmore would have embraced the future inmate of the Chartreuse; but he meekly drew back, saying :

" You might hereafter regret it."

Still, as Lord Stanmore turned to give a last look, on leaving the vessel, he caught so beaming an expression of heavenly hope issuing from the woe-cut lines of the stranger's face, that he passed on rejoicing in spirit, and completely occupied by the occurrence of the day, till, guided by a porter, he entered the hotel at Folkestone.

CHAPTER XXXIII.

THE RESPONSIBILITIES OF SERVANTS.

REFRESHMENT to the poor body was at length greatly needed; and Lord Stanmore, having thrown himself on a sofa, was rejoicing that he was not likely to be disturbed in any way, when the master of the hotel entered, and, respectfully placing before him a packet of sealed papers, said:

"This packet of letters, or papers, my lord, was enclosed in an envelope to myself, some days ago, with instructions to present it to your lordship immediately on your arrival from France— Lord Edwin Fitzjames, I presume?"

A pause of utter astonishment and dismay.

"I presume I have the honor of addressing Lord Edwin Fitzjames?"

"Certainly not," at length replied our hero. "I refer you, sir, to my valet, Mr. Temple, to know who I am; and as I feel extremely fatigued, I request to be left in perfect quiet until to-morrow."

The mystified master of the hotel withdrew in silence, consulted Mr. Temple; and it was agreed to postpone any further reference to Lord Stanmore until the morrow.   In the mean time our young nobleman began to feel such agitating suspicions that he started up and rang the bell.   A waiter obeyed the summons :

"I wish to see my servant."

The waiter vanished ; — Mr. Temple appeared.

"Who was that gentleman with whom I was conversing nearly the whole day, and whom I accompanied on board the other steamer ?"

"Lord Edwin Fitzjames, my lord."

"Is it possible?   Are you perfectly certain ?"

"Yes, my lord; perfectly certain.   But I knew as well that you were quite ignorant of his person. They say that unfortunate nobleman is so gifted with eloquence, and a certain fascination, that few can withstand him.   This excuses his victims."

"Oh! if I could but sleep!" exclaimed Lord Stanmore, tossing on the sofa.   "I am becoming so excited, so feverish.   Temple, you believe in true repentance?"

"Of course, my lord; I believe in the grace of God, and in faithful correspondence to grace.   But Lord Edwin has consented to be followed and flattered as the fashionable poet of the day; and to be pitied for his sorrows, as if he were the victim of fate.   There is no true repentance in this."

"It is exactly the conviction of how much this conduct must offend God," said Lord Stanmore, "that has induced Lord Edwin Fitzjames to seek a religious seclusion on the continent."

" Indeed ! " exclaimed Mr. Temple.   " Then it is through your influence, my lord.   You will have a rich reward for converting so dangerous a man. But about this packet of letters, my lord ; it is in consequence of Lord Edwin's taking your good advice that he has lost it."

" You can inform the master of the hotel," said Lord Stanmore, " that Lord Edwin Fitzjames will sleep at Boulogne to-night.   Whether he can be reached in time by the next steamer ; or whether, if he shall have left Boulogne, the police can trace his further course, these officials will know far better than I.   And, now, Temple, for the future, never mention that unfortunate nobleman to me.   As a true penitent, seeking to make reparation for the past, by the sacred effusions of his poetic genius, withdrawn from a seductive world, and persevering in a modest retirement, he will have my prayers ; but let his name never pass your lips."

" You may perfectly rely, my lord, on my never intruding such a name on you.   To others, as I have already said, I had resolved to keep the secret of this wonderful and unexpected meeting, which I must say, my lord, I looked upon as a most striking event.   You have rescued Lord Edwin from a relapse, in which he might have lost the grace of God forever.   I know, through authentic sources, that the most killing beauty of the London aristocracy has taken a wager that she will make ' the poet

Edwin' smile every time he meets her.   From what a snare you, Lord Stanmore, have been the instrument to save him."

" Temple," said Lord Stanmore, " I believe you upper and confidential servants of the aristocracy have a mission to fulfil, far beyond what is ever dreamed of.   You surpass the very police in your knowledge of family secrets ; and knowledge thus gained involves responsibility.   Of course it is through the servants of this foolish beauty, or those of the house in which she uttered this boast, that you possess the knowledge of her interest in Lord Edwin.   Perhaps this packet is from her ?"

" My lord, I believe it is, and I hope it may never reach him."

" I fervently hope so too.   But to return to the responsibility involved in the knowledge gained by servants of family secrets ; has the subject ever occurred to your own mind ?"

" It has, my lord.   I hope I should feel as much the honor and delicacy of such a trust, as if I myself were a nobleman ; for noble sentiments are gained more by association than original by birth."

" Ha !   Well, perhaps, you are right.   At any rate, I am much pleased to find you are yourself possessed by such a loyal spirit.   I am placed in a difficult and painful position, as the future son-in-law of the Marquis of Seaham ; and I think you felt this when you assured me that after this day's conversation the name of Lord Edwin Fitzjames should never be intruded on me."

"Yes, my lord; it was exactly from that feeling I made the promise."

"One point more, Temple. Family secrets become known, and the more painful, alas! the more widely spread the scandal. But other secrets are divulged — other scandals occupy public attention, till the old story is but faintly remembered. I therefore think it the duty of every one who believes himself my friend, to act as if the painful event of former years in the Seaham family had never occurred."

"I perfectly understand — perfectly agree with you, my lord," responded Mr. Temple.

25

CHAPTER XXXIV.

THE VISITORS AT MARSDEN PARK.

THE London season is truly considered to be the most open demonstration of the world, the flesh, and the devil; but there is a private world still more dangerous to a mind and heart that, not rising above the claims of earth, must feed on earthly excitement. The young beauty is less fatally engaged in following with enthusiasm the strains of vocal genius at the opera,. or enjoying the festive scene and exercise of a ball-room, than in wandering in sylvan bowers, with a romantic tendency towards the companion of her solitude, however worthless he may be. In the country there is more liberty, more private means of escape from worldly trammels, the which trammels act usefully when a higher restraint is ignored; therefore, the country mansion, containing a " select coterie," who can discuss the past London season, can lounge about, read enervating poetry, act charades, lose themselves by couples in charming labyrinths and copse-woods, — that country mansion becomes a more dangerous ally to the enemy of souls than all the squares, streets, and parks of the polite end of London, to the refined, tender, and unsuspecting female heart. Thus fell the young Marchioness of Seaham, the hitherto pearl of the aristocracy, and thus fall many, entangled in the snares laid for hearts, in these arcadian bowers; losing the first instinctive perception of wrong by the scales of the sanctuary, making heroic sacrifices for the creature, while forgetting the Creator, till a false conscience supervenes, and all is lost, save bitterness. Ah! bitterness — bitterness!

During the August just past, while Lord Stanmore was in the south of France, Marsden Park was full of visitors, who with the exception of Sir Henry and Lady Clara Moorland, might fitly represent the " select coterie" described above; comprising also a few statesmen who, amid the more serious and absorbing interests of guiding England, were not insensible to the attractions of lovely amateurs in all the softening influences of the fine arts, 'mid balmy weather, luxurious living, constantly varying amusement, and good news from the Crimea.

Lady Violet, like her aunt, lived unharmed amid these scenes. She had received permission to decline any active part in the sometimes doubtful amusement of the passing hour. On her arm constantly hung her conscience beads, unsuspected, in their brilliancy, to be what, to her, they were, — a silent record of the failings or self-conquest of the day. She had the privilege of some minutes each morning with

Lady Clara: these were happy interviews; but not
to last. General Sir Henry Moorland was sum-
moned to attend an important court-martial, and left
Marsden with his devoted wife and attendants, some
days before the return of Miss Campion from a visit
to her own family; the marquis had already been
compelled to meet the prime minister at a spot con-
veniently found between their country residences, so
that the Lady Violet was left, with all her father's
fair guests, in the false position of being considered
too young to exercise any authority. The leader
of the revels was a certain Lady Cecily, commonly
called Lady Cis-Dorel, — unfortunately a near cousin to the marquis, who, like the father of St. The-
resa, could not " handsomely " refuse the self-invited
visits of his kinswoman. The " memosa," Lady
Violet, shrank from the eager advances of her lively
relative; but not so the temporary inmates of Marsden Park. To the passive lovers of excitement, Lady
Cis-Dorel, as the personification of active excitement,
was a treasure to be hailed; and the departure of
Lady Clara Moorland, within a few hours of the
arrival of her cousin, seemed to emancipate from all
restraint the followers of the latter wild witty and
mischievous lady; so that the lord of misrule was
rapidly gaining the ascendant at Marsden Park.

To whom should the young Violet return? Not
even the near expected arrival of Miss Campion
would avail her, except as a personal companion and

protectress. She would be powerless to stay the torrent of folly that was each hour increasing in the house. Violet prayed long and earnestly; and, on rising from her knees, requested an interview with the family chaplain and her esteemed confessor, Dr. Rollings. The reverend gentleman was happily soon found; and responding instantly to the invitation, received the first outpourings of her confidence.

"Oh! Dr. Rollings," she added, "this house has known such sorrow, that if joy and merriment are again to be heard within its walls, it ought to be a joy sanctified by Heaven. My cousin and the rest never come into the chapel for Mass, or the night prayers. Lady Cecily ought to sing sometimes for God, she has so beautiful a voice. Dr. Rollings, you know the Church forbids that women should be dressed in men's clothes; yet my cousin has brought with her an equipment of armor, to act as Tancredi, in the gardens of Armida. They teased me to be Armida, which I have to repeat to you out of confession, and I received your consent and support to refuse everything of the kind. Oh! Dr. Rollings, you are so wise and full of expedients, as well as of hope, that I have, under God, confidence only in you."

"Go and pray, my dear child, and I will act," was the reply of the venerable chaplain.

The morning after this interview, Lady Cecily, unfolding at the breakfast-table an official looking document, exclaimed:

" Well, God bless the war in Sicily ! It has done wonderful things for me. It has just taken off the head of a most worthless husband. Yes, ye noblemen and gentlemen, here assembled, — ' Preux chevaliers !' behold a charming widow, breaking bread with you, sipping coffee, actually brought into the contact of common life with you, who can now be gained with her three thousand a year ! Wonderful position of things ! I propose a tournament in the park. We will all go together to select the spot, and have workmen directly to enclose the grounds for the lists. What if the marquis himself should prove the victor ? I beseech ye, gallant knights, permit my noble cousin to obtain the prize !"

On leaving the park to flutter about with innumerable orders, Lady Cecily was surprised by a request from Dr. Rollings, to speak to her immediately in his private study ; a request with which she complied, concluding that the object of the interview was an arrangement for requiem Masses. After a few words of condolence, however, Dr. Rollings led Lady Cecily to the chapel ; the door of which he locked, and thus addressed her :

" Madam, having from God, and the noble owner of this house, charge of the souls herein contained, I forbid you, with all the authority I possess, to further endanger or scandalize those souls by your conduct. The news you have just received, will form to your associated visitors an admirable plea for some days, at least, of more seclusion. Before these days are over, the marquis will have returned, — my responsibility will have ceased. I now distinctly forbid a tournament in the park. I have already stopped the preparations. I also forbid all theatricals, and, during these early days of your bereavement, all dancing and music ; of course, excepting the sacred music of this chapel. Let us now pray, Lady Cecily, that this short suspension from folly and sin may be blest to you. You are a Catholic. You know in Whose Presence I thus speak."

Dr. Rollings here approached the altar and knelt, but Lady Cecily only screamed with laughter, exclaiming :

" You delicious old man ! you are worth all the theatricals, dancing, and music, to be found round the globe. Where *did* you drop from ? Ha ! you said you were the chaplain. Well, you shall figure as such at the tournament. You shall shrive the vanquished knights, while I will crown the victor."

A little pause, and the following thoughts :

" What a fine study of the back of an old man's head. I wonder whether he could be coaxed to kneel in a *tableau vivant*. If I had but a pencil I could sketch it off. Truly a fine old man for the chaplain at my tournament !"

Aloud :

" You dear good creature, that is quite enough of the praying scene. What are you praying for at this time of day? Is it for me, or the rascal gone to kingdom come? Pray out loud, cannot you?"

A pause, and the following thoughts:

"I cannot lose any more time here, looking at that picturesque old man, I must tell the people to get on as fast as possible. How fortunate I chose the piece of ground directly after breakfast; a beautifully smooth, long, flat piece. I will write to that fool, Algernon Dorel, to come and compete for my hand, as nearest of kin to the *treasure* I have lost, and to bring with him half-a-dozen good riders and tilters, as handsome as himself."

Aloud:

"Come, you good old soul, I saw you lock the door, and pocket the key; but there is a time for all things, and with all due respects for your good intentions." Thoughts. "Perhaps he is deaf. I will go nearer. Oh! what an expression on that old saint's face. I cannot disturb him just yet."

During the next pause, Lady Cecily observed that the altar stood about four feet from the wall, and that a small door in that wall, temptingly ajar, would enable her to make her quiet escape. She, therefore, with some feeling of awe, passed behind the altar, and, gliding through the door-way, entered, as she expected, the sacristy. A glance around discovered two additional doors; one of these was locked, but the other opened into a modest suite of rooms, that must belong, she concluded, to the chaplain. The

last of these was a small reception parlor, the one in
which the Rev. Dr. Rollings had requested an interview.   Lady Cecily identified it by a remarkably
fine bust in marble of his present holiness, Pius IX.
She had then, she remembered, but to repass a short
corridor into the great hall : but no ; the door was
locked.   Retracing, with some impatience, the four
rooms to the sacristy, Lady Cecily, again involuntarily slackening her pace, re-entered the chapel from
behind the altar ; resolved to obtain the key from the
aged priest by screams, or even a personal struggle.
But the hitherto immovable priest was gone.   He
had passed through the great door of their first entrance, and had locked it, leaving Lady Cecily a
prisoner.

Although the afternoon was not advanced beyond
four o'clock, yet the chapel was dark from the effect
of an approaching thunder-storm.   Lady Cecily felt
nervous, but rallied her courage.

" A heavy fall of rain," thought she, " will be
good for the turf. How long does that fanatic
intend to detain me here !   He expects, I suppose,
that I shall while away the time by repeating all the
prayers I can remember ; but I will not stay here in
this gloom.   I will go back to the rooms, and ring
the bell, — a good peal, too."

At that instant the previous low rumble of the
storm, was succeeded by one of those near and crack-
ling bursts overhead, that follow immediately the

vivid flash.   An unusual sound was in the midst of the tumult, — the fall of the thunder-bolt!

On the floor of the chapel that guilty woman had fallen, exclaiming: "Judgment."   There she lay, writhing in the throes and pangs of an awaking conscience, while the storm, to her thrilling nerves, continued at its height.   Ah! yes; lie there, guilty woman!   Far more guilty in the sight of God than the former hapless lady of the mansion!   Lie there, while conscience recapitulates your many triumphs of caprice and infidelity towards God and man; your schemes, so artfully laid, to keep well with the world; your resistance to the grace that so often would have mercifully recalled you, and has now caused that thunder-bolt to fall within nine feet of your cunning head and selfish heart!

The storm had really been, of course, subsiding since the fall of the thunder-bolt; but the clouds, still thick and black, had advanced the night, and the chapel was illumined solely by the lamp of the sanctuary.   Lady Cecily dared not approach the altar. On rising, she sought a corner prie-dieu, and there sat, faint and bewildered, scarcely recognizing her own identity.

CHAPTER XXXV.

A LITTLE LIGHT IN THE HORIZON.

From the stupor into which Lady Cecily had fallen, she was roused by a gentle voice, saying, close to her ear:

" It is now your usual dinner-hour, my lady; you had best lean on me out of the chapel, to have some refreshment."

" Refreshment,—dinner-hour! Oh, yes, certainly. Who are you?"

" I am the housekeeper, my lady. I am called Mrs. Parker."

With some difficulty Lady Cecily arose, and, assisted by her new companion, approached the door behind the altar: Mrs. Parker devoutly knelt in passing. Lady Cecily, weak, and leaning heavily, was suddenly deprived of her prop; so that she not only knelt, but fell prostrate on the step of the altar, where she was again left alone; for Mrs. Parker, believing the attitude intentional, stepped on to prepare the immediate service of the repast.

Once more alone, and now fully conscious of how close she was to the tabernacle, this prostrate sinner had already received graces to feel that, being thus close, there was no other posture she could dare assume. More softened feelings began to respond to renewed grace. She wept long — sincerely; at first bitterly, with remorse; then sweetly, with repentance. She wept, and felt forgiven !—Forgiven, yes; but as a well-instructed, though erring Catholic, she well knew and trembled at the expiatory life before her — the life of practical repentance. Some long-disused words of prayer passed her lips. Again she wept—again she prayed; and now a courage was infused — a courage for God, that made her kiss the ground and rise to her knees, where she beheld Mrs. Parker patiently awaiting her good pleasure, to be assisted to her solitary repast in the reverend chaplain's private study.

" Why am I here ? " demanded Lady Cecily.

" My lady," responded Mrs. Parker, " this is the only suite of rooms — this one next the chapel — that is distinct from the rest of the house; and on your great bereavement — being suddenly left a widow — away from your own home, and in the midst of all this gay company, the Rev. Dr. Rollings has given up his rooms to your ladyship, that you may have the proper respect paid to your situation, without casting a gloom on the visitors."

Lady Cecily's keen intelligence was alive to the marked distinction between the severity with which Dr. Rollings treated her personally, and the respect he showed outwardly to her own position, and as the first cousin to the Marquis of Seaham, whose guests they were.   She restrained the utterance of this sentiment, and merely observed:

" But the house is so full, that I cannot hope the good doctor is himself well lodged.   I am sure he has not entered amid all the luxuries and profanations of *my* rooms."

" The reverend doctor, my lady, is in the room that once belonged to the late marchioness, and is never opened to visitors."

" Really !" cried Lady Cecily, with something in the tone that did not please Mrs. Parker ; " then he is not afraid of contamination in *that* room ? "

" Certainly not, my lady : the late marchioness was a most virtuous and exemplary wife and mother, so long as she remained at Marsden ; — a model to all !   When she fled with that fatal tempter, no one would believe in it.   Indeed, she again fled, in the right way, and was in the out-quarters of a convent, before any of the household knew of her fall.   The Rev. Dr. Rollings was afterwards in correspondence with the chaplain of the convent in Italy, where the holy penitent, through the merciful grace of her Redeemer, expiated her fault ; and I know his reverence's opinion to be that her purgatory was fulfilled on earth.   Why, Lady Cecily, our good God requires no more of any of His children, than that they shall repent, when they have done amiss.   He is a tender Father, and says of Himself, that He is more tender

26

than even a mother. But you are eating nothing, my lady. I must stop talking, and tempt you to a little of this delicate cutlet: the sauce is my own invention; and it is so much liked that whenever I send it to table the dish comes down empty, or nearly so."

"It is really excellent, Mrs. Parker. I feel getting better. Pray, does Dr. Rollings intend to pay me a visit?"

"As you please, my lady."

"Well, I think to-morrow. I am very tired: I will trouble you to send my maid directly."

"Miss Stokes, my lady, is gone to Chester, and is not to return till the day after to-morrow. Dr. Rollings told her, that no one knew your ladyship's tastes so well as herself, for the purchase of proper widow's mourning; so he wrote by Miss Stokes herself a letter of introduction to a family in Chester, where she will be hospitably received, and the best shops pointed out to her; also, a cheque on the bank."

"What a farce is this widow's mourning!" thought Lady Cecily; "but I will not scandalize this good old soul, by saying so. Pray, Mrs. Parker, where am I to sleep?"

"There is a spare room in this suite, my lady, that is generally kept locked. It is used a few times in the year, when Dr. Rollings has a brother-priest to visit him. I have had more pillows brought, and a proper toilet-table, and all your own little comforts placed in the room.   Now, a *little* jelly — orange jelly, and a little blancmange; some curaçoa, too, for a winding-up — George the Fourth's curaçoa; that is right; then I will show you your room."

"Are you to officiate as lady's maid, my good Mrs. Parker?"

" My niece has happened to come on a visit to me, my lady.   She is a dressmaker, but was once a lady's maid.   She has only to be rung for.   She'll be charmed to have the honor.   As for me, my lady, I should put you out of all patience, with my bad eyesight and want of dexterity."

" What are those voices?" suddenly exclaimed Lady Cecily.

" The servants' night prayers," replied Mrs. Parker.   " If you please, my lady, I will ring for my niece, Susan Dellet, and go to my place in the chapel."

" Pray, do so.   I will await your entrance just where I am.   Dellet, did you say?   Miss Dellet, milliner?"

" Exactly so, my lady; Upper Bond-street, London, number fifty-two, Miss Dellet, milliner."

Mrs. Parker retired to the chapel, and Lady Cecily remained occupied with some thoughts connected with the said milliner, of Bond-street, interspersed with mental comments on the devotions in the chapel; and at length joining in spirit, so that the quiet entrance of Miss Dellet was unperceived.

The night prayers were all in English; and at the
close the united voices sang, not in simple unison,
but in good harmony, an oratory hymn, of which
Lady Cecily, who had crept to the little door behind
the altar, heard distinctly the fourth and fifth verses,
thus :

> "Oh! how I fear thee, living God,
>   With deepest, tenderest fears!
> And worship thee with trembling hope
>   And penitential tears.
>
> "Yet may I love thee, too, O Lord!
>   Almighty as thou art;
> For thou hast stooped to ask of me
>   The love of my poor heart."

"*I* love God?" thought Lady Cecily, despond-
ingly. "I who cannot even love man but for my
own selfish ends, — my own advantage! God has
stooped to ask the love of my poor heart. Poor
heart, indeed! Does it deserve the name of one?
Why, I ought to feel for the soul just gone to perdition, for anything *I* have done to save. And this
Miss Dellet! What a part I acted towards her
young mistress. I just sent her to her grave. And
did I care for the man I seduced from her? No; it
was all vanity, — love of conquest, — love of excitement. I have not seen him these five years. Have
I ever really repented having broken off their engagement, and all my career at Florence and Lucca?
Lord, be merciful to me a sinner!"

Lady Cecily again lay prostrate behind the altar. These thoughts had been so rapid, that the domestic congregation were still singing the same hymn, the closing lines of which came distinctly thus :

.   .   .   .   .

"What rapture will it be,
Prostrate before Thy throne to lie,
And gaze, and gaze on Thee!"

"*I* gaze on God! Oh! never. I am unworthy to lie crouching down here behind the hidden Presence in the tabernacle. Oh! what a long life of penance mine ought to be, before I could sing those lines!"

The now real penitent, concealed in her self-condemnation from herself; ignorant of the progress she was truly making in the expiatory career, — that career so dreaded, — worn and exhausted, fell asleep at the back of the altar.

26*

CHAPTER XXXVI.

BENEFICIAL ARRANGEMENTS.

THE long prostration of Lady Cecily, prolonged beyond the intentions of the prostrator, had a softening and beneficial effect on the worthy and somewhat sternly-virtuous Miss Dellet, who, to oblige her aunt, and the reverend chaplain, had entered the rooms of one who, "in pride of power and beauty's bloom," had ruthlessly destroyed the happiness and at length the life of the lovely young creature, whom she had venerated as a saint, and mourned with deep affection. On the death of this young lady at Pisa, Miss Dellet returned to her kindred in England, by whose powerful interest in their own line she commenced business as a milliner, under the requested patronage of the Marchioness of Penzance, first lady of the bed-chamber. Miss Dellet consequently became the fashion, and took pains to preserve her renown. She now stood watching the prostrate form of Lady Cecily, who, at length, roused by the departing footsteps of the family congregation and the locking the great door of the chapel, arose and re-entered the room, where stood her temporary attendant.

"Miss Dellet, I believe?"

"Yes, Lady Cecily."

"A tLunder-bolt fell this evening."

"So I understand, my lady."

"*You* are a second thunder-bolt to me, Miss Dellet; but if you are willing to assist a person, who has caused you and your friends much sorrow, I will accept your services in the spirit of humility and contrition."

Miss Dellet bowed, and the night-toilet proceeded in silence.

The following day the recluse was visited by her inexorable guardian, Dr. Rollings. The interview was long, and terminated by a promise exacted to prepare for a general confession. This mental employment, assisted by written memoranda, enabled Lady Cecily to endure the solitude of the rest of the day; enlivened in the evening by the sole presence of Miss Dellet. The veneration, and even awe, with which she regarded the Rev. Dr. Rollings was chiefly owing to the conviction that his fervent prayer, in the midst of her levity, had drawn down the thunder-bolt to within a few feet of her erring life. As Lady Cecily has revealed this conviction to but few persons, who never contradict the feeling, it remains with her beneficially through life.

Mrs. Parker informed Lady Cecily the next day of the return of the marquis, and of the expected arrival of Lord Stanmore, the affianced husband of the Lady Violet.

"This will be his lordship's last visit," added Mrs. Parker, "before he comes to take our angel from us, to his own beautiful home in Westmorland."

It was from the lips of the Rev. Dr. Rollings that the marquis heard of the forced seclusion of his lively cousin, and of the combined motives for a step that every hour had rendered more imperative.

"I have now a favor to request, my lord marquis," continued the reverend chaplain: "I have, by the favor of God, obtained a wonderful power over that hitherto reckless lady. To-morrow her widow's mourning will arrive. On the following day I have proposed that she shall depart from Marsden Park; and the favor I have to request is, that I may resign the peaceful and honorable office I hold here as domestic chaplain, and may devote myself to the labor of turning the energies of this dangerous lady into a safe and useful channel?"

"Dr. Rollings, you propose to me a great sacrifice; and one that will fall too heavily on my daughter."

"In a few months, my lord marquis, the Lady Violet will have found another home and another chaplain."

"That is true; but you promised her to perform the ceremony."

"And I will fulfil that promise. I will return, my lord, for that event; and, as the time is too short, at this first departure, to pack my library and pictures, I can do so when I return for the marriage. Let me now, therefore, only return my thanks, my lord marquis, for the truly devout and noble consideration you have always shown, in my person, to the *office* of the priest of God."

The marquis sighed :

" I am truly grieved, Rev. sir. This is to me a very heavy loss. I little thought," added he, trying to smile, " that my gay cousin would have bewitched even you !"

Dr. Rollings replied :

" My lord marquis, I must own to you that I consider your cousin, Lady Cecily Dorel, to have been a most wicked woman. I doubt the stability of her repentance, without a dominant power constantly over her, such as she recognizes in me. I leave all to which my heart dare attach itself, in leaving Marsden Park, especially that angelic child, Lady Violet."

Tears stood in the eyes of the marquis, and a short silence ensued. He then said :

" Are you not giving the term ' wicked woman ' to my cousin Cis, as an indignant refutation of my accusation that *you*, even, were bewitched by her?"

" My lord, I had known the career of Lady Cecily Dorel from painfully authentic sources, before her arrival here. She has been a wicked woman, not in the estimation of the world, that she has loved, feared, and flattered, but before God. She has broken hearts, ruined family peace, led others to perdition, but has preserved her own reputation. A restless craving for admiration and excitement, has been the hidden propeller of all this mischief and sin. I feel called on to turn these natural and impetuous qualities into the straight path."

"But you must not make that straight path too narrow or too steep, Dr. Rollings, or she will go mad. What do you propose?"

"Lady Cecily Dorel, although a Catholic from her birth, has hitherto done nothing for the Church, or for the poor. I, therefore, propose," said Dr. Rollings, "that her expiatory life shall be so actively useful, as scarcely to leave her an hour's relaxation. And as she must be amused and praised and excited, I will take care that she becomes the patroness and benefactress of schools and reformatories, and widows' almshouses, and orphanages, and poor religious congregations, with annual meetings and banquets and complimentary speeches and bands of music and processions and bonfires and fireworks, to light up, propel, and recreate in the straight and narrow way."

"Admirable!" cried the marquis. "You have the gift of discernment of spirits, Rev. sir. I fear not for the good result."

On the second morning after this conversation, the elegant equipages of Lady Cecily Dorel conveyed herself, in due widow's attire, the Rev. Dr. Rollings, and the attendants, to a temporary residence she had selected, near Tunbridge Wells. The ecclesiastic who had succeeded as chaplain at Marsden Park had occasionally supplied for Dr. Rollings, and had, therefore, become known to and esteemed by the family.

CHAPTER XXXVII.

MATRIMONIAL ARRANGEMENTS AND A DEATH.

ON the 2d of September, a small, confidential, and happy circle were together rejoicing at Marsden Park, with much to recount, and still more to anticipate. The following day business was transacted in the marquis' private study between himself and Lord Stanmore, the open letters of the Earl of Charleton lying on the table before them, with legal documents, already signed by the earl. In the afternoon of that day, in the presence of witnesses, and in due form, other signatures were attached. Business thus over, all hearts were ready to enjoy the brief fortnight of Lord Stanmore's visit, and the joyful news of the fall of Sebastopol on the fifth. Then came a parting, in which hope forbade sorrow, and our hero was *en route* for Westmorland, until the twentieth of the following month, when he was to return and claim his bride.

Two years only had passed since the scenes our hero was approaching were all new, and of interest to him chiefly on his grandfather's account. He had had no personal memories, at that date, connected with Woolton Court.   But how much of thought and feeling had been crowded into those two years! What mental vicissitudes connected with the halls of his sires!   Therefore, on the first evening of his return, when the earl and his grandson sat alone, watching the varied outline of the circling mountains against the sunset glow, the deep hereditary love, so felt by the grandsire, passed into the breast of the heir, and he exclaimed:

"Yes! it is the *return* to a place that makes one love it.   It is the remembrances clinging round favored spots that so endears them.   I could not have believed that I should ever love this place as now I do.   I valued it for your sake, my lord; but my own heart was more on the shores of Provence.

"You have hitherto, you say, my dear Arthur, loved this property for my sake.   I can almost say the same with respect to you.   My earthly hopes have been and are in you.   Very soon they will be also in the sweet girl who is to become my grand-daughter.   You could not have made a choice more acceptable to me."

"Thank you, my dear lord.   Heaven has made the choice, it seems, not I.   But after many way-ward feelings, I can at length say with you, that a choice more acceptable to me could not have been made."

"These are precious assurances to my heart," said Lord Charleton.   "Lady Violet would have attracted you at once, had not your admiration been previously engaged by her aunt. The circumstance of your having first known Lady Clara involves no fault on your part. You have suffered; but you have not sinned. From all that I have observed, or known, you have been faithful to your engagement. You have done your duty. God will reward you by a constantly increasing affection for your lovely and faithful Violet."

"Yes!" exclaimed Arthur, "she has, indeed, been faithful. More faithful than I to her. I do not here refer to my worship of Lady Clara; but to the horror I felt when the blot on the family was made known to me—a blot, a stain that could affect Lady Violet alone, of the whole family; for she only had the blood of the unfortunate Marchioness of Seaham. I felt so indignant at the apparent concealment practised towards me, that I determined to break off the engagement. I was withheld solely by the power Lady Clara possessed over me. *She,* more than the Duchess of Peterworth, has made this marriage. Still was I hoping for some honorable means of escape, when the attempt became serious of our younger branch to nullify my existence as your heir, and turn me into a foreign peasant. At that crisis the constancy of Violet's attachment, the fidelity of her heart to me, in my adversity, so won my admiration and my gratitude that I renewed, before God, my betrothal by vow."

" And now," inquired the grandsire, as he looked his full approval, "when ' the elder and the younger angel' are together before you, to whom does your heart incline?"

" I have not dared to investigate too closely," replied Lord Stanmore, " but, as you have so well observed, to comfort me, *I can suffer without sin!*"

" And, during the short interval that will now occur before your marriage," continued . the earl, " were you to find that Lady Clara had become a widow, how would you relish the having renewed your betrothal by vow?"

" Lady Clara," replied Lord Stanmore, " considers me so truly as if already united to her treasured niece, and is so assured of Violet's affection for, and trust in me, that the event of Sir Henry's death would arrive too late to cause any change in my position. Even were I capable of deserting Violet, I should find no sympathy in the aunt: for she would accept no tribute to herself at the expense of my honor, and the happiness of her niece."

" I am comforted to be thus reassured," said Lord Charleton ; "for the life of Sir Henry Moorland has been considered most precarious."

" You mean that there still exists a tendency to blood in the head?"

" Yes. You are aware that a court-martial has been held on a Major Roderic, and that Sir Henry's opinion was unfavorable to the acquittal?"

"I have simply known of the court-martial; and that Sir Henry and Lady Clara quitted Marsden about a week before my arrival there from France."

"Then I have to announce to you the fact of a second stroke of apoplexy."

"How strange!" exclaimed Lord Stanmore, "that I should thus, by one day, have missed hearing the bad news at Marsden, to be informed of it here, so far north."

"The news reached me," said Lord Charleton, "just when I was expecting your arrival. The son of our nearest neighbor, Captain Gelliot, on leaving the court-martial, travelled direct to his father, to remain with him some weeks. Squire Gelliot immediately wrote to announce to me the fatal termination of the attack."

"The fatal termination! Then General Sir Henry Moorland is really dead? Then Lady Clara is actually a widow?"

"Yes, my dear Arthur, it is really thus. The Mass to-morrow will be for the repose of his soul."

"Oh!" cried Lord Stanmore, "I must go to her. Where is she?"

"Squire Gelliot's letter does not mention; but we will send Grainger to ascertain."

Accordingly, in one of the lighter carriages, and driven swiftly, Mr. Grainger, the butler, visited Gelliot Manor, and returned within two hours, accompanied by Captain Gelliot. This young officer recounted, with much animation and feeling, the scene of the court-martial; the investigation; General Sir Henry Moorland's vote of disapprobation of the conduct of Major Roderic; the stroke of apoplexy; the being bled immediately and copiously, but without return of consciousness till a few hours before his death, which had taken place in the early morning of that very day. Lady Clara Moorland was in a villa near Chatham, awaiting the funeral, which was to be at the royal expense, and on a munificent scale. Captain Gelliot had seen Lady Clara on the previous evening. He had been the youngest of three officers sent from head-quarters to congratulate her on the return of consciousness to Sir Henry.

"Her ladyship received us most courteously," continued Captain Gelliot, "and with great calm of manner. She expressed her gratitude for the return of reason; because Sir Henry would then fulfil all those religious duties that he had desired should occupy his last moments. She had herself no hope of his recovery. There were two fine babies seated on the table before her — twin girls of a year old. They were literally ' pulling caps ' and frolicking till they made us all smile. On Colonel Fanshaw's lamenting that one was not a boy, to carry on the baronetcy, Lady Clara informed us that her husband's heir and namesake was the little son of a cousin lately deceased. Then Colonel Fanshaw asked the little beauties which of them would smile on the cousin, and wed without changing her name: when each seized a moustache till he laughed outright — for he was in high spirits, taking quite a different view of Sir Henry's case to the true result foreseen by the wife. Colonel Fanshaw and the general had been old brothers in arms; and when he awoke this very morning, to be told that the general had been dead some hours, he was nearly having a stroke himself, and had to be bled."

CHAPTER XXXVIII.

A FUNERAL, AND THE MARRIAGE OF ARTHUR AND VIOLET.

AT daybreak Lord Stanmore and his faithful attendant, Mr. Temple, were on the cross-road to meet the London train, and to be conveyed as far as the Chatham line. This immediate arrival, from so great a distance, was duly appreciated by the mourner; and as the Marquis of Seaham, whom Lord Stanmore met at the villa, could not remain with his sister more than a few hours, our hero devoted himself to her plans and wishes in every respect, until, within a week. The funeral being over, he escorted the mother, children, and servants to their cordially-invited home at Marsden Park.

"Let not my widow's weeds defer the date of the marriage," pleaded Lady Clara. "I shall not be visible, but shall view the ceremony from the chapel gallery. Our Violet's other aunt has accepted the invitation, and will be the chief lady present."

The request was sincere, like everything proceeding from Lady Clara; and at length the marquis, who had proposed to add the delay of a month to the first

date assigned, compromised for a fortnight's addition
to the interval before Lord Stanmore's return to
Marsden. This would bring the wedding-day to the
20th of November, 1855.

On the young viscount's return to Woolton Court,
he found that his grandfather had carried out his
long-proposed plan of a division, into two parts, of
the mansion of Woolton Court. The great entrance
remained to both divisions, but different sides of the
court conducted to the now separated habitations of
the Earl of Charleton and Viscount Stanmore. No
exterior sign of this division appeared, excepting that
it explained the occupation of a hitherto small court
by a magnificent flight of steps on the eastern side
of the mansion, destined for the bride and bridegroom. The long picture-gallery of the north façade, with its door at either end, was the medium
of communication between the dwellings. The south
front, to the gardens and lake, was divided equally
to both families. The earl retained the dining-room
and library, but ceded the great banquet-hall, for a
dining-room, to Lord Stanmore, and suite of drawing-rooms. Arthur found that his grandsire had
relinquished too much ; but Lord Charleton assured
him that the division thus made was the result of
deliberate thought, adding :

"When you wish to give a ball in the banquet-
hall, you and your friends must dine with me ; you
are also invited to dine with me every Sunday and

great festival, while I will accept your invitations four times in a year."

Lord Stanmore laughed, and gayly accepted this most methodical arrangement, that reminded him of the punctual habits of Marseilles. He was himself fully occupied in directing fancy artists and other work-people in renewed decorations for the drawing-rooms and the Lady Violet's own boudoir, and had the satisfaction of seeing all fully to his taste, on the eve of his departure, with the Earl of Charleton, for Marsden Park, where, on their arrival, they found a really " select party " assembled for the bridal ceremony.

The customs of the continent, more than those of England, prevailed, in one respect, at the marriage of Viscount Stanmore and the Lady Violet Chamberlayne. Instead of the maiden bridesmaids, was the one especial matron to support and counsel the bride. This matron was the younger Duchess of Peterworth. Fifteen years before she had herself stood a bride in that very chapel, the same reverend celebrant officiating, when the supporting matron was her own sister, the late Marchioness of Seaham. The duchess had never revisited Marsden Park since the flight of her unfortunate Ethel; yet the same devoted attachment to the memory of her sister, that had aroused her from her sick couch, in London, to present Lady Violet at court, now braced her nerves to venture once more to Marsden Park.

Violet felt and appreciated all this energetic love in her usually languid aunt. She also, and still more gratefully remembered, with tender confiding affection, the widowed aunt concealed, but fondly gazing on her from the trellised gallery of the chapel. Her father, however, was paramount in her thoughts. She was now old enough, and had read and pondered enough to be aware of how acutely, how intensely, he had suffered; and she was to leave him! But he wished this marriage. He loved Arthur almost as paternally as he loved herself; and she had begun to perceive how, apart from his appreciation of Lord Stanmore, her father must feel consoled to see the daughter of the wife who had fled from him well married. These were Violet's precursive thoughts; but when the Rev. Dr. Rollings commenced the introit of the Mass—the bridal Mass—her whole attention was concentrated on the sacrament of marriage : its indissoluble character, comprising much of suffering as of joy; ardent prayer that all the graces bestowed might fall on the good ground of a prepared heart. All these for Arthur as for herself; while he, concentrated on the sacred obligations contracted by the ceremony, deserved, like herself, the nuptial benediction that closed the function.

CHAPTER XXXIX.

LONG-DEFERRED HOPES FULFILLED.

AFTER the departure of the bridal pair from Marsden Park to St. Leonards, on the Sussex coast, the Earl of Charleton returned to Woolton Court. The day following he ordered his close carriage-and-four, and was conducted, without further expression of his wishes, to Eagle Crag, the residence of the dowager Duchess of Peterworth. On entering the accustomed sitting-room, he found his old friend seated before an open letter, with a handkerchief to her eyes.

"How is this?" said he.

"Ah!" cried the duchess, "for the first time, these nearly fifty years, I must refuse my good George his Christmas invitation. I cannot invite him here; because he scrupulously remains at Polhill Towers throughout the Christmas holidays, to give the example of a good lord of the manor to all on that estate, for the love of God and man. I can no longer make long journeys; I must remain here. But it is not the corporeal weakness I lament. I am ashamed that I, who so much love solitude, do not love the solitude that old age procures; I am humiliated to find that I, who ought to have resources at all seasons, yearn for the cheerful circle of bright eyes and loving hearts at these great festivals."

"Woolton Court is not a long journey from Eagle Crag," said Lord Charleton: "I have come to fetch you to spend the Christmas in a circle, where Arthur and Violet can supply the bright eyes, and your poor old Charleton the loving heart."

"I would accept this kind invitation," replied the duchesss, "but for the following difficulties: I have always had with me two lady companions, and two lady's maids; for this reason, that the one lady companion and the one lady's maid, not having received the same education, could not be proper associates for each other; and would either each seek me, when I wished to be alone, or would endeavor to find sympathy of tastes abroad. When on a visit, I have had my two maids only, leaving my two ladies together, or permitting them to visit their friends. But in visiting you, Lord Charleton, who have made yourself a separate dwelling from the young couple, I should be compelled, for propriety's sake, old as we both are, to bring with me four women, who each like a separate room. Can you accommodate such a party?"

"Perfectly well," replied the earl. "Remember the size of two sides of a square, such as Woolton Court. The suit of rooms prepared for you, is on the first floor: it consists of ante-room, drawing-room, bedroom, dressing-room, bathroom, before which, to the south, is a little conservatory, opening to a terrace on the leads, which will be good for exercise in damp weather. There is also in this suite, the room of your immediate personal attendant. The two ladies and the other maids, will be on the floor above. Will you come with me now in my carriage, and order that your own shall follow before night with the ladies and maids, and whatever comforts you may require?"

" Can you wait an hour?" demanded she.

" Have I not waited at Eagle Crag many an hour?" returned he, smiling.

" Well, then, I will give my orders, write my letter to George, and do as you wish."

In little more than an hour, the carriage of the Earl of Charleton was slowly ascending a short but steep hill, at the top of which a high landmark notified the boundary of Eagle Crag. Often, as the occupants of the carriage had each gazed separately on that well-remembered spot,—the scene of the parting described by the old gardener,—they had never, till now, viewed it together.

" Fifty years ago, Charleton."

" Yes, Emma; on this very day, by the calendar month, the 22d of November."

" And now, Emma, I am, at length, bearing you away from Eagle Crag to Woolton Court, never to leave it, as your home."

28

" My dear Lord Charleton, what are you saying?"

" That I trust in the constancy of your friendship and affection, as I prove my own. That as Divine Providence has permitted me to conquer the adversity of our parting, and has left you without ties, and even desolate, we may never again part. I bring you to Woolton Court as absolute mistress of all I have retained of the mansion, before the arrival of our young bride, that you may receive her, not be received by her. Your high rank, your venerable age, and your title to her respect, as her godmother, will induce Lady Violet to feel, that when she visits me, as her grandfather, she is second to *her* whom I delight to honor, as first in my house, as in my heart."

These were the last words spoken, until they reached the avenue of the causeway, that led direct to the great gateway of the court. There, in addition to the usual line of servants, in their gala liveries, presented themselves James Turner and Thomas Jenkins.

" Why, how is this?" said the butler; " there is no great number of visitors to-day to require a number of servers. Dinner is laid for only four persons."

" Ha! Mr. Grainger," replied Turner, the usual spokesman of the two friends. " Just consider what a day it is. Here is the young earl, as was, bringing home the duchess as is."

" Home !" cried Grainger. " What, is this going to be her home?"

" Now just you watch and see," returned Jenkins, " whether she ever leaves this, except for a drive, before she goes to heaven."

No more could be said. The carriage passed through the entrance tower. The earl alighted, and, with stately tenderness, alone assisted the Duchess of Peterworth from the carriage; who, still in silence more eloquent than words, lent passively on the arm of her old friend till they entered the hall.

" Perhaps you had better not mount the stairs just yet," said he. " Shall we go into the library, or to the chapel?"

" To the chapel," was the reply.

In the evening the female followers arrived, and arranged her grace's suite, as well as their own rooms, till they felt at home. The duchess had fore-seen the difficulty and incongruity of bringing the liveries of the Dukes of Peterworth under the obe-dience of the butler of the Earl of Charleton, or of keeping three men independent of all control but her own. The men-servants of her grace were, there-fore, rewarded and discharged, and two new footmen hired for the service of herself and ladies, who were to wear the livery of Woolton Court. All things proceeded thus in perfect order and harmony, while awaiting the arrival of the bridal pair, who, after a little tour by the Sussex coast, reached Woolton

Court early in December, the weather having proved most propitious.

Perhaps a happier young being than Violet could not be found, while folded alternately in the arms of her new grandfather and her ancient godmother.

"Oh, duchess!" cried she, while looking like a newly-descended angel from above, "what joy to find you here. It makes all look so like home. Arthur promised me that our first ride should be up to Eagle Crag; but how far better to find you here!"

"And to find her always here," added Lord Charleton. "The duchess has long wished to yield her hereditary property to her nephew, Lord Dartfort. She has also the generosity to consent to take compassion on my old age, and be my valued companion during the intervals of the Sunday visits of my grandchildren."

Lord Stanmore instantly perceived the whole truth. He gracefully took the hand of his grandfather and that of the duchess, and, bending, pressed them to his lips, while the Earl of Charleton passed the disengaged hand on his grandson's head, saying:

"Duty and fidelity, whether in youth or age, God loves graciously to reward!"

CHAPTER XL.

A HAPPY HOUSEHOLD.

It was a merry Christmas and a happy New Year, both to peer and peasant, at Woolton Court. A devout Lent followed; then the joyful alleluias of Easter. With the autumn came the occupation of the "holyday cottage," on the lake of Windermere — Violet's dowry — by the Marquis of Seaham, his sister, Lady Clara Moorland, with the little twin girls and the attendants. The aged and young couples from Woolton Court were there to greet their arrival, and the latter remained during some happy weeks in the scenes of sweet remembrance; the more endeared, because of the many vicissitudes that had followed the betrothed, and had terminated so blissfully in their marriage. Before the anniversary of that marriage, it became a question whether Lady Violet Stanmore was to venture any more visits to Rockley Cottage; therefore, the same happy party assembled in the eastern half of Woolton Court, where, on the 10th of October, the Earl of Charleton was invited with his venerable companion, the Duchess of Peterworth, to pass by the long picture-gallery, from their western residence, to the Lady Violet's private suite

of rooms.   On arriving in the drawing-room, Lord
Stanmore advanced from an inner-room, and placed
his infant son in the arms of his grandfather, saying:

"Bless him, and he shall be blessed!" adding
with emotion, "Oh! it seems that for the first time
I am really able to know and appreciate all the love
you have had for me, my dear grandfather."

Lady Violet had a short convalescence, in reward
for the courage with which she had borne the maternal pangs.   Very soon, with little Philip Henry in
her arms, she glided through the long gallery, to
make him return the visits of his grandfather, and of
"Grandworth," the hereditary abbreviation of all
grandmamma's Peterworth, by the children of Polhill Towers.   No wet-nurse, no foster-brother, no
sister, was permitted to approach the little Henry.
Good and affable as the Lady Violet had ever proved
to the poor on the estates of her father, — a reputation that had preceded her to Woolton Court, and
had hitherto been sustained — it was now sufficient
for the poor applicant to have an infant in her arms,
for Lady Violet to refuse the shortest audience ; and
until she was assured that the peasant child had
quitted the house, her own precious babe was nestled
to her bosom.

"Oh, papa!" cried she, in reply to some playful
comments of the marquis, "how can I be too cau-
tious?   How can I help seeing a 'Léon Bauvin,' in
every infant that approaches my Henry?   Ah! how

grateful I feel that I am strong and healthy enough to be his only nurse."

"Violet, shall I row you and baby on the lake?" said Lord Stanmore, fully expecting an assent, as he took the little heir in his arms.

"Thank you, Arthur; yes. It will be very refreshing."

"Come, then; I have sent the nursery servants down to the boat-house, to amuse themselves there; but I wish to have only ourselves on the water."

Away went the youthful pair; and the marquis, who had strolled from them at the first mention of boating, for which he had no fancy, gave an arm to his sister, Lady Clara, whom he met on the terrace; and they bent their steps to a pleasant walk, overlooking the lake, whence they saw the boat and its precious freight glide from the boat-house along the bowery and varied shades. They continued thus to watch in pleased silence, till the sounds arose, in perfect harmony of the strain

"I know a bank whereon the wild thyme grows."

"Ah! Clara," said the marquis, when the sounds were lost in distance, "under heaven, all this happiness is your affecting. Had you deviated from your perfect line of conduct, by one smile or one look of evil fascination, you might have dragged Lord Stanmore at your triumphal car, till you had made desolate the now happy and congenial hearts of my Violet and her husband. You are one who could have done evil, and did it not. *Qui poterit transgredi et non est transgressus, facere mala et non fecit!* Therefore shall your fidelity be found good in the sight of the Lord, as it is in that of your approving and grateful brother."

While this tribute was paid to the exalted and solid virtue of his sister, by the penetrating Marquis of Seaham, the venerable Earl of Charleton, while strictly keeping his grandson's secret, had received with consolation the confidence of the duchess, on her observation of the mild dignity, the unobtrusive firmness, and rectitude of Lady Clara Moorland, as opposed to the love of conquest but too prevalent in her sex. On this day the aged couple had descended to the pleasure-grounds for the usual two hours, destined to air and exercise after breakfast. The duchess in a light wheel chair, drawn alternately by Thomas Jenkins and James Turner; while Lord Charleton, resting a hand on the side of the little carriage, regulated the pace of the charioteers, to suit his step when in exercise. By this arrangement, the vigorous frame of the earl was enabled to continue the healthy custom of long walks, without losing the society of his more delicate companion.

Sometimes, when by some rustic seat, they would dismiss for awhile the attendants, and converse or meditate, while Lord Charleton rested. On this day, perceiving the Marquis of Seaham walking with his sister, and engaged in deep discourse, they began to converse on the happy state of those who like themselves, being advanced beyond the meridian of life, might laudibly retire into calm shades with those of a like frame of mind.

" They must have served God and man first in active life, before they can thus retire with congenial spirits," observed the earl. " Our friend, the marquis, and his admirable sister, are fit types of the meridian time of the great toil of life. He minister of state, and she, courted as his sister, the female head of his house, with known influence from the respect he bears her, with responsibilities as such in the accepting or refusing to patronize the applications made through her. She also may be said to have become a public character. It is well she has strength of mind to bear the weight, as well as to despise the glitter, of her position."

" There is another fair relation of the Marquis of Seaham," observed the duchess, " who would have turned all the astute diplomacy of her character to supplant Lady Clara Moorland in St. James'-square and Marsden Park ; but who has been providentially carried far from the scene of temptation, by the family chaplain, Rev. Dr. Rollings, and made the centre of a vast and admirable field of usefulness, whence she doubtless writes to all her former acquaintances, as she writes to me, to assist her in converting the

world by the means laid down to convert herself.   I
speak of Lady Cecily Dorel — a woman powerful in
her energy and activity; once a notorious votary of
Satan, now turned to the service of God, and another
type of the heat and toil of meridian life."

The marquis and his sister had now arrived sufficiently near the speaker for her to add :

"I am recounting to Lord Charleton the perseverance as well as zeal of Lady Cecily Dorel, who
writes, I conclude, to interest her cousins in every
good work under her patronage."

"You have conjectured with your usual penetration and accuracy, duchess," replied Lord Seaham.
"I can already produce a mighty packet of letters,
sermons, pamphlets, prospectus, architectural draw-
ings of chapels and school-houses, lists of deserving
school-masters, and other candidates for my patronage; although the focus of these admirable doings is
in the heart of England, while I am now at the head
of Foreign Affairs."

"But still, marquis, I conclude, from your great
interest with your colleagues in the ministry, you
have done something for Lady Cecily?"

"I have compromised with my dear little cousin,
that she shall be paid partly in her own coin.   I
have pushed on, successfully, two of her plans, and
one of her school-masters; while, in return, I have
sent her the repentent Mademoiselle Lucille Brontel,
escorted by Monsieur Julien, to be her chief assistant

in forming the Congregation of the Holy Tongue.
May God speed these two pious foxes! They require
it: not that I wish them the wisdom of the serpent!
They must serve God according to the characters He
has given them."

"Yes," responded Lord Charleton; "the character given originally by the Creator we should never
attempt to crush and destroy; it is a presumptuous,
a vain attempt. We perceive some characters to be
naturally more lovely and attractive than others; but,
doubtless, if we watch the career of the originally less
amiable, we shall recognize a gift of courage to conquer their defects, which, with an enlightened conscience, is certain to meet with deserved success, and
form in the end most estimable and pleasing characters. I think also, in watching the Providence of
God, respecting those to whom have been granted
by nature lovely and attractive dispositions, we shall
perceive a constant demand on them for generosity
and self-sacrifice. If they respond to these calls,
they will be cheered, even in this life, by peace of
heart amid trial, and will hereafter have their glorious eternal reward. I need not seek far to illustrate
my theory. As maiden, wife, and widow, I have
recognized this spirit of generosity and self-sacrifice
in Lady Clara Moorland; and, as perseverance in
well-doing is in itself virtue, and gives increased
value to every charming act, I wind up to a culminating point in the testimony I bear, through a

long life, to the tried virtues of the Duchess of Peterworth.”

“ I thought, duchess, you had left off rouge,” said the marquis, smiling, to his old friend.

“ Here come the hopes of Woolton Court ! ” cried she, as Lord Stanmore, advancing slowly from the lake, with his wife on one arm and his sleeping babe on the other, took the path that led direct to our group of friends. The nurses, who at present led an easy life, went towards the house.

“ Lay the little Philip Henry on the knees of his ‘ grandworth,’ ” said Lord Charleton, “ and we will follow at their chariot-wheels.”

“ I beg pardon of all the lords and ladies present, for my observation,” said the charioteer, James Turner. “ But this here blessed baby will grow up to be the perfect image of his great-grandfather, the young earl as was; and it is a fine day for me to see him in the lap of her as should have been his great-grandmother, the beautiful young lady of Eagle Crag.”

It was during that happy autumn of 1856 that, at his evening toilet, Lord Stanmore said to his valet :

“ Temple, I release you, during the next half-hour, from the promise I exacted from you, never to let the name of Lord Edwin Fitzjames pass your lips. He *has* been faithful to grace. He *has* persevered. He is professed. He signs himself Brother Bruno of Mercy ; but reveals his real name. He has written

a thick volume of sacred poetry, in the spirit of expiation for his former loves of earth. His expressions
are most edifying and affecting. He feels convinced
of the continuance of my prayers, and promises his
own; but he can never write again."

"I feel extremely grateful to you, my lord," said
Mr. Temple, "for imparting to me this gratifying
news. You will receive an additional joy throughout
eternity each time you meet this repentant sinner,—
this now holy penitent." After a little pause, Mr.
Temple resumed: "Has it ever occurred to you, my
lord, that some innocent, but tepid souls, would be
lost but for some startling fall, that has publicly disgraced them, and opened their eyes to their own
previous state?"

"I think, Temple, you must mean to say, those
apparently innocent souls; for 'tepid' and 'innocent'
cannot hold together. A soul so tepid as not to love
God, sins by omission, even mortally; that soul is
just ripe for mortal sin by action. And now that we
understand each other's terms, I will assure you I
quite agree with you, that a public fall,—a public
disgrace, may possibly be the only means to save
many such souls. Still, even here, we must not
generalize too much. God does not limit His means
of grace. It was through you alone, while at Marsden Park, that I heard the details of the wonderful
conversion of Lady Cecil Dorel. There was no
moral fall, no public disgrace. The family chap-

lain," continued Lord Stanmore, smiling, " caught a tepid lady in a trap, locked her up, prayed with such fervor that, like the tears of St. Scholastica, he drew down a thunder-storm ; then persevered with his holy sacrifice and his prayers, till contrition succeeded to remorse, love to fear."

CHAPTER XLI.

THE FAMILY JEWELS.

It was on one of those clear still winter mornings that proclaim a walk or a drive, that the duchess, having been as usual handed into her little carriage by Lord Charleton, had to await his return from an audience he had promised to a tenant in his private study. This awaiting the earl seemed to be an opportunity long desired by the two humble friends who drew the carriage ; for the usual spokesman immediately commenced with :

" Honorable Miss Sedley, of Eagle Crag, as was, and grand duchess as is, we have, that is Tom Jenkins and me, has still a secret, and it is to you, that's still prettier in our eyes, and more right to be here than any one else, that we wishes to confide it." He then whispered : " In the ceiling of the chamber supposed to be haunted by the Honorable Tristam Woolton, there be something else besides the music tubes. There be a casket — a jewel casket — the family jewels, marm. Now that the blessed baby, Philip Henry, is born, and we now really believes the dark young man is Viscount Stanmore, we gives up the secret."

" What could induce you to suppose Lord Stanmore to be otherwise than the real heir to Woolton Court?" demanded the duchess.

" We was always afeared he had to do with the branch in the West Injees; for about twenty years ago, a fine handsome gentleman, but very dark, a Mr. Woolton, grandson of the Honorable Gilbert, came here to see if the old place was likely to be sold; and he talked freely about his being the heir to all after the earl's death. When Lord Stanmore came to prepare for the return of the earl, we took him for the son of this dark gentleman, and did not give him no confidence. The two valets, Mr. Julien and Mr. Temple, have taken great pains to make us understand all the rights of it; and now the blessed baby is born, so fair, like all the true Wooltons, we gives in. So here's the last of the secrets, marm ; and sure if any one had a right to wear them jewels, marm, it's yourself."

" Do you wish that I should be the one to inform Lord Charleton of the safety of these family jewels ?" asked the duchess.

" Why, then, marm, that is my lady duchess, if you please; if you will soften to the earl that we kept the secret so long, all on account of Viscount Stanmore's dark eyes, and the West Injees."

" Ah! my poor Arthur," silently mused the duchess; " those brilliant orbs, with their black fringes, have had to pay the tax of beauty; first in lending themselves to the machinations to turn you into Léon Bauvin, then to the belief that you were of the family of the machinators."

Here the return of Lord Charleton enabled her grace, after some desultory conversation, to impart to him the fact that the family jewels he had believed to be sacrificed to the creditors had been rescued, and were under the hereditary roof with himself.

"If they have been saved in an honorable manner," said the earl, "I must, of course, be gratified to retain them, for the remembrance they bring of the virtuous and beautiful ladies of my house, now departed to a better life, and as affording the happy occasion of presenting them to the acceptance of the present elder and younger lady of Woolton Court. Can they be reached by portable steps, Jenkins?"

"My lord, it will require not only steps but tools. But as I was the only one employed to hide them under the cornice, by the Hon. Tristam Woolton, I shall want no one but my friend here to help me, after the ride of my lady duchess; but if we might bring them ourselves to your lordship, and have a sight of them, it would do our eyes good; for I hear such a constant talk of jewels in sermons, and read, too, about them in good books, that I would like to see a lot all at once, such as must be in that 'ere casket."

"I am sure, my lord, you will permit our two faithful friends to have this treat," said the duchess;

"they have earned it well. But you must be prepared, Turner and Jenkins, to find all the gold of the setting discolored, and even the jewels dimmed by time and damp. No real damage, however, can be done. Both gold and jewels are brought forward by preachers and spiritual writers, because of their enduring qualities, as well as their extreme beauty. They are the most valuable of all lifeless works of creation, and the Holy Scriptures mention them perpetually ; so if Lord Charleton will permit, you shall bring them to him, in my drawing-room, at whatever time his lordship pleases, this afternoon."

"And now for a good pull at the little carriage, and a good step forth," said Lord Charleton, suiting the action to the word, and silence ensued.

While the fact just announced occupied his thoughts, in the various conjectures they suggested, some not unmixed with dread of dishonorable concealment from creditors, the servants' dinner-bell sounded on their return home, and the two humble friends announced it to be the most propitious time possible to perform their task. Accordingly, between three and four o'clock, it was announced to the duchess that the two servants who drew her garden chair had something they wished to show her grace. They were admitted ; but the casket, in many folds of paper, was not touched until the arrival of Lord Charleton.

"There was a coarse cloth outside of all," said

Jenkins, "that I remember to have helped to sew on with twine, after I had laid the music pipes in the ceiling; but it is so full of lime and dust, I have just now ripped it off agin, my lord."

The casket was at length placed on the table, free from wrappers. It was, in itself, valuable from its antiquity, the costliness of the materials, and the intricate and delicate workmanship.

"Do you remember this casket?" asked the duchess.

"I do," returned his lordship. "It used to stand within an outer case, that let down on all sides, so as to display the casket, while my mother finished her toilet on great occasions. The outer case, when doubled together and fastened, was immensely strong. I remember having been told, as a child, that an attempt to force that iron case would break any tool."

Lord Charleton, as he turned to inquire of the two friends whether they had ever seen that case, observed a look of intelligence pass between them, while to his lordship's plain question they found it difficult to reply. Reserving to another time any further questions, Lord Charleton took from one of the handles of the casket the suspended key, and raised the lid. Tray upon tray of valuable contents, in silver-paper and cotton-wool, were removed from the casket, and laid upon the table before the duchess. But a discovery awaited Lord Charleton of more interest to him than any jewel. At the bottom of the casket lay a manuscript of several pages. Glancing at the signature, his emotion increased, and he said, in a low voice, to the duchess : ·

" Emma, I must retire to read this paper, at least to the other end of the room. It is written by the so-long-recluse uncle, Tristam Woolton. Open and look at all you please ; select what you prefer, and reserve the rest for Violet. Let our two honest friends have the treat of beholding that which they have so long guarded."

CHAPTER XLII.

TYPES AND ANTITYPES.

Lord Charleton having seated himself at a further window, became absorbed by the manuscript, while the duchess unrolled silver-paper and cotton-wool, and laid rows of brilliants on the table to the gaze of her humble friends. To her surprise, no injury seemed to have dimmed their lustre. The setting of some, especially the diamonds, was very antique, but in perfectly good preservation.

"So, my lady duchess," said Turner, " it's with these here things we 's to be rewarded up in heaven for doing our duty all our lives on earth. They are pretty things, Tom."

"My good friends," said the duchess, "you see before you the most precious of minerals and metals —jewels and gold ; and because they are such, God, who condescends to our notions and to our language, speaks of them as types of the spiritual blessings and shining graces He will bestow on those who love Him."

"But we shall have the real things — the jewels themselves, marm, I hopes, in our crowns — real crowns? 'Twont be all make-believe and moon-shine up above, I hopes and trusts?" cried Jenkins.

"You see, my lady duchess," interposed Turner, " him and me we be accustomed to touch and handle the things we sees. He's been knocking into hard wood all his life, and I striking into the ground with my spade; so, when we hears and reads of nothing but clouds and music, we gets a little downcast, to think that the reward we's to have for serving God, and turning our backs to the devil, is to be in a life we can't no how comprehend."

" There's the banquets," suggested Jenkins.

" Ha! yes, there's the banquets," responded Tur-ner. " Perhaps there's nothing the poor man un-derstands better than that blessedness of sitting down at the table of the King of Heaven. But if that blessed rest and refreshment, and all the beautiful saintly ladies, and the rich garments, and the wine and delicious food, and crowns, and jewels, are all to be types, which to us two, marm, means moon-shine, why we prefers, Jenkins and me, to live on here at Woolton Court, with the earl and you, my lady duchess, and the blessed babe, Philip Henry, and the prayers in the chapel, and the actual real jewels too, here right before us."

" My good friends," said the duchess, " you have, in your own way, expressed the sentiment of a worldly nobleman, who declared he could fancy no joy in eternally sitting on a wet cloud singing Alleluia. Even a Catholic — one of the grand dukes of Florence — being, during his last illness, exhorted, by his confessor, to turn his thoughts to the joys of heaven, replied: 'Ah, dear friend, I am contented with the joys of my own ducal palace!' Literally, — 'Caro amigo, sou contento del pallazzo pitté!' Yet, both to these personages and to yourselves have been given these precious words: 'Eye hath not seen, nor ear heard, neither hath the heart of man been given to conceive what God hath prepared for these who love Him.' You may, therefore, safely trust this Heavenly Father, who loves you, Turner, and you, Jenkins, far beyond what you have ever felt for Him; — you may trust Him, that you will not be put off with what you call 'moonshine,' but will have, in reward for your long life of fidelity, all that you now so well comprehend of the repose and refreshment, as well as the honor of being seated at the banquet-table of the King of kings: the delicious viands, the beauty of the heavenly company, the graceful garments, the dazzling jewels; I fully believe all these will be real, although but types, and, therefore, inferior to the antitypes, which are spiritual. You are aware, my friends, that the Old Testament is pronounced to be both historical and typical; that is, the events recorded did actually take place, the personages represented did really exist, and their good or bad actions are noted as historical facts. Still, these events, these personages, are types of something superior. In the same way, you, Turner, and you Jenkins, will, I hope, be seated at a real banquet, where you will truly feel the repose of being seated, will taste and enjoy the viands and beverage, will really hear the exquisite music, will behold the beauty of the saints, and the glory of the Divine Royalty; while, at the same time, you will receive the antitypes, which are spiritual; that is, an increase, by every sense, of the knowledge and love of God. Let us now take the example of these very jewels and of a crown: how seldom, in these modern times, does a king wear his jewelled crown! He is a king by his coronation, whether he afterwards' wears his crown or not; whether it be on his head or in the treasury of the regalia, he is equally king: still the crown is the type of his royalty, and is a thing that can be seen and handled. A crown, Jenkins, is a substantial object: it is not 'moonshine.' Tell me whether you now understand, that if a king be greater than his crown, which he decidedly is, and yet admires and values his type, which he can see and touch, and all the spectators can perceive to be a tangible object, it will be the same in heaven? The eye will really see, the ear hear, the mouth taste, the whole body repose, or delight in movement; and yet these rewards to *the senses that have been mortified on earth*, will be but types of the greater spiritual joys bestowed."

" I understands and I likes your sermon, my lady

duchess, better than all the sermons ever I heard; because it goes right with my own mind."

"I quite agree with you, my good friend," said the earl, returning from his solitary window, where he had heard the explanation on types; "you have heard a very good sermon, and, as a remembrance of it, you must each select a jewel, which you can wear on state occasions, and leave to your heirs, when you go to receive the jewels of heaven. Are there not some single ones?" continued he to the duchess.

"There are broaches and pins," replied she, turning over and arranging the single stones.

"Go, then, Turner and Jenkins, round to the side of the table, and choose just what you please," said Lord Charleton.

"We humbly thanks you, my lord," said Turner; "it will be very encouraging to wear the type, and feel it to be a real thing. If we might be so bold, we would like to have exactly the same size and color, to prevent coveting, jealousy, and disputes."

While the two friends were absorbed by their unexpected acquisition, Lord Charleton seated himself by the duchess, saying, in a low tone:

"I, too, have had a good and deeply interesting sermon, which I will impart when alone together."

CHAPTER XLIII.

THE MANUSCRIPT IN THE JEWEL CASKET.

" I think, Emma, I can ensure a couple of hours now, without interruption," said Lord Charleton, on the following day. " I therefore request you to give orders to be left in the same peaceful retirement, that I may read you this paper, found yesterday in the recovered box of jewels. The last date is forty-two years ago."

The duchess gave the required orders, and listened with the deepest interest to the manuscript of the unfortunate captive, Tristam Woolton.

" I write these lines in the spirit with which I now offer everything to Thee, Oh, my God! I know not whether they will ever be read by my own flesh and blood, but I know, and I accept, that I am taken for a suicidal, for a lost soul, for a bad ghost. This is not my fault — this does not touch the conscience. But to have helped to lose the halls of my ancestors; to have the place of my birth and happy youth bought over my head; to be prisoner in a small space, contrived by the ingenuity of humble friends, whence I dare not show myself for fear of creditors : this is painful to the sensitive part of the soul, — this demands prayer for grace.

" I thank thee, Oh ! Lord, for many alleviations to my sufferings.   First, in having inspired these young workmen with such feelings of devotion for me, that I have become the one object of their respectful service.   I thank Thee, also, that a separate sale of the family library and pictures has not been necessary.   They are included in the purchase of the estate.   I have hitherto gone into the library at night, to exchange the books I required, and twice in passing have I heard screams of terror.   This belief in my supernatural appearance saves me from the creditors ; but at how heavy a tax on health and spirits, Thou alone knowest, Oh ! Lord God.   I am but thirty-four, with an impatient love of freedom, of the charms of cultivated society, conversation, music, delicate food, choice wines.   In the indulgence of these tastes and habits, my brother Gilbert and I helped to ruin our house.   It is well he should expiate by exile, and I by imprisonment, this careless and selfish career.   Should my young nephew ever read these lines, I entreat his pardon.   He is driven into exile ; but not by his own fault.   He has a strong mind ; and, as God helps those who help themselves, he may return a rich man."

[*At another date.*]   " My only solace, when wearied of reading, has been the flute, and this only at night. My humble friends now inform me that the sounds being so stifled, and in the dead of night, are taken to be my wailing soul, and that the new proprietors are resolved to sell the place and depart. This has given me an extraordinary feeling of hope that, perhaps, my brother Gilbert, or my nephew Charleton, may repurchase the place."

[*At another date.*]   " My hopes have proved fallacious, and my own life seems wasting away. O Lord ! I accept all this in expiation of my dissipated youth, and for the wrong done to my nephew.

" Jim Turner and Tom Jenkins have brought me a medical practitioner from Kendal. He forbids the flute, and commands air and exercise. As the new possessors of Woolton do not reside here at present, my life may be prolonged by passing through the upper rooms, with the windows open. Last year I could get into the pleasure-grounds at night ; but I have no longer the strength."

[*At another date.*]   " I have invented a substitute for the flute. It is even superior. I have written a description of this instrument. Tom has placed this, my invention, in the ceiling, that no one may deprive me of it, should my hiding-place be discovered. I can pull the cord of the bellows, as I lie on my bed."

[*Another date.*]   " The confidential doctor has, at my desire, sent me a priest. These visits are always contrived by Jim Turner, the gardener, who conducts the visitor from the roof of the conservatory to the flat leads hidden by the roof of the chapel, and through a window, to my retreat.   Both this ecclesiastic and the doctor assure me that they believe all the debts are paid ; and that, at all events, they will ensure me as perfect a retreat elsewhere.   But I no longer desire movement and variety, and I cannot leave my musical instrument for any other advantage."

[*Another date.*]   " I am, at length, happier here than I could be anywhere else on earth.   I love to die here, where I was born.   I am near, very near to the portals of eternity.   I have no longer strength to pull the chord of the bellows, which is a great privation.   I have to await the leisure of my two friends.   They tell me that the terror in the neighborhood, since my instrument has been played, is so increased that the new owners are not expected to remain.   Again some vague hopes of the return of the exiled lords of Woolton."

[*Another date.*]   " Jim and Tom have brought me, to-day, the casket of family jewels, separated from its ribbed iron case, which I perfectly remember was placed in the hall to be taken by the guard of the mail coach to London, and placed in the hands of the family lawyer, Mr. Oldham.   They tell me the iron case was conveyed to London, as directed, but the jewel casket has just been discovered in the powdered bark of the pine-apple bed, in the hothouse.   Who has thus defrauded the creditors ? and

30*

how has Mr. Oldham satisfied all demands without these jewels?

[*Another date.*] "Tom Jenkins has just related to me the whole history. Gilbert had the casket beneath his cloak when departing at night from the saw-pit of Tom's daily work; but that he gave it to the young man to carry for him to the turn of the road, where a friend was to meet him. This friend was accompanied by another gentleman of, perhaps, sterner moral principle; for on recognizing him Gilbert turned to Tom, saying: "Oh! that casket will ruin me. God bless you, Tom; good bye. Hide it —take it back. Do not come a step farther with me. Accept this guinea." But Tom would not deprive the poor fugitive nobleman of his guinea. He kissed his hand, and then ran back, hiding the casket by tying his handkerchief round it. Not knowing the nature of the contents, but concluding they belonged to the family, he took it next morning privately to his friend Jim Turner, and they agreed to bury it in the dry bark of the pine-apple bed, where they both forgot it, till yesterday, talking over the past, they recalled the casket and the hiding. I have now informed them both of the real nature of the contents of this casket, and have desired them, at my death to open it, and lay this explanation inside; together with my regret that I have not strength left of mind, or body, or social position, to communicate in any other way with the heir, my nephew."

"May Almighty God have compassion on Gilbert, my brother, and teach him that without moral rectitude, the finest abilities and endowments of grace and beauty will avail nought, but to increase the danger of the soul's damnation.

"I have received the last rites of the Church. I offer this imprisoned life, thus shortened, the undeserved stigma of my death by suicide, and my actual death here, alone, in expiation of my brother's and my own guilty career.

"Lord Jesus, have mercy. Sweet lady, smile on me.

"HENRY PHILIP TRISTAM WOOLTON,
"Aged forty-one.

"February 18th, 1814."

As the earl finished this truly contrite and resigned document, he became, although at the second reading, much affected, and his sole auditor the same. At length the duchess inquired:

"What step shall you take respecting the subtraction of the jewels from the creditors?"

"Last night, for this day's post, I have written to Mr. Oldham," replied the earl, "to search among his uncle's papers for a notice of that fact. This reply will be interesting, as containing details of the reason for my having had to transmit to him annual sums, up to the date of 1832, when I received his receipt for the whole of the payments made."

In a few days the answer arrived from Mr. Old-ham, as follows :

"My lord, on reference to the papers of my uncle, I find recorded the fact of the arrival of an iron case, containing an oblong stone, enveloped in several papers, the exterior one being sealed with the arms of the Wooltons ; also noticed a prosecution commenced against the guard of the mail coach, but stopped ; and a compromise made with the creditors ; also noted a correspondence with yourself, my lord, stating that, as the value of the jewels was unknown, the creditors were content to place them at four thousand pounds. To this last letter no reply having been received, the copy of a second letter merely urges an immediate acknowledgment of the first, and states that four thousand pounds in small instalments would satisfy the remaining creditors. This letter was duly received, and each year your lordship remitted a sum, till in June, 1832, the whole, with the interest, was liquidated."

"Never were jewels more worthily redeemed," observed the duchess.

"And now you will wear them ; will you not ?" said Lord Charleton. "Not that you require any addition to the superb jewels you retain for life, as dowager Duchess of Peterworth ; but for my sake."

"Ah ! dear Charleton," replied she, "I have other remembrances of you. Give them all to Violet. I am thinking, like our humble friends, of the typical jewels of the New Jerusalem."

CHAPTER XLIV.

THAT evening's post brought the announcement to the duchess, from her beloved step-daughter, Lady Emily Whynne, that the colonel and herself were about to start for Vienna, in consequence of a communication from Mrs. Bligh, the companion of Lady Claud Chamberlayne, of a very unsatisfactory nature. Mrs. Bligh recorded a new friendship of nearly the same ardent nature as with the fascinating Hortense. This new friend was a German lady, married to an Englishman, closely united in office, as in esteem, to the ambassador, Lord Claud Chamberlayne. The especial temptation of this lady was, not ambition, but gambling; into which dangerous folly the weak Georgina had been drawn, to the already loss of several hundreds. Lady Emily entreated the duchess to receive her second daughter, Leonora, under her roof, until their return from Vienna.

"Thank God," wrote the duchess, in reply, "that Georgina has with her a person who was chosen by yourself, who possesses your confidence, and knows where to turn for prompt and effective assistance.

God speed the journey ! Send me Leonora : Lord Charleton joins me in this warm invitation ; yes, send me Leonora ; I value her more than you have ever done. You have made an idol of Georgina ; and you are now punished by having to play second to every friend, or rather female seducer, who crosses her path. Remember that *I* never permitted my preference for you should give pain to others. Do not resent my warm expressions, Emily, my dearest child. I am anxious to save the post. Once more, God speed the journey !— Love to Charles.

> "Your devoted mother,
>
> "EMMA PETERWORTH."

About a week after this rapid exchange of letters, Miss Whynne, accompanied by the housekeeper and one of the footmen, in addition to her own maid, arrived at Woolton Court, — an intelligent, loving creature ; perhaps, too much so for the slender form and hectic cheek. When folded in the arms of her step-grandmother, she trembled so much, that she was gently laid on a sofa by that same grandmamma, and the hands locked in each other.

"My poor child," at length said the duchess, "weep on ; it will relieve you. You have had partings ; you are far from home."

"Oh, no, grandmamma !" cried Leonora, starting up ; "it is not *that* ; I am weeping for joy, I believe ; and I feel very much exhausted. How long it is since I saw you, grandmamma : you look so well, — younger than ever, and *so* loving !"

" But do not weep on that account," said the duchess, herself holding the handkerchief to her eyes, " my little Nora is to become quite strong and gay at Woolton Court.

" Oh ! yes, grandmamma. Anywhere near *you;* and I hear this is such a beautiful place. How happy are those who live in the country ! How wearied I am of London and of watering-places; yet, there are gardens in and about Belgrave-square, and the sea is ever magnificent; but there is always such constraint. I am told there is a small lake in these grounds, and banks of wild flowers ? Oh ! grandmamma, did I ever see wild flowers ? I do not think I have ever seen them. And to see and inhale them with you, grandmamma, and to sit amongst them on those banks ! "

Here a salver of sandwiches, fruit, and wine and water caused an opportune pause, during which Lord Charleton entered, and received the thanks of his young visitor, for the invitation conveyed by the duchess. The two ladies-companion, Mrs. Bentley and Miss Telford, now offered to conduct Leonora to the rooms destined for her use; and the happy girl was soon prattling to them both, and admiring everything she saw around her.

Thus passed a week, when Lord Stanmore proposed to Lady Violet to arrange some party of pleasure for their young friend, having previously ascertained the bent of her tastes and wishes. Therefore, at Leonora's next visit, Violet soon found a good opening for saying :

"What is the most congenial to you, Leonora? What gives you the most pleasure, of all your pursuits and amusements?"

A little pause, a smile, a blush, and the reply was :

"High Mass and Benediction."

"O! dearest Leonora," cried Violet, "what happiness this gives me; for ours will be a holy friendship. And to be so merry and pious! Why, this is just like the duchess!"

"Now it is my turn," said Leonora, "to exclaim 'Oh, dearest Violet! what happiness this gives me!' for nothing—that is," added she, laughing, "nothing after High Mass and Benediction—makes me so happy as to be thought like grandmamma; especially by you, Violet, whom I admire and esteem so much. In short, what can exceed the happiness of being always with those one loves and admires; and to be loved by them," added she, in a lower voice, while a diffident, hidden expression stole over her hitherto animated countenance, and a tear rose in the large bright eyes.

"Dearest Leonora," said Violet, "*I* love you, *all* love you,—from your grandmamma to the peasant women who weed the walks in the pleasure-grounds. How can you doubt?"

"I do not doubt exactly," replied she ; "but

Violet,"—and the little head was on the shoulder of her friend,—" I have been an unloved child !——"

Some tears fell on both sides, of which Leonora was aware : and this effect of soothing sympathetic friendship was greater balm to her heart than the most eloquent flow of words from the lips of Violet.

" O ! you sweet blessed creature," said Leonora, " do not weep for me : this adversity in my home has been blessed to me; for I have fled into the sacred heart of my divine Redeemer : and *His* Mother has become mine. Still, as faith is weak, and the unseen is but too apt to be forgotten in things visible, I wish it were my duty to live always at Woolton Court, or to live somewhere near you, Violet."

A sudden thought struck Lady Violet. She gently raised the head of Leonora, and said :

" After emotion of a painful nature, it is very beneficial to have a little recreation; therefore, I wish to include you, dear Leonora, in a short drive, which my aunt and I are going to take, by appointment, to bring a picture, which Lord Stanmore has requested her to copy before she returns to London. I think you will enjoy this little trip, provided the duchess has no other plan for you."

" I will run directly and ascertain," said Leonora. " At what hour must I be ready?"

" At eleven, and it is now past ten. We must not lose this bright sun ?"

The duchess was engaged in writing when Leo-
31

nora entered to ask permission to dine out with her
friends, Clara and Violet, and she merely smiled and
nodded her assent, without inquiry.   Neither did
Leonora inquire, nor give heed to aught beyond the
happiness of being with congenial spirits, in the
midst of scenery so far surpassing all she had ever
viewed in her excursions from her London home.
Lord Stanmore was on horseback, the carriage was
open; he was, therefore, able to communicate all the
local information he had gradually acquired to the
ardent visitor.

CHAPTER XLV.

THE LORD OF THE MANOR.

HALF-AN-HOUR's drive brought our party to the entrance-gate of Gelliot Manor; and Leonora was then informed that the picture — object of their drive — was that of a certain Lady Maude Woolton, who had been espoused, in the middle ages, to a Squire Gelliot; but that the best picture to be seen at the manor-house was the present squire. This soon proved to be true, although the rooms contained some good and rare paintings. The especial object of the drive had been already taken from its place, and a modern painting substituted, which latter sufficiently inspired Leonora to exclaim, "O! surely this is the most beautiful of all. If *I* could paint, this would be my choice! Lady Clara, is my taste correct?"

Turning round to her friends she perceived a smile on each one's countenance, and observing the squire more in detail, she smiled also, saying, "I begin to be aware that the picture is a likeness of Squire Gelliot in his youth."

"A very correct supposition," said the old gentleman, bowing, "considering the original is not here. This painting is a portrait of my son, Captain Gelliot, of the Life Guards. A better man than his father, but thought very like him. If God spare his life, he will be the forty-seventh squire of Gelliot Manor, since the grant of the lands, by William the Conqueror, in 1066."

"Ah! yes, squire," said Lord Stanmore, "you are the most ancient here on English ground. We had no land till Agincourt; and to prove ourselves as ancient as you, have to trace back to Dauphiné in France."

"Your grant of lands," observed the squire, "was first under the title of Baron Woolton of Woolton. 'T is a pity you ever accepted anything beyond. You intermarried with the Gelliots in 1380, and again in 1638, the title up to the last date being still Lord Woolton of Woolton. It is therefore incorrect, according to modern times, to label the picture I am lending you, 'the Lady Maude Woolton;' for you were not then earls. But the label was on before my birth, and may therefore remain; for doubtless such was then the usage. But now let me show you a fine picture of what in the London catalogues at exhibitions is termed 'dead life!'" and the squire humorously introduced the party to a substantial luncheon, in a room commanding, as he informed them, the best mountain view to be obtained in the neighborhood. In the mean time the servants and horses were regaling to their full satisfaction. The squire had expected his friends to spend the day, and would not let them depart. So after the luncheon they wandered in the pleasure-grounds, and rested awhile in hermitages, and in a grotto with a fine echo; in the latter of which the Ladies Clara and Violet sang with Lord Stanmore.

"Do you sing?" said the old gentleman, with complacent looks, to Leonora.

"Not at present," replied she. "I have been forbidden; for my chest is rather delicate. But after a few more weeks in this fine mountain air, I shall be stronger, and then I will sing to you. I suppose you prefer everything English?"

"I do," said he; "but above all things I prefer to get you strong and well. This air and this soil are far more healthy than at Woolton Court. I am such an old man that you can very well come and regain your health here with me, without wagging evil tongues. I have an old housekeeper, who once knew better days: she shall sit in the drawing-room while you are here. I will go now and arrange with Lord Stanmore."

"O, no!" cried Leonora, laughing; "I cannot give myself permission. I must ask it of grandmamma."

"Who is grandmamma?"

"The dowager Duchess of Peterworth."

"Ho, ho! You are perched up at Eagles Crag! Too bleak! You must come here directly."

31*

"I am not at Eagles Crag, for grandmamma now lives entirely at Woolton Court."

"Ho! so the old lovers are privately married at last," thought he; then aloud, "Now, do you not think this much the finest place?"

"I think," replied Leonora, "that the mountain scenery is really more grand and extensive. But you have no lake."

"Very bad for you that still water; the less you are near it the better. You shall see the Gelliot cascade,—far beyond any lake. Perhaps we have time even now."

The squire looked at his watch, just as Lord Stanmore came to represent, that when a lady undertakes to act the true mother's part to her infant, she must submit to the trammels of that duty, and not remain too many hours from home.

"I must, therefore," continued Lord Stanmore, "return to Woolton Court with Lady Violet; but if you, squire, will convey Lady Clara and Miss Whynne in your own carriage, and spend a few days at Woolton Court, it will make us all very happy."

"O, *do* say yes!" exclaimed Leonora.

"Then I *will* say yes," responded the gallant old squire. "And we shall soon follow you on the road, Lord Stanmore; for this little lady must not be out after sunset. But I must take with me the remedies that will begin her cure."

These remedies for Leonora consisted in home-brewed ale and home-baked bread; a small provision of which was placed in a hidden receptacle of the carriage for her supper that night; and a light cart from the farm was to convey a cask of the ale; while the home-baked loaf involved a ride each morning of some farm-servant from Gelliot Manor.

"My powers!" exclaimed the highly offended housekeeper of the western-half of Woolton Court. "To think of Squire Gelliot despising in this way, the hospitable care of this noble house for the invalid young lady. Cannot *we* brew, I should be glad to know! Cannot *we* bake!"

As reported speeches gliding up stairs and through corridors soon arrive at the supreme lady of the mansion; so, in the like manner, a softening influence, through the medium of Mrs. Bentley, descended with equal speed to the worthy Mrs. Tartson, to induce her to modify her expressions, and even her feelings, because the duchess wished to humor the good old squire, and prevail on him to become a more frequent visitor at Woolton Court; as in the olden times, when the ladies of Woolton wedded the squires of Gelliot; also because Lord Stanmore had so true a regard for Captain Gelliot, the only son of the squire. Peace, therefore, preserved; Squire Gelliot remained a whole week the guest of the Earl of Charleton, — effecting, by the united powers of fatherly affection, home-brewed ale, home-baked bread, and teaching her picquet and backgammon, a marked improvement in the health of the sensitive and too studious Leonora. Quite astonished to become the object of so much affectionate attention, her gratitude evinced itself in all those little nameless effusions of looks and smiles, and little services, that give equal happiness to the active as to the passive participator.

The day before the departure of Squire Gelliot, the duchess gave her consent, after private conversation with him, that Leonora, accompanied by Mrs. Bentley, as lady-companion, and by her own maid, should pass a fortnight at Gelliot Manor. This consent was received with equal joy by the squire and Leonora. Mrs. Bentley raised no objection ; and after a short farewell to all at Woolton, and a glistening tear to her grandmother, the adopted father and daughter, duly escorted, entered the old manor-house.

CHAPTER XLVI.

DIPLOMACY AT VIENNA—LIFE AT THE OLD MANOR-
HOUSE.

DURING these last weeks letters had passed from
Vienna, not only from Lady Emily to the Duchess
of Peterworth, but also from Lord Claud Chamberlayne to his brother, the Marquis of Seaham; avowing that he was placed in a position from which that
brother alone could extricate him. Lord Claud described the exemplary life, first-rate abilities, and
hitherto good understanding with himself of the unfortunate husband of an unprincipled woman, who,
if not removed from Vienna, by some master-stroke
of diplomacy, would ruin his domestic happiness, and
even his good reputation as a prompt payer of all
claims. Lord Claud tried to write playfully, but his
brother saw he was cut to the heart. The marquis
had left Westmorland for Cheshire, where he was
conferring with brother ministers, previous to the
approaching parliamentary season. A fortnight
elapsed, at the end of which Mr. Sidney Cameroll became Sir Sidney Cameroll, with promotion,
from a subordinate post at Vienna, to the first rank

as envoy to an inferior court; while Mr. Pemble, the hitherto secretary of the marquis, was promoted to the vacant post under Lord Claud.

At the hour when a heart-rending parting between the ambassadress and the cunning friend, whose coffers contained all her disposable money, took place at Vienna, — while the thoughts of the parents were exclusively occupied with the painful past, and more hopeful future, of their weak, but amiable and idolized eldest daughter, the forgotten Leonora was playing backgammon in the quaint old parlor of Gelliot Manor; — already more rosy, with dimpled cheek and laughing eye, — the more dimpled and the more archly mirthful because Mrs. Bentley was required to assure the squire, every morning at breakfast, and to re-assure him every evening, at Leonora's supper of the home-brewed and the home-baked, that no place could possibly equal Gelliot Manor, in the effect produced on the health and calm spirits of Miss Whynne. After breakfast, Leonora, well wrapped-up, always walked alone with the squire to the cascade — a really magnificent specimen of the kind, and in that season approaching the sublime.

" This is the water," said he, " that circulates and purifies the air, and, therefore, braces the human frame; — the water-fall — the running water. Our cascade is considered to be the finest in this season; but it has, perhaps, a more beautiful effect in summer, from the contrast of the dark rock now hidden in the torrent."

Leonora repeated :

> " ' In winter from the mountain,
>   The stream like a torrent flows ;
>   In summer the same fountain
>   Is calm as a child's repose.
>
> " ' Thus in grief the first pangs wound us,
>   And our tears in despair roll on ;
>   Time brings sweet peace around us,
>   And the flood of our grief is gone.' "

" These lines are very beautiful," said the squire, " and beautifully repeated. As you are still too weak to sing, I shall be quite content to hear the recitation of good poetry : I, indeed, prefer it. I care but little for young ladies' accomplishments, but I appreciate what is mental ; and your mind, as I perceived the first day we met, has been originally well formed by the Creator, and wonderfully culti-vated for so young a person. How old are you ? "

" Very nearly eighteen," was the reply.

" That is always the way with very young girls," said the squire, smiling : " they mention the date by anticipation. But we must keep in exercise, and reserve the poetry for the evening. You have been brought up in the midst of the frivolities of London life, fashionable watering-places, in the shadow of the court, and yet how congenial you appear with all that is retired, and even solitary. Is it the poetry within you that makes you so blithe and gay, without young companions, or amusement of any kind ? "

"How can you say that I have no amusement," replied Leonora, "when I walk out with you amidst all those varied beauties of scenery, so new to me? Some of the wild flowers here are different from those at Woolton Court: I made a book of them; that is, I placed them to dry in the blank leaves of a book, and labelled them. I have commenced a book of Gelliot Manor's wild flowers to-day; then, when our walk is over, sir, and we return to the house, on what interesting subjects do we not converse? Young as I am, I am quite aware of how deeply read you are, and that your magnificent library is not one merely of show, but has been received into the mind of the owner. Then I am making a purse, when I rest on the sofa after my walk; and because it is for you, whom I so greatly love and respect, I am quite agreeably interested in the actual work, endeavoring to make the row of stitches as even as possible. I shall have just finished the purse for you, and the scarf for the housekeeper, before they fetch me back to Woolton Court."

"So you have actually made, not only a purse for me, that I shall prize all the rest of my days, but also a keepsake for good old Mrs. Coventry?"

"You mentioned once," explained Leonora, "that she had known better days; and I feared that if you had told her of my expected arrival, and of her permission to sit in the drawing-room, she might be hurt that grandmamma would not permit me to come without Mrs. Bentley."

" Just what I saw that first day in those loving eyes and thoughtful brow," mused the squire. "What delicacy of thought and feeling for another in a girl not yet eighteen !"

To Leonora's great surprise and joy, Squire Gelliot consented to accompany her back to Woolton Court, and to remain there some days the guest of Lord Stanmore, in the eastern residence. It was then made known to her that her young friends had prepared for her, as the treat she loved best, a grand High Mass and Benediction in the chapel, for the eighth of December, the feast of the Immaculate Conception.

82

CHAPTER XLVII.

DURING Leonora's visit at Gelliot Manor, Lord Stanmore, his wife, Lady Clara, and Miss Campion, had been steadily practising and rehearsing a Mass, simplified from Mozart, and a beautiful modern offertory. They found, however, that a bass voice was required to support Lord Stanmore's tenor, Miss Campion's contralto, and the two sopranos. This they happily obtained from the same religious congregation that supplied the deacon and subdeacon of the Mass. The organist was a young and modest genius, who taught in the neighborhood and performed on Sundays and other festivals in the chapel of Woolton Court.

Leonora had returned on the sixth of December, and the few remaining touches to be made to the decorations in the chapel she watched with delight, from the private gallery tribune of the duchess. This, so kindly and secretly " taking her at her word," respecting High Mass and Benediction, seemed also to explain a fact, that, with her penetration, she could not fail to perceive, that the whole family, in league with Squire Gelliot, had some secret withheld from her. While she feared bad news from Vienna, this preoccupation of mind, from which she was excluded, had caused her anxiety; but a letter that morning from Lady Clara Chamberlayne, full of minute family details, addressed in confidence to herself, set her heart at rest, and enabled her gratefully to enjoy her favorite and holy recreation.

The early Mass of the feast, with holy communion, was attended, as usual, by the silently devout congregation of the household of Woolton Court. The High Mass was at eleven o'clock; and the happy Leonora, by the side of her treasured grandmother in the gallery above, was there with missal and office of the feast, long before the time appointed.

" My divine Redeemer," thus arose part of her aspirations; " how I thank Thee for the grace that makes me love Thee supremely. But for that grace what would become of me, who so much love Thy creatures ! "

At the first rising of the united voices in the " Kyrie eleeson," Leonora was not the only one to weep. The expressive and devout singing, and the effective organ, in solemn yet modulated tones, seemed to render just the sweet homage due, on that day, to heaven.

" What a pity it is all over ! " said Leonora, on re-entering the drawing room of her grandmother's suite of rooms. " But in the evening there will be the function of the Benediction; so that I shall look forward to that happiness."

"Between the two holy functions," said the duchess, "we are requested to receive our now valued friend the squire of Gelliot Manor, who wishes to introduce his son, Captain Gelliot. This estimable young officer arrived last night, with leave of absence for a month, and will proceed to-morrow, with his father, to the manor-house."

"Grandmamma," said Leonora, after a little pause, "is Captain Gelliot *really* 'estimable' as you term him? Because during the whole time I stayed at the manor-house, the squire never would speak of his son. This seemed so mysterious, that I feared it must proceed from that sad conflict of love and displeasure that takes refuge in silence."

The duchess smiled, and thought within herself: "Overcaution is the characteristic of open-hearted persons, schooled into prudence." She then said: "I can safely say I know Lord Stanmore, and esteem those he esteems. Young men are judges of each other. These two have become personally acquainted but a few months since; but the qualities of mind and heart being similar, they have become congenial friends. Captain Gelliot has not only a proper filial regard for his father, but admires him, and delights in his society. This month at home will prove a real holiday to him."

This little explanation occurred just in seasonable

time; for a ring at the western door of the long gallery was followed by the inquiry, whether her grace the Duchess of Peterworth, was at leisure to receive a visit from Lord Stanmore, accompanied by Squire Gelliot and his son, Captain Gelliot, of the Life Guards. On the return of a favorable message, the trio entered. Leonora recognized in Captain Gelliot the portrait at the manor-house, and blushed; Captain Gelliot, who had felt so diffident and nervous before the visit, that his father related the anecdote, blushed also; then all the party talked at once. First the amateur choir of the chapel were praised, especially the Offertory, and the soft echo of the word "Immaculata."

The draperies and ornaments then received their share of encomium, during which subordinate topic Captain Gelliot ventured a few words to Leonora, in the inquiry whether the two families united at dinner on such a festival? Leonora informed him that Lord Stanmore and his friends always dined with the Earl of Charleton on Sundays and festivals; and, therefore, they were all expected by him and the duchess, at seven o'clock, after Benediction. This opening made, the conversation continued, and was interrupted only by the squire claiming his usual companion for a walk. Leonora's look towards the old gentleman, as she gracefully accepted his escort, was so expressively beautiful, that the son began to consider himself in the way to become a very happy

32*

man, provided he could prove himself worthy of the prize placed within his reach. So, after a few words of compliment to the duchess, he quickly followed his father to the gardens.

Before the month's leave of absence was over, Captain Gelliot and Leonora were engaged, conditionally on the consent of the parents. To obtain this consent, it is well known that the duchess had only to write one of her emphatic and persuasive letters, and full consent would arrive. This proved true with one stipulation; that the granddaughter of Sir Howard Whynne and of the Dukes of Peterworth should not be married from the roof of any, however respected, nobleman, who was not of her own blood. The parents, therefore, requested the duchess to return for the marriage to her own property of Eagle Crag. For although the step-grandmother, she was the dowager duchess, and descended from the same ancestors as the Dukes of Peterworth. Colonel and Lady Emily Whynne regretted their inability to return at present to England; and each wrote a letter of parental affection to Leonora, as " their good child, who had never, from her birth, given them one moment's uneasiness but from her delicate health!" What wonderful tenderness a marriage brings forth! These letters bedewed with tears, were laid beneath the pillow of the neglected child, and brought balm to her timid heart.

CHAPTER XLVIII.

BETWEEN the feast of the eighth of December and Christmas, the Marquis of Seaham, Lady Clara Moorland and family, according to good old custom, were to be at their residence, Marsden Park. On the twentieth, therefore, all the inmates of Woolton Court dined together in the eastern residence; and as partings belonged exclusively to this vale of tears, and are, however salutary, but little festive, Lady Clara, for the first time, arranged that the little twins, Claudia and Violet, should enter with the dessert to keep up the gayety of the family party. They were now two years old, and presented themselves with an almost exact cast of features, to which likeness the similarity of their pretty baby toilet contributed.. They were soon each on a knee of their uncle; the one shy, but merry; the other calmly regarding the circle of faces. They soon began, however, to play and laugh with each other, and create the merriment desired.

"Duchess," said their uncle, "which of these little beauties is to be the youngest Duchess of Peterworth?"

"Any daughter of Lady Clara," replied she, "would be welcomed for her mother's sake; but she alone can know the, perhaps, opposite dispositions of these dear infants. George is like his father, a fine, warm-hearted boy, and at present warm-tempered. He studies well, and has a great sense of duty. He is ten years old; just eight years in advance of these pets. Truly, a royal betrothal of the middle ages! Anna would prize a niece of yours, marquis."

"Well, Clara," said he, "which is the best tempered of these two babies? For, as our little Marquis of Cheshunt is excitable, he must marry his contrast."

"You mean to ask me, I conclude," replied Lady Clara, "which of the two has naturally the wildest temper? but that will not prove that at seventeen or eighteen she will possess that advantage over her sister; for I have observed that where God permits, by nature, certain defects, He bestows strength of mind — moral courage to conquer these defects; so that, even here below, a reward is given in the love and approval of those who can appreciate the conquest."

"Come, Clara," persisted the marquis, "which is to be the conqueror?"

"I never will reveal to any one," said she, "the natural dispositions of my children, for the reasons I have already mentioned. I think it cruel that certain tendencies, which fidelity to grace would conquer or turn to good, should be known in childhood, and remembered in after life, by persons who could not have a mother's feeling, and who might mar the happiness of a young girl, by whispering, ' I knew her as a child, and was told she had such or such a fault.' "

" Very right, Clara. I have been saying, ' very right, Clara,' half my life." Still the scrutinizing uncle endeavored to penetrate the secrets of the soft brown eyes that looked confidingly on him.

" Yes, marquis, your sister *is* quite right," said the duchess; " and I will perfectly trust to her decision, should God prolong my life fifteen years, which of your beautiful, accomplished, and virtuous nieces is at seventeen to marry the future Duke of Peterworth, and which Sir Henry Moorland."

" How old is the little baronet?" asked Lord Stanmore.

" He is nearly eight years old," replied Lady Clara.

" Claudia and Violet, look at this," said the duchess, holding up a jewelled bauble to attract their attention. The infant girls looked first at the speaker, then at the jewels, while she looked steadily at each.

All the dinner party then moved to the drawing-rooms, where the duchess said, in a low tone, to Lady Clara, " To you alone I utter the prophecy, that you will train Claudia to become Duchess of Peterworth, and Violet, Lady Moorland."

"You know them apart, then," said the mother, taking Claudia in her arms.

"Yes; not perhaps in features, but the expression. Claudia is the most calm; she is also the eldest, by ten minutes. These united claims fit her to become the wife of my impetuous George, Marquis of Cheshunt, and future Duke of Peterworth."

"Oh, you lovely and loving little godchild!" exclaimed Lady Violet, taking her little namesake a joyous dance in her arms through the rooms. "What a smile, and what dimples, you little beauty! Oh, papa, what early betrothals! They far exceed mine. We should be arranging matrimonially for Philip Henry, were not his future wife in the chaos of expectation. This is my first godchild. I am so proud of the honor — an honor most honorary; for, with such a mother, what has a godmother to do, but to dance and kiss her dearest little cousin."

"Violet, tell me," said the persevering diplomatist, "how do you distinguish between these very young children? I see clearly their mother does."

"I cannot read as deeply, papa; but it seems to me that this, my little namesake, is more sensitive than Claudia. She will, therefore, have more to suffer."

"Ah! just so," said the marquis; "now I have a clue."

The sleepy little innocents were then taken to their beds, and the father and daughter remained in confidential interchange of parting words.

It was well for Lady Violet, the following day, that she was called upon, almost immediately on the departure of her father, to attend to the approaching Christmas festivities, which were celebrated with due honor, and brought joy into the hearts of all.

After New-Year's Day, the duchess, her ladies, the bride elect, and suite, removed to Eagles Crag, where, after the Epiphany, the bridal guests assembled from Woolton Court and Gelliot Manor; the squire being welcomed with honor day and night, but the affianced son being compelled, by etiquette, to be received, at night, into the best room of the nearest farm-house. The wedding of Leonard Whynne was just suited to the pious, affectionate, and unambitious bent of her disposition. Surrounded by high titles, she was content to become Mrs. Willoughby Gelliot, and to anticipate a life chiefly spent in the routine of the old manor house, where, loving and beloved, she hopes to render her duties worthy to become a store for heaven.

On the return of the inmates of Woolton Court, they dined together in the western residence, and in the evening Lord Stanmore and Lady Violet received the congratulations of the venerable couple, on the skill and prudence with which they had united two persons so well suited to each other.

"This is not the only inspiration Violet has had, the credit of which she either shares with, or totally resigns to, others," said Lord Stanmore, looking beamingly towards his wife. ,"The Rev. Dr. Rollings has assured me that, shocked as he was at the wild revels at Marsden Park, he could not see his way in the least, till after an interview, which Violet requested, — an interview which she had sought, by inspiration, after fervent prayer."

" But Arthur," said Violet, " *I* could only introduce Leonora and the squire together. It must have been her good angel who caused her to make that pretty little blunder about the picture, that ended so well. And it was you who carried on the correspondence with Captain Galliot, and who not only so appreciated Leonora's character, but were also able, from your gift of eloquence, to place all her characteristics in the fairest light, so that highly valuing *your* opinion, he came resolved to gain the prize."

" And now, Violet, my dear child," said Lord Charleton, " that you have mentioned your husband's gift of eloquence, has it occurred to you that, for him, this happy country life must be drawing to a close? Do you wish to remain here with our little Philip Henry, until the real London season commences, and the weather becomes more genial for travelling?"

" O, grandpapa," she exclaimed, " is it not my first duty to follow my husband?"

" Unless he should decree otherwise," replied the earl.

" Arthur," said she, " you never could decree our separation."

" Not for my own sake," replied he.

" For whose sake, then ?"

" I feel it to be a pity to take you now to London, where, although nominally with me, you would have to pass so many lonely hours, for Miss Campion expects no release from her uncle's death-bed. You have wished me to enter public life under your father; this is now the case, and you well know that no one working for the Marquis of Seaham is permitted to be idle. If he have complimented me on the possession of good brains, he takes care they shall not become inert. His holiday time here included many working hours, both for himself and me; and when, on parting, he said, — 'I foresee hard work for us both to prepare for parliament,' I also foresaw, by that speech, enough to make an idle man tremble. Were all my work to be like that of the secretaries, plain before me, you could still be with me; but half my time will be spent on the railroad to Marsden, or driving to Bayswater, to assist in consultations, for the Marquis will be in St. James'-square as late as possible. He cannot bear to be alone in that house; he told me this; so that without the power to do otherwise, I should seem to neglect and desert you. Then, Violet, think of all my grandfather has done and suffered for me. I must leave him; but he sees me in little Henry, and loves *you* as his true granddaughter. He thinks that the child had better travel in more genial weather to Carlton Gardens ; the

Easter holidays are short, but they would give me time to fetch you to London.”

“ But you forget, Arthur, that papa expects us for the Easter holidays at Marsden.” ·

“ Does he? Was any promise made? I was not aware.”

“ I thought it so natural, so likely that you would say ‘ yes,’ that I answered for you to papa. Poor papa ! People only know him as the great orator, the great statesman, who is to sway cabinets, and keep the equipoise of Europe. Few know his good, his wounded heart. He said it would comfort him to welcome his grandson to Marsden Park. Philip Henry is his grandson, his only,—only grandson, grandpapa.”

“ You must go to Marsden, my child,” said Lord Charleton.

“ Can it not be thus arranged?” interposed the duchess. “ Lord Stanmore fetches Lady Violet and the infant, at the Easter recess ; but he conducts them to Marsden Park, till—those short holidays being over—the whole party must necessarily remove to London: the already great statesman, the future great statesman, and Philip Henry; the latter being little aware of his consequence in any relation of life.”

“ That seems a very good arrangement,” observed Lord Stanmore.

“ Oh !” cried Lady Violet. “ Were I a poor

woman, with but one house, — one little cottage, I should be compelled to live there, and there alone with you, Arthur. Sweet obligation! But now I must yield for these few weeks, before Easter; and God, who sees the anguish of this parting, will accept the sacrifice, and will guard and preserve you to me, Arthur. You will not forget me; you will not wander from me!"

"*I* forget *you*, Violet!—I wander from you! Oh! how have I deserved these last words!"

More followed, during which the venerable witnesses to the scene, dropped a tear or two of remembranced sympathy, and the earl whispered:

"Our young days, Emma."

These first moments of disappointment over, however, Lady Violet recovered the heroism of her character, even through the parting moments. She accepted, for the first fortnight of her bereavement, the paternal invitation, with the precious babe, to the western mansion, after which she returned to her usual duties in the eastern half, with the additional one of a punctual and detailed correspondence with her husband.

CHAPTER XLIX.

VIOLET's solitude was cheered by visits from Leonora; and she soon became vividly interested in a scientific competition, communicated to her by her friend, in which Captain Gelliot received the prize, for a greater extension of light. On Violet's next return of visit to Gelliot Manor, however, she found that a scientific gentleman, who had expected to receive the prize, and who possessed great interest, was exerting himself to have the awardment annulled, as a mere pretended improvement on that which he himself invented. Captain Gelliot very naturally vented his indignant feelings in letters to his wife, who communicated them to her friend; and the two young, but intelligent heads, combined to frustrate the plot. Violet drove home, and that night commenced an earnest correspondence with her father, which, in the end, procured a full acknowledgment of the genius and signal services of Captain Gelliot, by both houses of parliament.

But the interest which the Marquis of Seaham had taken in the intelligent young officer, did not terminate in a vote of thanks: he sent for Captain Gelliot;

the anterooms were filled with greater people, but the secretary came forth from the inner focus of excitement, and, guided by the groom of the chambers, approached the outer door, near which sat the patient and modest young officer.

" Captain Gelliot, I believe."

On receiving the bow of assent, the secretary said, that instead of returning through the rooms, he would conduct him by the private door to the minister.

" Captain Gelliot," said the Marquis of Seaham, " colonels and majors do not die off to oblige the friends of a deserving young subaltern officer, whom they wish to promote. You cannot expect to rise, under our present system, except by purchase into another regiment. Perhaps you are too justly proud of your present corps, to desire to take that step?"

" Very true, my lord," was the reply.

" Your father, Mr. Gelliot of Gelliot Manor, is, I understand, of very ancient family, and is naturally proud of the happy accident of birth?"

" He is my lord."

" You are married to a young lady, who, although not herself titled, is closely allied to the first nobility of England?"

A wondering " yes," was the sole reply.

" She is, by the mother, granddaughter to the late Duke of Peterworth; by the father, granddaughter to an ancient baronet, Sir Howard Waltham Whynne. Her sister will be Marchioness of Seaham."

An expectant silence was all the young officer could bestow.

"Antiquity of family," pursued the marquis, "is deservedly considered; and when merit and distinguished talent are combined to demand a recompense from a grateful country, it facilitates the bestowal of honor. We offer you, Captain Gelliot, a baronetcy."

"My lord marquis, I feel most truly grateful," at length replied the astonished young officer. "I have followed your arguments. I am aware that the noble relations of my wife wish for my exaltation, for her sake, or, more correctly speaking, for their own sake; but I am not the less obliged to you, my lord."

"Then you do not refuse to become Sir Willoughby Gelliot?"

"I should prefer that it were offered to my father, my lord marquis."

"Well, write to the old squire," said the marquis, with an approving look, "although I know what his answer will be. In the first place, he did not invent the Gelliot light. In the second place, he is antagonistic to all new creations; not considering that to those placed above pecuniary recompense, her gracious Majesty has but the reward of elevation to bestow. When you shall have received the reply from Gelliot Manor, write to me, or rather come and dine with me. My dinner-hour is seven o'clock."

In a few days Captain Gelliot, with his father's reply, presented himself, rather before the rest of the guests, in St. James'-square. He was immediately shown into Lord Seaham's private study, to whom, with a smile, he handed his father's letter, saying :

" Your lordship predicted rightly ; almost to the very letter."

" DEAR WILLOUGHBY, — These new titles are very well for naval and military men, especially when they have deserved them. *I* have deserved nothing, either by warlike exploit, or scientific discovery. Do not, from filial piety, wish me to accept the offered baronetcy, and so keep it merely hovering over your head for, perhaps, many years. To my mind, it will be only a pretty second title to the lords of the Manor of Gelliot. Lands held from father to son during eight hundred years : the round tower, that first stood on the lands, for our crest to this day, with the two owls for supporters. The right to supporters cannot be lightly granted. All this will be yours some day : and if, in addition, you like to be Sir Willoughby, why, in your case, 't is well enough. My little bird, Leonora, is the blessing of my life. We are together nearly all the day long. I tell her that I am the best husband she has ; but she looks significantly towards a packet of your letters, smiles, and shakes her head.

" Your affectionate father,
JOHN HILDEBRAND GELLIOT."

The marquis looked at the seal.

" Ah ! truly a fine specimen of armorial bearings. Call on me this day week, and I shall then greet you as Sir Willoughby."

This took place just before the Easter recess, and was the last of the London dinners given by the Minister for Foreign Affairs, before the holidays."

Directly he was free, by the departure of his chief, Lord Stanmore faithful to his promise, passed rapidly into Westmorland, to fetch his wife and child to Marsden Park. Amid smiles and tears, Lady Violet departed with husband and infant from Woolton Court, while the aged couple watched the retreating carriages with resignation.

"Thank you, Emma," said Lord Charleton, "for sharing my solitude. We shall, please God, welcome them back in July or August; and Philip Henry will then be a stout little champion."

The venerable nobleman's hopes were fulfilled. Early in August, the whole family of Woolton Court were again assembled in cheerful and loving greetings, the circle being agreeably enlarged by the arrival from the manor-house of Sir Willoughby and Lady Gelliot.

Philip Henry, now ten months old, stood unaided in the centre of the group, looking steadfastly at his great-grandfather, whom he at length recognized by a smile.

"Ah!" said the earl, "he is, thank God, loving, beautiful, and intelligent, as he ought to be with such parents; and such prayers, ever ascending to the throne of grace, for the heir of Woolton Court!"